W9-BDI-843

BRAINDRAIN

It was happening.

Nothing would come out of her mouth. But that was the least of the horror beginning to run through her in time with her quickening pulse. She was losing it. She could literally feel the clarity going out of the way she saw things, seeping away like blood from a wound.

It was draining out of her. And not painlessly. She felt it going, felt every scruple of herself boiling off against the terrible heat inside her. Time sense going. Memory. Even recognition of the faces now crowding over her. Everything was going but the horror.

Something was wrong.

Terribly wrong.

Don't Miss the Next Exciting Adventure of the
SPACE COPS
Coming Soon from Avon Books

KILL STATION
*by Diane Duane and
Peter Morwood*

Avon Books are available at special quantity discounts for bulk purchases for sales promotions, premiums, fund raising or educational use. Special books, or book excerpts, can also be created to fit specific needs.

For details write or telephone the office of the Director of Special Markets, Avon Books, Dept. FP, 1350 Avenue of the Americas, New York, New York 10019.

SPACE COPS
MINDBLAST

DIANE DUANE & PETER MORWOOD

AVON BOOKS ◆ NEW YORK

If you purchased this book without a cover, you should be aware that this book is stolen property. It was reported as "unsold and destroyed" to the publisher, and neither the author nor the publisher has received any payment for this "stripped book."

SPACE COPS: MINDBLAST is an original publication of Avon Books. This work has never before appeared in book form. This work is a novel. Any similarity to actual persons or events is purely coincidental.

AVON BOOKS
A division of
The Hearst Corporation
1350 Avenue of the Americas
New York, New York 10019

Copyright © 1991 by Bill Fawcett & Associates
Cover art by Dorian Vallejo
Published by arrangement with Bill Fawcett & Associates
Library of Congress Catalog Card Number: 91-91772
ISBN: 0-380-75852-0

All rights reserved, which includes the right to reproduce this book or portions thereof in any form whatsoever except as provided by the U.S. Copyright Law. For information address Bill Fawcett & Associates, 388 Hickory, Lake Zurich, Illinois 60047.

First Avon Books Printing: July 1991

AVON TRADEMARK REG. U.S. PAT. OFF. AND IN OTHER COUNTRIES, MARCA REGISTRADA, HECHO EN U.S.A.

Printed in the U.S.A.

RA 10 9 8 7 6 5 4 3 2 1

For Colm and our friends at The Grove Bar,
of The Willow Grove, Greystones,
County Wicklow, Ireland,
who keep asking the one question
we never get tired of hearing:

"And where've you been
these ten thousand years?"

Law stops at atmosphere

       —old criminal axiom, c. 2010

HE PUT HIS BACK UP AGAINST THE GRIMY
corridor wall and just held himself there, breathing hard.
There was nothing else he could do at the moment. Sweat
trickled down his back, tickled him. He didn't move. He
didn't dare. The wrong move, the wrong sound, would get
him killed.

Their voices were loud, farther down. They knew they
had nothing to be afraid of. They were in their element,
in the dark, in corridors they knew well—better than he
did. He cursed himself softly for that. He should never
have let his curiosity drive him down here. His "overset-
ting sin," Evan had always called it.

He breathed out once more, thinking about Evan. Things
would be a lot easier if he were here.

"T'not be here," a voice said down the corridor, after
a quiet moment. *Yes,* he thought. *You think that. Just this
once, you think that, smart boy.* There was rustling, shuffling, down at their end of the corridor. *Not the slightest
idea of how to be quiet,* he thought. Or perhaps that was
just their contempt for him showing—that they didn't feel
the need to move quietly, not when a slug was involved,
a grounder.

He looked up and down the part of the corridor closest
to him. It was typical of the more neglected downlevels—
dirty, the panels chipping, all sprayed over with the intri-
cate twined sigils of the local inrunners; a messy heraldry,

1

one crest defacing another, others altered to reflect deaths and changes in leadership. He thought of all the weeks he had spent deciphering that language so as to understand the shifts in the business he was following: who was holding, who was bought, who was pitching. But something had gone wrong. He had been careless—he might as well admit it to himself now. He hadn't been able to admit to himself that there might be someone here capable of figuring out what he was up to.

And now he was going to pay for that blind spot, unless he got very lucky. He eyed those smeared, peeling composite panels in desperation. There had to be one that could be used as a bolthole. The basic structure of the fiver usually left one in three panels nonsolid, not backed by the service conduits or the ducts. But which one?

"Muf went gone downside," someone said from down the corridor, where they huddled together. The voice seemed faintly hopeful—some younger blood in the group, by the sound. "Leav'm get'm where'e lives."

That would be much preferable. There was enough weaponry in his flat to make any attack that followed interesting to watch. Meanwhile, all he could hope was that they *would* think he had gone downside. But even if they did, they would come down here to find out how he had done it. He had this advantage, only this: he was better armed than they were. But not by much, and not for long. There were no more than twenty of them, no less than ten—that much he had been able to judge by the sound of footsteps alone when they first came on him about a kilometer back. They were being cautious now, hoping that they wouldn't need to be cautious later. He had led them a nasty chase, but they had refused to be put off the trail. He wondered what they had been offered for him . . . or threatened with if they let him get away.

Never mind that. Calm, now. Consider the options. There were always options—that was the first lesson they taught you in the force—options and the assessment of them. The dark end of the corridor, the panels to either side of him; those were his options at the moment. None of the panels were accessible, by the look of them—the "easies" always had old repaired pry marks left on them this far down, where money was scarce to put in new ones. There probably wasn't one panel in this part of the fiver that hadn't had a prytool into it at one time or another, for there was an active black market down here in copper cabling and stolen datasolids. The only problem was that none of these panels had the hobomarks on them that he could recognize as an inrunner group's sign that the panel could be used to *get* anywhere.

"No outs, no downs," someone said from down the way, a hard, dark voice with that particular nasal turn to the vowels that meant someone born and raised here. It was the voice that had called up this particular gang of inrunners and set them on his trail in that other shadowy corridor. He had known his danger, trespassing into inrun ground that he hadn't yet researched. He had thought that just for a few minutes, just this once, he would get away with it—

The bolt burned hot down the corridor, its range failing well before him, but still managing to leave a panel about fifty yards down from him bubbling and stinking black. He did nothing, made not a move. The shot was certainly meant as a flush. They were not going to have him that easily. He thought about more of the options. *Floor?* Hopeless: here he was down to bare metal. Underneath him were nothing but engineering levels like this one, some converted to squats as this one was, but all alike, nothing but hard bare cubic with no windows or open spaces. *Ceiling?* The upward glance told him this was a waste of time too—the same bare-panelled stuff as the floor, the corrugated texture of its underside clearly visible, stamped out on some press on one of the orbital smelting facilities, a solid inch of steel. He had better things to do with his gun than try to burn through that.

"N'wast'm'time," said the dark voice, "get'm." Footsteps moved right then, shuffling, reluctant. Perhaps that shot had been meant for one of them after all? Never mind that now. Options. *Further down the corridor—* It was a T-junction, he could see it clearly enough, even in this gloom. One side of it dead-ended. He knew that, having walked a clone of this corridor on another level higher up, last week. The other end ran down to an L-junction and then to another corridor parallel to this one. He knew there were easies in that corridor: he had passed one on the way to where he was now. Five seconds, that was all it would take him to get it open. After that he would be safely into the duct system. They might know that better than he did, but there the advantage turned to him. They couldn't come at him in numbers, there—only one by one.

Another bolt screamed out and fried a panel just down from him. *A little too close,* he thought, but he really had nothing to complain about as far as that went: he couldn't hope for a clearer indication of their weapons' range. And the characteristic whine of the bolt told him clearly that the stuff was nothing military, just Webley 16's— rechargeable from the mains but not from packs. Limited range, limited power, and the charge on these was running low. That was just fine by him.

He listened, let the footsteps fall into pattern—they always did that sooner or later in this kind of situation, the multiple nervous minds taking refuge in pack-behavior— and then stepped out from the door-alcove, sighted, shot. Two of them went right down, one swearing, the other with an extra hole burnt in his head that was no good for cursing with, or anything else. He aimed another shot at one of the panels down by the runners and held the beam there for a second, just long enough to make a good deal of smoke. Coughs and curses and howls of rage and pain came floating out of the murk as he dove and rolled, came up running, headed down the corridor as fast as he could, looking over his shoulder as he went. A couple more bolts came lancing out of the smoke, but he saw them coming and was untroubled. They were poorly aimed, and no wonder, considering what the fumes from burning panel- ing were like.

"Get'm, get'm, y'furgs!" screamed the dark voice from somewhere in the smoke.

He spared himself one breath of laughter: this kind of confusion was what he liked to hear. There was one more alcove between him and the end of the corridor. Use it for another moment's cover, or go straight on down? The footsteps sounded like they were getting closer; he decided against the alcove. A bolt burned past his ear just as he dove again, for prudence's sake. He rolled again, came up on his feet again, and then dodged down the right-hand turning of the T-junction, the one that would get him out of all this—

—and found it a dead end—

No downs, no outs, the dark voice had said. The footsteps were coming in a rush now, and the screams of rage with them, as he looked around him in desperation for an easy, anything that would get him out of here. Walls, ceiling, floor, all solid—

But this should have been a through corridor, part of his mind screamed at him. And another part said, more quietly, *You've been driven. Herded like cattle. This whole thing, from that first chance meeting two levels down, it was nothing but a planned trap. You're dealing with something here that's a lot more dangerous than a few inrunners with murder on their minds. How long have they been waiting for you to walk into this? And worse . . . who in this fiver knows exactly what you're thinking, days before you think it yourself?*

The only other thought he had time left for was the memory of his notes, all the slowly garnered information, which EssPat would now never get its hands on. Only he knew where it was. And there was not going to be time to get it to anyone else. All his careful work, wasted.

A moment later, there was a dark bulge at the corner of the corridor in front of him: someone just barely peering around it. Not barely enough, of course. He fried the side of the inrunner's head, and the side of the next head that peered around, lower. His charge was going to run out soon, but they didn't know that yet.

More bolts came, not aimed at him now, but at the corridor panels. They smoked and bubbled and fumed, and he started coughing, unable to help himself. What were they doing? Didn't they know they were killing themselves by standing in this stuff and breathing it—

The coughing got worse, so bad that he couldn't hold still to aim. His lungs were on fire. A moment with his eyes squeezed shut against the burning, that was all it took for someone to step in, kick the Webley out of his hand, scoop it up. Eyes streaming, throat swelling, he looked up and saw them standing over him: saw the noseplugs and mouth filters; knew that his herding had been much more purposeful and complete than he had suspected. No question, he felt suddenly certain, of any of his work even *surviving*, now. If they had known his movements this well, they must know where all his collected evidence was.

He had just time to feel bitterly sorry for his replacement before they killed him.

JOSS O'BANNION LOOKED AT THE PADSCREEN with a mixture of pleasure and annoyance. He hated enforced vacations: he had just been telling himself so. Now his vacation was over, and his first reaction to the discovery was to be annoyed.

The notification sitting there on the padscreen in his lap looked like any other dispatch from the Solar Police executive, the usual account numbers and routing strings at the top of the screen, and then Joss's name, and then the bad news. But the routings caught his eye first: they were peculiar. *Since when are they bouncing Moonbound messages through an L5? What's wrong with the Endymion cynthiosynch satellite? Busted again, probably. So much for machinery built by the lowest bidder. . . .*

The message under the routing codes said: REPORT ASAP TO COMMISSIONER'S OFFICE SOUTHERN LUNA/MARE SERENITATIS FOR BRIEFING AND TEAM ASSIGNMENT. And that was that. No explanations, no hints. That was pretty much their style, though. And under that, a private-flagged note from his comms rep: TOO BAD, KID. T.

Joss sighed and stretched, and looked out the non-opaqued part of the dome. It was midafternoon on the near side of the Moon, as it had been for several days, and would be for a few more. The shadows stretched long and black and razor-edged behind every rock and pooled inside every craterlet. Despite the fact that there was no air to soften it, the light still had that quality that said "afternoon." It made him want to get into his pressure suit and go do a little more rock collecting, but there was really no time for it now. The rest of the research for the paper on compression factors in lunar minerals would have to wait till the next holiday.

Joss sighed as he read the message on the screen again, thinking, *They said it was going to be some time yet before they partnered me. Oh well.* . . . The rest of his mind was still muttering over the loss of the rest of his holiday. He had intended to keep the cottage for at least a couple of weeks, and he had been here only how many days now? Three? It was a good thing he had taken the rental insurance—it would cover the loss of his air deposit and the penalty for the early departure.

Another partner. . . .

It had been a while since his first partnership. He and Maura had parted amicably after half a year together, she to take on an enforcement job on Pluto, of all places, and he heading back to the Moon to assist with a statistical study on the shifting of patterns of Lunar crime over the past decade. Joss had missed Maura, but not for long. He had to admit to himself, in retrospect, that their partnership had not really worked. He wasn't clear about the whys of it all, but the occasional niggling thought came up for examination that someone had *gladly* left him to go to Pluto.

It made him wonder whether he was really fit to be partnered at all.

But the head office seems to think so, he thought. *Not that the head office has a monopoly on being right.* . . .

Joss sighed and tossed the padscreen aside. The message had been receipted: Communications knew he had read it, and when. There would be problems if he delayed too long in showing up for a briefing. He didn't even have the excuse of having to pack up his things. Three days into the holiday, he hadn't even gotten around to taking things out of the cases yet. The only thing that needed packing was the twenty-pound bag of sealed and tagged rocks that he had collected so far.

Joss stood up and headed for the closet built into the central service module of the dome. He really did dislike leaving on such short notice. He was just getting used to the comfort and charm of the place. It had been tastefully furnished in antiques—genuine Danish Modern brought up from Earth—and the cool chaste lines of the furniture, all whites and greys, went well with the milk-white opacity of the dome or the unremitting blacks and whites outside. Joss stepped around the prize of the collection, a genuine Saarinen chair, and whistled the closet open.

Pants, uniform singlet, boots— He studied himself a moment in the full-length mirror behind the closet door, straightened the shouldertabs on the singlet and wondered if he needed a haircut. *Oh, never mind—if they want me right away, they can deal with the extra hair.* The image in the mirror was quite presentable enough: a man in his late thirties, of mixed heritage, the red hair betraying his Irish blood, his light wiry build and the slight epicanthic fold to his eyes a gift from his mother's side of the family, mixed Polynesian and oriental. A face not too innocent and not too hard; cool eyes and an amiable set to the face; someone who didn't look particularly like a policeman, or like anything else specific, as Maura used to say. That had proven to be an advantage, once or twice, when Joss was out of uniform but on business. Heaven only knew if it would be of any use to him wherever he was going.

Joss lifted his eyebrows at himself in resignation, then hauled his still-packed bags out and told the closet to shut itself. He cracked open the biggest of the bags and spent a few minutes tossing rocks into it, then sealed it up again, evacuated both bags, and put them out into the airlock.

His pressure suit was hanging there. He ran his eyes over the gauges and telltales for a few seconds, doing the checks the ritual three times, air, regulator, structural fitness, material fatigue, polarizer, water and survival rations, ballast. Everything was on green or on the up-and-up, though some people might have been surprised at how little ballast he used, even for someone born on the Moon. Well, let them be surprised. No use in carrying extra mass around or overworking your muscles, no matter what the weight was supposed to do for your maneuverability or your traction, and no matter what some people said about the degenerate quality of most human muscle these days. Joss was not one of your exercise nuts. He trusted the drugs that kept the intermuscular electrolyte balance in shape at low gravities, and simply enjoyed being weightless or a little more than weightless as much of the time as possible.

He pulled the suit on and did up the seals, checked his air flow and temperature maintenance, and then—the traditional last thing, for him—turned the badge on. Before settling the helm in place, he bent over his chestplate, craning his neck a little to make sure it was working. The hologram gleamed with the golden star and nine concentric circles, and his badge number. Turning the thing on was more than a matter of pride. Any sop could deadhead anywhere in the system, and Joss intended to hop a scheduled carrier rather than taking public transport. There was no point in getting yourself onto a shuttle with a limited launch window and then being thrown off by some tin can from automated security because you'd forgotten to turn your badge on.

He sighed as he put the helm on, polarized it, and completed the final seals. *A new partner,* he thought, shutting and locking the dome's main access with the keycard, then dropping it into the coded receptacle by the door. *Am I going to get stuck with another Maura? And where are they going to send us? Not Pluto, I hope. I hate the cold.*

Joss loaded the luggage onto the follow-me carrier and opened the outer airlock, looking out at the path that wound away among the low dusty hillocks toward the partly-concealed domes of the other holiday cottages, and past them, into the foothills of the Appenines. No more rambles for him; this time just the short walk to the bus stop, and the ride to the shuttle port. At least the walk would be comfortable. It wasn't more than a hundred cee below at the moment, well within the suit's comfort range: a pleasant stroll in the warm Lunar afternoon.

Joss sighed and bounced off down the path to the bus stop, and the luggage carrier put out its pogo sticks and followed him, leaving small bright dustclouds hanging in the vacuum behind it.

DESPITE ITS IMPORTANCE, THE SOLAR PATROL's HQ was not a prepossessing-looking building. It was dwarfed by Eagle Base Museum nearby—a fact that fiercely annoyed most of the locals. Eagle Base was mostly considered an architectural eyesore, with its huge barren spires sticking up and out in all directions; an aberrance of the Non-Functional school of architecture of the late '20s, all mirrored plastic film and stays and guywires. At the time it had seemed like a good idea to cover the whole Tranquility Base site over and "preserve it for the ages," though some people had at the time pointed out that in the Lunar environment, where there was no erosion or wind, the ages would take care of themselves very nicely, and a fence or a forcefield would do the job. But then others had reminded the protesters what had happened to Stonehenge, and reluctantly the new Lunar government had given in and covered the place over with what some people claimed was a design approved more in spite than anything else, sometimes described as "a coathangers' orgy staged in a mylar tent."

EssPat HQ huddled (or seemed to) under a dome in the northern shadow of Eagle Base, between it and the single clean-lined spire of the Houses of Legislature. There was, of course, a lot more to it than that one dome. Extensive tunnelling had been done in all directions, and was still being done, leading to the joke that the first place where human beings had gone when initially arriving on another world was the top of a police station.

The dome proper wore only one external sign of what it was: the Solar Police sigil, nine concentric circles and the central Sun-in-eclipse. There was one other indication. Graven several feet deep in the Lunar sandstone in front of the main entrance, and inlaid with sand-brushed steel, were the words *CEDANT ARMA TOGAE*. None of the sops used that way in, of course; it was for tourists doing the staged tour of the facility, or official visitors. Joss was privately a little abashed by the fact that every time he passed by the front entrance, he got a bit of a shiver. It was not something he would have admitted to anyone, but sometimes he found himself suspecting that more than a few of his fellow sops shared the reaction.

Today, though, he headed for the "back door," the small domed access nearest Eagle Base. He got out of the bus from the shuttle terminal and almost immediately found himself tangled up in a p-suited group of tourists queueing outside the Base. Working his way through them, he had to stop at least twice to let his poor luggage catch up with him when it lost his signal in the crowd. A few of the tourists pointed at him as he passed, or put their helmets together to comment on his badge—complimentarily, he hoped. Joss had heard some of those comments on occasion, and they tended to be of the "you-can-never-find-one-when-you-need-one" variety.

Joss got free of them and headed for the back-door dome's access lock. There was something to that line, of course. With millions of cubic miles of space to patrol, just in the inner System—let alone the wilder outer reaches past the Asteroids—you could hardly have a sop posted on every rock, no matter how many people you trained and equipped. The whole population of the Earth could go through the three-year basic course—after first doing their "affiliate training," the master's level work and psych work—and still not be able to cover the "high ground" by more than one sop per hundred thousand cubic kilometers.

The access read his badge and hissed open for him. Joss bounced inside, closely followed by his luggage, which brought a little cloud of dust in with it as the door sealed. *The programmer who taught this thing to jump was an Earthling for sure,* Joss thought, dusting himself off as the lock pressurized. *It's got no grace.*

Sound came back, the hissing of the entering air tapering off, then stopping, and the inner lock opened for him. Past the lock was the usual public unsuiting room: headheight hooks and helmet clamps on a conveyor, the "meat rack," which led back into the suit storage area. Joss slipped out of the suit, puffing a bit and wondering whether he had put on some weight while on vacation, then hung the suit up, stowed the luggage in the rack under it, and waved at the rack's sensor to start the conveyor going. It clanked off, and Joss headed through the door out of the unsuiting room.

The big room just beyond unsuiting was comms: under its own small dome, perhaps a third of a klick across, full of a scatter of desks and consoles and computers and other machinery about which Joss knew nothing whatsoever. Every sop knew the voice of comms, though, and every independent officer knew at least one of its representatives by voice, though rarely by looks. There was always a voice that passed on data and orders through your pad or your radio or on the phone; that took your reports, and sometimes said a word of encouragement or made a bad joke; always the same voice for a given officer. Joss's voice was named Telya—a slightly abrasive, usually cheerful voice, with a weird accent that smacked both of the old Slavic bloc and of the Southern Pacific drawl. She always accused Joss of slacking off, and typically passed on orders and information with an air of disgusted disbelief that Joss found hilarious. As he strolled through the room toward the lifts, Joss gazed around him at the several hundred uniformed people hammering on consoles or talking to hushed voice connections, and wondered which of them Telya was. Not that there was time to find out, at the moment—

One of the lifts in the center of the dome was waiting open, as usual. Joss stepped in. "Fourteen," he said.

The lift thanked him, shut its doors, and sank with a suddenness that left Joss hanging several inches above the floor for a moment. He grabbed the railing and pushed himself down until he felt the deceleration begin, only a few seconds. At least it was a short ride, as opposed to the ninety-level run down to the sops' own offices, the "Inns." The Commissioners had precious few perks besides quarters inside HQ, and offices fairly near the top level. It seemed to be the Chief Commissioner's opinion that competence in handling a crushing workload should be primarily rewarded by more work.

"Fourteen," the lift said, and slid its door open. Joss stepped out into the central reception area, waved hello at the young gent managing the hot seat—the comms post for the Commissioners' offices—and headed past his big circular desk down the hall to the Area Commissioner's office.

The door was locked in the open position, as usual. Joss peered in for a moment before entering. No one else was waiting in the outer office. There was nothing but the tangle of plants and potted trees that Joss remembered from his last time in here, when he had been sent off with Maura. The Area Commissioner was raised somewhere in the Caribbean, and took her plants seriously.

He sat down on one of the seats—backweb canvas, for the Commissioner was fond of antiques as well—and had no sooner gotten himself comfortable before the door to the inner office slid open and her voice said, "Come on in, O'Bannion."

He went in. "Take a seat," she said. "How was the rock-collecting?"

How does she do it? Joss thought. Lucretia Esterhazy leaned back in her chair and eyed him with that disturbing black gaze of hers. One of the nicknames for her around HQ was "Borgia" and it seemed to fit. There was something Sicilian in her makeup, or at least some derivation from south of Earth's Alps, to judge by the blue-black hair and olive complexion, and the fierce, sharp face. Esterhazy had a reputation for being able to find anything out about anybody. It had doubtless contributed to her rapid ascent from Independent Officer, to Senior Investigator, to Assistant Commissioner and then to Area Commissioner, all in the space of just six years. But it was still unnerving to have that wily mind digging around in your *own* past and present doings, and finding out heaven knew what.

"Not too bad," Joss said. "The gariotites were a little disappointing, but then it wouldn't be any fun if they were just lying around on the ground waiting to be picked up."

Lucretia raised her eyebrows at him and flicked a glance over at one of her screens. Her desk had more padscreens on it than Joss had ever seen in one place at one time, as well as several 3-d boxes, genuine boxes, not synthesized stereo platforms. Now she tapped at the input pad for one and gave it the cool look of someone seeing news that doesn't please her, but is beyond doing anything about.

"I dislike interrupting people's holidays, even if they consist entirely of picking up rocks and drinking imported wines at ridiculously overpriced restaurants," she said, "but something came up."

"Getting me partnered?"

She looked over the screen at him and sighed, pushed the input away. "The computer keeps tabs of these things for me, usually," she said. "Its compatibility-judgment programming is more expert than mine: I have to make do with hunches. But there are people it doesn't mind me leaving unpartnered for long periods of time, and people it resists my leaving unpartnered for more than five minutes or so."

"And I'm one of the ones it can't leave alone?"

"You're one of the ones it could care less about," she said. Joss kept his reaction to himself; Lucretia smiled a sour little "gotcha" smile.

"One of the other Lunar Area Commissioner's people has come unpartnered just now," she said. Joss repressed the desire to shiver: the euphemism never quite succeeded in derailing his images of the worst thing he could imagine having happened to the "unpartner." How had it happened? Explosive decompression? A slug or a bolt out of nowhere? A blunt object? Bare hands?

"The partner was shot on Freedom II," Lucretia said.

This time Joss's eyebrows went up. "I lived there for a while when I was still in college," he said. "Pre-grad work for Cornell High."

"I know. The murder looks gang-related, but the IO wasn't working on gangs. His former opposite number is a must-partner—"

"—and I happened to be free—," Joss said.

Lucretia looked at him. "You must be worth *something* to this force," she said, "because you obviously think well enough of yourself. The live half of the team is an exosuit specialist of a very high caliber. The computer finds your basic profile and his fairly well matched. It's not high enough a percentile to make it a must-match, beyond my authority to contravene, but—"

She stared at another of the screens for a moment, then said, apparently to her comms implant, "Not now, Gyorgi, I've got a headache." Then Lucretia looked up at Joss and scowled. "The match is good enough," she said. "I want to see you make it work. You understand me, Joss? I want to know what killed our IO on Freedom. He was an extraordinarily talented man, not a careless type at all. Very intelligent . . . but apparently not intelligent enough to stay alive there by himself. Let's see if the two of you together can manage it."

Joss nodded. "Who am I being partnered with?"

"He's down the hall. You'll go down and meet him shortly." She scowled again and chewed her lip, then said, "We are not completely sure what his partner was working on. Originally he was one of the free-floating enforcement people who move around the L5's and LunOrb colonies to catch trouble before it starts. We have some early reports from him that indicate that he thought there was. He was paying a great deal of attention to the pharmaceutical companies headquartered there."

"Drugs?" Joss said.

"He didn't think so, though I find myself wondering whether he had changed his mind. His original brief was to look into various communications leaks that some of the drug companies were having trouble with."

"Industrial espionage? That's hardly our business."

"It is if it's BurJohn or MSD that's shouting for help. Those companies have too many political connections on Earth to ignore, and not just any one country, either. EssPat has found it 'appropriate' to examine the situation itself rather than to leave it to the private security companies." Lucretia leaned over to look at another screen, tapped a character or two on its input. "All the relevant files are stored with comms: have your rep offload them to you when you have your pad handy.

"Anyway, the dead man's reports started getting very, well, *sparse* over the past couple of months or so. None too communicative, by and large. One message contained one of the code groups that indicates he thought perhaps his comms were being tapped."

Joss was surprised. "I thought that wasn't possible."

"So did we. I want to find out if it is. Part of our effectiveness as a law enforcement organization lies in secure communications. If someone has found a way to compromise comms, I want to know about it before the High Commissioner does. You get my drift?"

"I do."

Lucretia sat back in the seat a bit. "One more thing.

Glyndower—that's the man you're being partnered with—is a bit on the conservative side by your standards. A bit stodgy. Don't let it bother you, but don't leave it out of your reckoning, either. You'll see the psych evaluation with the rest of his service history.''

Joss smiled a half-smile, since Glyndower, wherever he was, was certainly looking at Joss's profile right now, if he hadn't been earlier. Joss knew what had been in it when he was working with Maura—your partner was allowed to show you, if he or she pleased—but heaven only knew what might be in it *now*. WOMAN FLEES TO PLUTO TO ESCAPE PARTNER— ''Is this partnership a permanent assignment?'' Joss said.

Lucretia looked at him for a moment without saying anything. ''Optional,'' she said at last. ''The computer says there are some idiosyncrasies.'' And she snorted. ''As if I need a machine to tell me that, especially about you. See how it works, Joss. My main concern is for this particular operation. Afterwards—I'm willing to let it be gentlemen's choice. Settle it yourselves. But find out what killed Glyndower's partner. The people Upstairs—'' she rolled her eyes expressively at the ceiling ''—are anxious to find out what killed a man so smart and so productive of results that he was ready to be promoted to Senior. And I want to find out, too. Not just because I like this office, or because you like your IO status, either.''

Joss nodded.

''I suspect you're big enough to make your own introductions,'' Lucretia said. ''Glyndower's in 18A, down the hall. Make sure your groundwork is solid before you leave. When you're ready to start, call me and tell me what you think you'll need. I'll okay it with Supplies. Now get out of here and leave me to my sordid lonely existence.''

Joss stood up and headed out without saluting. Lucretia was not that kind of supervisor. ''And O'Bannion?'' she shouted after him.

He turned.

She was scowling again. ''You watch your expense account this time. I don't want to be faced again with the prospect of explaining to Xibeng upstairs about any

Buddha-be-damned half-dozen bottles of Chateau Fancy-Pants 2016!''

Joss found it hard to look sheepish for more than a second or so. ''But they *worked*,'' he said.

''That's why *you're* still working for *me*,'' Lucretia said, making a face as if she had just had a long pull off a bottle turned to vinegar. ''Now you go on away.''

He went.

HE ACTUALLY PAUSED OUTSIDE 18A, DISCOV-ering that his palms were sweating. He laughed softly to himself, just a breath or so. The conditioning an IO went through usually included things like being shot at or tortured; one was supposed to be able to meet people for the first time without too much trauma. *The next time they condition me, I should make some suggestions about improvements in the operant conditioning program. . . .*

He knocked. ''Come,'' said a rough voice from inside, and the door opened.

18A was one of the lounge rooms, comfortably set up with couches and an infoterminal, and a pseudowindow that at the moment was looking out on a young crescent Saturn as seen from one of its nearer moons, the rings nearly edge-on, the dusty pink soil in the foreground lightly dusted with methane snow. Sitting to one side of the room, the input pad of the infoterminal in his lap, was a man so big and tall and somehow *rough* looking that at first Joss had trouble putting him together with the cool smooth decor of the room. It wasn't the man's dress that threw him off; that was EssPat uniform of the ''long'' or outdoor type, favored by those working onplanet or in other places where the climate was uncontrolled.

The man simply seemed too big for the room. *Earthling*, was Joss's first thought, for ever since there had been several generations born in space, there had been a general decline in height among the spaceborn. People conceived and born in low gravity tended to have heavier bone structure rather than lighter—their bones needed to manufacture more red blood cells than Earthlings'—and to be generally smaller, though their muscular bulk might be some ten percent greater than an Earthling's due to increased amounts of blood plasma and other factors. No, this man was not just Earthling born, but he came from somewhere where Earthlings were built larger than usual, even by the standards of a couple of hundred years ago.

He looked up at Joss. The man's face had been through bad times in the course of some duty or other. There were scars, and a couple of old burns, and his nose looked to have been broken at least twice. A greater than usual asymmetry about the face spoke of a cheekbone broken, too. But the eyes distracted you. They were piercing grey, quite clear, the effect augmented by dark rims around the irises—seeing eyes, and not at all cold, as one might have thought. The grey was hot, interested, and involving, so that Joss found himself becoming curious, against his will, to know what the man was seeing as he looked at him. That face stayed quite still, but the eyes, as the man got up, seemed to become more interested—

"You must be O'Bannion," he said, and held out a hand not much shy of the size of a ham.

"Joss," Joss said, and was surprised at himself, since it had taken something like three months for him and Maura to get to first names. They had spent all that while in the partner-myth that it was somehow more adult and exciting to call each other by last names. But, "You're Glyndower," he said anyway, not wanting to presume.

Glyndower nodded. "Close enough," he said. "Evan is my name. Do sit down, man."

Joss sat down on the arm of the couch. "Evan," he said. "Sorry, did I mispronounce it?"

Glyndower gave him a wry look. "Not as badly as some have," he said. "No matter, it comes with time. Have you had any time to get at my records?"

Joss shook his head. "Lucretia just tossed me in here."

"Ah," Glyndower said. "That one, she'll never slow down till they pile the rocks on her." He frowned to one side at the screen of the infoterminal for a moment, then shut it down with a dismissing flick of a finger. "I take it," he said, "that she told you about Lon. My old partner."

"Only a little about what happened to him."

Glyndower sat back in the hard little terminal chair, and it creaked slightly, as if in protest, at his weight. "A bad death," he said.

"Not sure I know any good ones."

Glyndower looked up at Joss from under his brows.

"Better ones there are," he said, "I'm sure. But Lon was a sharp lad. Too sharp to be hunted down by a pack of grubbers."

The slang caught Joss's interest. "You've been out in the Belts?" he said.

Glyndower nodded, stretched a little. "A year on the off-Jupiter patrol," he said. "Lon was my ship-and-base liaison. I was the suit."

Joss nodded, suddenly very interested indeed. *So Lucretia's picked me to be the brain half of a brain-and-brawn team.* It was a signal that this assignment was likely to be dangerous as well as a cause for career advancement, since the use of suits—powered exoskeleta—was strictly limited to the Solar Police and the various groundbound military organizations. And not every sop got to wear a suit: it took a very particular kind of officer.

"I was in AED," Glyndower said, "in the British part of the EurUnion. Special armed intervention—you know the kind of thing."

Joss nodded, more than slightly impressed. AED, the Armed Enforcement Department of Greater Britain's Ministry of Defense, was descended from a long line of intervention forces with a reputation for toughness and getting the job done. By old tradition, they were the only police force armed in Britain: hence the name. "Why did you leave?" Joss said.

"Mandatory retirement," said Glyndower, with a humorous look. "Yes, at forty. Now who ever heard of such a thing? But they're old-fashioned, some ways, and they never quite believe that time teaches you things that not even a young man's reflexes can make up for." He grinned, and all his face creased itself into a map of smile lines, totally at odds with the rather dour look of him when his face was at rest. "So I took up another line of work."

His face went still again. "In AED," he said, "they

trained us to be loners. You know the line: 'You and your suit can't afford to depend on anyone else.' It took a while for me to start breaking that training. And no sooner do I start to get the hang of it—''

Joss held himself quiet for a moment until Glyndower turned back to him. "Have you ever been in an L5?" he said.

"Not in the line of duty, no. I have a sister who emigrated to *Farflung* about ten years ago: I've visited her there a couple of times." He shrugged a bit. "Didn't care for the feel of the place. A bit too processed for me, it was."

Joss nodded. "Do you mind if I use this?"

"Be welcome."

Joss pulled another light chair over to the infoterminal, pulled the input over and let it take his fingerprints.

"You again," Telya's voice said. "What's all this garbage they sent me for you? Don't tell me you're going to one of those tin cans.''

"All true, I'm afraid."

"I went there on a package tour once," she said. "I was gee-sick all but the last week . . . and when I *could* eat, the food was terrible."

"So I won't eat anything. Have you got a precis of this stuff for me yet?"

"Several, but more are coming. Even *I* can in-key only so fast. What did you want, specifically?"

"A map might be helpful."

"That I have. Here. Evan, did you find everything you needed?"

"Yes, T-*bach.*"

Joss gazed over at Glyndower in interest. He mouthed at him, *You have her too?*

Evan nodded, with a slight rolling of the eyes.

Joss smiled.

The screen flickered to life with a map of Freedom II. It was one of the older L5 colonies, built on the old cylindrical pattern—two-thirds of it solid, one-third transparent, a reinforced "window" to space and the stars. There was an open central core, with an artificial sun to provide UV for the crops growing on the top "inside" layer, and then numerous "downlevels," more or less like an apartment building flattened out and curved into three-quarters of a cylinder. The whole structure was honeycombed with service levels, elevators, escalators, stairways, listed and unlisted accesses. *Not a place to have to be running for your life,* Joss thought.

"I spent some time there while I was at college," Joss said. "It's not exactly one of the best of the L5's any more. The newer ones are quite a bit more expensive to live or run an industry in . . . and only the biggest companies and the wealthiest people, or those with the most valuable talents to offer, can afford to degravitate to them. Now *this* one," and Joss tapped the screen, "has almost paid off its mortgage . . . but it's depreciated pretty badly over the past century. It's the usual thing: a lot of 'deferred maintenance,' or money spent by the maintenance contractors on 'life support' that should have been spent on amenities."

"You mean the contractors were raking off their usual percentage," Glyndower said.

Joss nodded. "The drug companies who moved in there in the mid-2000s are still mostly there. Their office facilities and other properties are all paid for by now, and there's no point in them moving. Their parts of Freedom are supposed to be pretty plush. But the rest of the place . . ." He shrugged. "Businesses just starting up locate there. Some of them are looking for a fast buck. Some of them are there to take advantage of the tax break—"

"Pardon me? 'Fast buck'?"

"Sorry. Fast credit."

Glyndower stretched again. "Oh. —But I take it that the place has become a haven for, ah, low-overhead, high-income businesses."

"Yes. The illicit drug trade is a problem—not as much as it used to be, since space to grow the organics is pretty limited. But custom-designed drugs still keep popping up. Other things—gambling-connected vice, and tax fraud, since the place is a tax haven. And so forth."

Glyndower looked at the map silently for a moment. "Where," he said, "would level twenty-six, corridor A-nineteen be?"

Joss touched the input pad to reduce the map to a cut-away diagram, realized that that wouldn't work, and touched it again to leave it a wire-outline diagram. He touched for the coordinates. One spot, buried far down in the substructure of the L5, began to pulse red.

Glyndower looked at it, his eyes hooded.

Joss breathed out. "Not the best of neighborhoods," he said. "In these places, as a rule, the more money you have, the closer you are to the 'surface.' The less you have, the further down you wind up. And a lot of people born there, working for the companies, don't have enough money to live in the nicer parts of the place . . . or even to leave. Gangs run loose in the underlevels. Freedom's security was never able to do much more than contain the situation."

Glyndower snorted. "You mean, fence the troublemakers down there and keep them from bothering proper folk up in the light and air."

"Something like that." Joss looked away from Glyndower for a moment, having caught a bitter look on the man's face.

But Glyndower was leaning in toward the screen, gazing at it. "Now, Lon, my lad," he said softly, "just what in bloody blue blazes were you doing down there?" Joss said nothing to the rhetorical question, just was quiet, listening to the man's breathing. It was even enough, but there was a raggedness about the edges of it. After a moment Glyndower straightened up and sighed.

"Well, we'll go and find out, shall we?" he said, turning to Joss.

"As soon as we decide we're ready," Joss said. "I want to do some research myself before we go . . . look into your partner's reports and so forth."

"How long will it take you, do you think?"

Joss considered; glanced at Glyndower's eyes.

"Tomorrow, I suspect. The next day, if you're not too rushed."

Glyndower nodded. "Not too much so. I want to get going . . . but on the other hand, my suit has been needing some downtime among techs who know which end of it I sit in. I'd be glad of an extra day to let them work on it."

"No problem with that," Joss said. "I have a flat here, over the other side of the city. Telya's got the address. Care to drop by tomorrow lunchtime? I should be finished with my reading by then."

"Done and done," Glyndower said, and held out his hand again. Joss took it, shook it, felt the strength in it. The man made no attempt to try any of the knuckle-cracking on him that Joss had run into among some other IO's.

Possibly because he knows there's no need, Joss thought. *He could break me in two with just that hand.*

"Tomorrow," Joss said, and went out feeling thoughtful.

HE WAS UP ALL NIGHT DOING HIS RESEARCH. Most of it was the same briefing Glyndower's partner Lon had been given before he left.

There was little enough to go on. It had all started, as Lucretia had mentioned, with complaints from the two big drug companies still quartered on Freedom—BurJohn S.A. and MSD Limited. They were among the forty or fifty remaining companies that still held multinational status under the old pre-unification laws. They were considered sovereign nations, represented in the U.N., and among the community of corporate entities were nearly royalty. Their holdings in almost every country on Earth made them powerful friends and allies, and when they complained, even the Solar Police, who were above politics as a rule, would pause to listen.

There was more to their influence than mere economic necessity, of course. MSD's investment and research over some thirty years had been responsible for the tailoring of the hunter-killer retrovirus that solved the awful auto-immune-deficiency plagues of the early twenty-first century. BurJohn had tailored "Ricketts' Folly," the neo-chlamyd "living gene-splicer" that had been spun off into cures for nearly every kind of cancer known to man. They, and many other drug companies by association, had a reputation now as saviors of humankind. When they complained about something, it was as often guilt or gratitude that caused a nation or another company to give them what they wanted.

BurJohn had started it all, with complaints that someone had been leaking classified information about drug development to one or another of the news services. Normally this would have been something for their own internal security, or the L5's security, to handle. But they proved unable to handle it. Information potentially worth tens of millions of credits was finding its way into the public eye— or worse, into the research departments of other drug companies—with great regularity. If this kind of thing was going on (said BurJohn to the other multinationals, and to the various national governments), then what was happening to *their* communications network could shortly be happening to other companies' nets, or to national banking or intelligence networks.

This caused enough of a ruckus in the U.N. for the Solar Police to find it appropriate to pay attention to the various petitions that made their way into its executive. Though most of Earth's national governments had eventually become subsumed into the supranational structure of the U.N., sharing a common monetary system and legislature (somewhat along the lines of old Great Europe after the EEC), most of them also still kept their own intelligence organizations, cherishing the idea that their *own* spying was better than the homogenized intelligence that came down to them through the U.N. structure. And the thought that intelligence on the "private" national level might be compromised was intolerable.

So EssPat had taken an interest, and had sent Evan's partner Lon Salonikis to look into things. They had wanted him to be inconspicuous, and so had deteamed him from Evan temporarily—a suit was anything but inconspicuous. For a long while there had been no significant results. Lon had taken a position in Freedom II's comms department, and found nothing specific at first—not surprising, since the industry and public usage alone of telecommunications in Freedom generated something like eighty thousand gigabytes of data per day; a haystack if ever one was, and a bad place to be hunting needles. But Salonikis had been carefully chosen, since comms was both a hobby for him, and an old job—he had been a systems designer for UT&T before coming to the Solar Police.

And sure enough, after several months, he had had a small breakthrough. Salonikis had written and hidden away in the L5's packet transmission software a small, unnoticed subroutine that checked the label of every transmission packet—the coded bytes that told the receiving system what alphabetic and numerical characters the packet contained, and how many bytes they totaled—against the number of bytes the packet actually contained. There was already a routine of this sort in the error-correction protocols for transfer between stations, so Lon had little difficulty disguising his mousetrap as part of the larger routine. And after a while, he caught a mouse or two. Packets turned up for transmission Earthside, every couple of weeks, that had an extra forty or fifty bytes apiece added to the end of the declared communications packet—no more than four or five letters' worth. But Lon knew a code group when he saw one. He recorded the code groups about the same time he stopped routing his reports home through the L5's usual connection to comms at EssPat. Then his reports stopped entirely. And then he was killed.

Joss sat back in his chair, home in his flat, late that night, and began to see the point of the weird routing strings on top of his summons from Lucretia. Someone quite knowledgeable had possibly caught Lon at what he was doing . . . and very cleanly, very quickly, had excised him, so that business as usual could continue. Whatever the business was. But EssPat had deemed it best to let the people on Freedom II know, more or less in the clear, that it was not going to let the matter lie.

Joss wasn't exactly ecstatic about that . . . but it made a sort of crooked sense, in that people frantically trying to cover up what they were doing would be that much more likely to make a mistake at the covering. *But still, I'm no comms expert. What does Lucretia expect* me *to do about this situation? Other than investigate it . . . and with a brawn, this time . . .*

He reached out for the cup of tea he had been drinking, found that it was cold, and got up to get some more from the pot. *I suppose I should be flattered,* Joss thought. *All my work so far for the force has been detective work . . . precious little physical stuff.* He made a wry face at himself as he poured his tea. He was as physically proficient as any sop had to be, to become a sop in the first place; all the usual armed and unarmed combat training, self-defense of six or seven different kinds—the whole nine yards. But he disliked using it, and he suspected someone in Assignments, or Lucretia herself, had noticed the preference and had let him work with his brains instead of his guns, whenever possible. Joss had to admit, even to himself, that even as sops went, he was pretty good at figuring things out: a "fixer."

And they want this problem fixed. So they've partnered me . . . with a brawn, to keep me out of trouble. I'm still new enough at all this that Lucretia wants an eye on the rookie. The thought would have annoyed him . . . except that Salonikis, a very talented man indeed from his record, multiply decorated in fact, had not survived his investigation, nor was there any further trace of what he had been working on. His flat had been rifled with unprofessional-looking but extremely professional thoroughness, and all his notes, tapes, and datasolids were gone, or wiped, or trashed. *Why didn't he just dump all his stuff to the network,* Joss thought for the thirtieth time. *This is all going to be a lot harder now. . . .*

Still, if the man had thought that the network itself was somehow being compromised . . . that would have been reason enough. And it was also more than enough reason to send a brain/brawn team along. Anyone who had found a way to break the ciphers and other internal and external security of the system's most secure communications web would gladly kill any number of people to keep the secret . . . or to keep the sops from doing something about it. Solving the situation was probably going to require a good deal of muscle. And that meant a suit.

Joss sat down at his terminal again and smiled at the

compliment that Lucretia had paid him. Being teamed with a brawn was quite a plum. On the other hand, in this particular case, he felt somewhat outclassed by the brawn.

He touched the input pad of the terminal and brought up Evan's record again. It was innocent enough in its early days: born and raised in Wales, a stockbroker's son, of all things—good enough in school to win a Treaty Organization scholarship to any university he fancied. Instead he went into the groundbound police, taking his degrees in sociology and police science in his spare time, via Open University courses. His commanding officers spotted his talent quickly: he rose through the ranks until AED noticed him. There he had found his niche.

Joss breathed out a small breath of laughter at the casual way Evan had mentioned his AED time, as if it was nothing special. But Evan's record mentioned Falklands III, and Prince Willems Land, and the Cap Uprising, and Bradford, and several other nasty criminal interventions, including the hostage situation in Southwark, almost the last of its kind on Earth, in which at first a whole building, then a whole city was held for ransom . . . and both were freed without any loss of life except among the terrorists. Every one of them had been killed, with a thoroughness which the local media had tried (not too successfully) to conceal, and which had been said to be a contributing factor in the great lessening of terrorism in that part of the world thereafter. Evan had led that assault, and had been chief among the tacticians who designed it.

And they retired him, Joss thought, shaking his head. And wondering a little. There had been an investigation after the Southwark siege. No one had had anything but good to say about the AED men involved in it. At that point in time, no one would have dared. After all, Evan and three other men had been awarded the O.B.E. for their part in the business. But then he and one other of them had been offered retirement. With pensions, of course, and with full honors, and completely voluntary— All the same, there were indications in the report that came out of the inquiry that some people in government were somewhat . . . *disturbed* by the relish that some of the AED people seemed to have shown when dealing with the terrorists. *Idiots,* Joss thought. *What were they supposed to do? Apologize to the terrorists as they killed them? Shoot them more in sorrow than in anger? The sons of bitches were prepared to nuke the city!* But it seemed possible, from that aspect of Evan's career, that one could do a job too well for the liking of one's political masters. Or had there been some fear in high places that such a hero, if left in civil service, might step too easily into one of *their* jobs? At any rate, Joss made a mental note to be very careful with "knight in shining armor" jokes around this man.

Joss paged down through the record. After the Solar Police recruited him—a matter of days—he had risen quickly through their ranks as well. No surprise there. There weren't anywhere near enough sops to do all the jobs that needed doing, and a man with Evan's brains and—admit it, ruthlessness—was too good to leave managing inner-planet customs or otherwise patrolling a desk. There were places in the solar system where ruthlessness was badly needed . . . there being so much of it running loose already.

So Evan had been in the Belts, hunting down claim-jump killers; and out around Uranus, looking into corporate racketeering in the methane-mining business; and on Mars, where he had helped break up a ring of thieves and blackmailers who had been preying on archaeological sites— Joss shook his head. This was high-powered company . . . and someone very good to have at your back in a nasty situation.

Which, he rather suspected, was where they were headed. . . .

I hope I can bring something *useful to this team,* he thought. *Glyndower must think I'm fairly wet behind the ears.* . . . But Joss *did* have the advantage of knowing Freedom II fairly well—both its physical layout and the psychology of the place, which was not nearly as straight-forward or easily understood as the rough-and-tumble of the asteroid Belts. *I won't be* completely *a rookie.*

He breathed out and tapped the pad one more time to bring up the picture that had been haunting him these past few hours: Salonikis, lying there crumpled in the cramped little downlevel corridor, after his killers had finished with him. The state in which his body had been left was plainly meant as a warning. Joss recognized some of the tribe marks that he had heard rumors about in college—ritual mutilations that meant one gang in particular was responsible for a murder. Apparently the tradition was still in force.

Joss hit the pad one last time to turn the terminal off. Here, of course, was the problem they warned every sop about in training: confusing which was more important—the assignment itself, or the fact that it had killed a fellow sop. The rage that came up at seeing something like that burned, torn shape on the corridor floor, was a tool, nothing more, toward solving the crime. It was a sop's business to make sure that it stayed that way, and well out of the range of vendetta.

Of course, it was also the sop's business to make sure that the idea of someone wanting to do the same to *him,* or *her,* didn't interfere with his investigation. The instructors had only been able to offer suggestions about how to manage that. It had not been one of the areas at which Joss had excelled so far.

He suspected he was going to get some practice.

EVAN CAME BY THE NEXT MORNING, AND THEY went over the information together, trying to arrive at some plan of attack. The problem (as Evan admitted to Joss immediately) was that Salonikis had left them very little to go on. There was really nothing to do, he agreed, but go up to Freedom, settle in, and start looking around. Through the whole morning, he deferred so consistently to Joss's opinions that Joss began to wonder whether something was extremely wrong. *What* have *they been telling him about me?* he wondered. But those grey eyes gave nothing away. They agreed to leave for Freedom the next day, and off Glyndower went, in something of a rush, Joss thought.

He spent the day packing what he thought he would need for an extended stay—after all, Salonikis had been in the place three months, and apparently had only begun to scratch the surface. Their stay wouldn't be all work, of course. There would be some time for recreation. And EssPat encouraged its independent operatives to have hobbies, the more the merrier, especially when their work was likely to take them out into space for extended periods. Not even the stabilization conditioning given to IO's as preparation for teaming could do much about the boredom that could set in while sitting a stakeout somewhere past Jupiter in a two-man ship.

Joss was fond of history. He had quite a collection of vidsolids, many of them holding archive-quality transfers of entertainments that few people alive had ever heard of, and that even fewer could understand. In among his leisure clothes were packed twenty or thirty of these; old "video" and "cable" entertainments, and some actually dubbed straight from mechanical film or tape. Wrapped in his spare uniform tunic was his viewer—professional quality, simply the best that money could buy, and certainly too expensive for even someone with *his* salary. Maura had teased him unmercifully about it, and until he had learned to tease her back about her needlepoint, and call her a throwback, he had had no peace. He found himself wondering idly, as he snugged the last few solids into place inside his spare boots, whether she was having any trouble getting that special crewel yarn out to Pluto.

A few taped journals went in on top of everything else. Joss had found in college that he had a flair for chemistry, leaning slightly toward the organic. His Lunar rock-collecting was a gesture towards keeping that interest alive. There had always been something fascinating for him, a hint of mystery, about the slight traces of organic compounds to be found in many extraterrestrial bodies. His interest in the Martian archaeological digs was more in terms of fossilized amino acids than in the hope of finding any artifacts. There wasn't going to be a lot of biogeology to do on an L5, but he could at least have his mail forwarded, and keep up with developments while he was gone.

And that was all there was to his packing. Their shuttle was due to leave around noon the next day. Joss went to bed early, got up early, and was uniformed when the door spoke to him.

"Glyndower—"

"Come on in," he said—and a giant entered.

He nearly dropped his last cup of tea onto his packed luggage; it squeaked and sidled over a foot or so to avoid the spillage. Joss had seen powered suits before, but never one quite like this. Most exosuits left some part of the wearer showing—arms and legs, mostly, exposed between the skeletal braces. This suit, though, looked all like one smooth shell—a matte-gloss carapace, solid graflar from the looks of it, with a dark gunmetal sheen. From helm to boots it was at least seven feet tall, perhaps a bit more. The upper-arm and leg armor seemed contoured to Glyndower's own muscle shape, which was impressive enough: the armor carapace increased the effect impressively. But the forearms were at least twice the thickness of Evan's, and there were smooth coverts at the end of down-jutting fairings that started at the elbow and ended an inch or so behind the wrists. The chest-shell was a smooth grey expanse broken only by a Solar Police badge that seemed to have been done in graflar to match the rest of the armoring . . . which made sense: it would have been ironic to have your badge be the most vulnerable part of your uniform. The suit helmet was one shining featureless curve of grey mirror—until suddenly it depolarized and the bottom half of it slipped up into the upper half.

Glyndower was grinning at him. "Man," he said, "you look like you're seeing ghosts. How about my new paint job, then?"

Joss laughed and put his teacup in the dish-handler to be cleaned and racked. "I thought graflar armor was supposed to be indestructible."

"Oh, no," Evan said, "if you get in the way of a carbon asteroid, you can be scratched up pretty fair. Some of those things are full of industrial-grade diamond. Bolts and slugs, those are problems too. Bad for the surface coating . . . ruins the looks." He grinned.

Joss shrugged into his uniform jacket and sealed it, glancing up and down at the suit. "You're not that tall," he said.

Glyndower lifted one of the boots, peering at it. "I know," he said. "It's all negative-feedback sensors and gyros and gravity compensators."

"Elevator shoes," Joss said, picking up the remote tag for his luggage.

"What?"

"Never mind."

"Here, I'll take that," Glyndower said, reaching for the luggage.

"No, it's all—"

Glyndower picked up the luggage and its carrier, which had to mass eighty kilos at least, and tucked it all under one arm. "Do tell it to stop kicking, man," he said, as the luggage carrier's little feet scrabbled helplessly in the air for a foothold. Joss made a wry look and deactivated the carrier. The legs slumped with a reproachful little sighing noise of relaxing servos.

"Ready?" Glyndower said.

"Yup."

Joss locked the place up, patted the doorsill goodbye, and together they headed out into the public corridors leading to the shuttle pads. He couldn't quite stop looking at the suit as they went. But then neither could anyone else, it seemed. Evan strode along like a giant with a toy suitcase under his arm, and people passing by on the slide-walks stared. Joss had a flash of feeling small and childish—a slight figure accompanying its huge armored daddyfigure out on a walk. But that feeling was something that the instructors had warned them about in training, too. Joss put it aside for the moment.

"Correct me if I'm wrong," he said, "but that's not a standard sop-issue suit, is it?"

"Indeed, no," Glyndower said as he strode along. "They haven't anything this good, in my opinion. Which is doubtless biased." That incongruous grin spread over his face again. "No, when they retired me, I managed to extract a few perks from them. They owed me that much. I told them I wanted to keep my AED suit. Oh, they made a mighty fuss, but when they found out that the Solar Pacification Treaty Organization wanted me"—and he pronounced the words in a tone half relish, half scorn at *them*—"then the Powers that Were said, Ah, well, nothing but the best for our Evan: let him take it. And so they did." There was a momentary frown. "After they stripped it, of course."

Joss's eyebrows went up. " 'Stripped it'? You had *more* guns in that thing than you have now?"

Evan threw Joss a sidelong look. "All I have at the moment," he said, "are two powerguns and an autocannon. And barely enough ammunition for that, let me tell you. And then this useless little substances storage—" He nodded at the hump on his back. "Heaven forbid I should need to carry more than a quart of alcohol, or acid, or tear gas." He frowned—then his face lightened, as if considering better days. "Now I *had,*" he said, lowering his voice conspiratorially, "a two terawatt GE particle-beamer, *and* a flame thrower, *and* a Vulcan-Gatling minicannon—oh, a nice little tool that was. You could open an armored vehicle like a tin of cocoa. Three thousand rounds a minute, and only a hundred and ten kilos with the cooling system and all."

"Nice," Joss said, slightly stunned at the idea of a man carrying around his own particle-beam weapon, let alone can-opening an unsuspecting tank. He had known such things existed, but it was different meeting someone who had used them.

"And the sensor array I had then," Evan went on. "The invisible-spectrum stuff—ah, it doesn't bear thinking of. They took it all out. Said they had to insist that the off-planet equipment-parity agreements be enforced. Bah." Joss had to smile; he had never heard anyone say "bah" before, outside of one of the old vids he had, something called *A Christmas Carol.* "So here I am in this monkey version of a real suit," Evan said. "Ah, well, I suppose it's well enough for where we're going."

"I certainly hope so," Joss said. "Strikes me that you could knock over a building with that kind of firepower."

Evan shot him a glance that looked, to Joss, slightly guarded. "Muscles might be enough," he said. "It would depend on the building."

Joss nodded.

Definitely, he thought, *a good man to have beside you in a bad place. Except for the ricochets . . .*

They got off the slidewalk and walked through the airlock of the departures dome for the shuttle pads. It was only a moment's work to confirm their identities and bookings to the people at the ticket counter and for Evan to hand over the luggage and its somnolent carrier. Then they waited for boarding. The shuttle sitting outside the clear dome was the standard dual-purpose beast that ran the triangular routes, Moon-Earth-space station. Chemical engines for the close maneuvering work, cyclonic "sublight" engines for the longer hauls—and aerodynamically designed for landing, the delta-wing design that had barely changed since the mid-twentieth century. This one was in the silver and red TPA livery, and sat there desultorily venting liquid nitrogen from the attitude jets' nozzles on its sides, while the cargo and baggage handlers tended to it.

Joss yawned a bit, as cover for noticing all the fascinated stares at Glyndower. "You seem to be attracting a lot of interest," he remarked.

"A good thing, do you think?" Glyndower said, glancing around.

"Someone knows we're coming anyway," Joss said. Lucretia saw to that. "No harm in word getting around a bit, I suppose."

"I wonder," Glyndower said, and gazed out at the shuttle being loaded.

Joss, itching with the stares *he* was getting, wondered too.

SHE WAS AT WORK WHEN SHE STARTED TO DIE.

She might have missed the early symptoms entirely, except that she had happened to miss breakfast that morning, and her blood sugar was a little on the low side. That was the reason she gave herself, at first, when she began to feel a little down, a little tired, just before the halfshift break. She paused just long enough to rummage around in her bag for a wrapped sweet; found one—rather grimy and crumpled, since it had probably been in there for about a month—and popped it absently into her mouth while she turned back to her work.

Her job had always been an absorbing one. That was why she had started using, originally; she began to dislike the fact that mere paperpushing was so absorbing. She had heard from some friends about hyper—how it gave you time to do other things while still getting your work done . . . getting it done better than before, in fact. The stuff was fairly expensive, but she had run out of interesting things to spend her money on a long time ago.

It had been a good move. Everything was interesting, now, and her life had become neatly divided into smoothly-working halves: the part that ran on automatic, and the part that sat back and assessed. The automatic part of her did her job with embarrassing ease. It was depressing, in retrospect, how much time she had used to spend wondering what comm call to make, how to make a set of work schedules come out right, how to get the computer to do what she wanted it to do. Now all that simply seemed to take care of itself, leaving her delightfully free to watch everything else.

And everything meant more. She understood, now, every casual frown of Carl's across the room, as he took calls from supervisors and employees, and she could reason out every word of the conversations on the other end of the line, just from his replies, even though his comm circuit was hushed. She could tell from a twitch of an eyelid what was going on in her boss Harv's mind, every dull or ambitious or lecherous thought—the ugly old pig. She could predict within a few minutes what files were going to turn up on her terminal, which employee was going to get called on the carpet, who was due for a raise, and why he would get it, or not, depending on whether her boss had had any the night before, or would have any tonight, or next week. The right two rumors put together could tell her how work in the office would be for the next month. And the delight of it was that no one else knew . . . and no one else suspected that she did. She sat on her own comfortable little promontory of the mind and watched all the people she worked with, watched their little doings, the toy loves and hates that possessed them so. And she was tempted sometimes to laugh, but she never did. It might have given the game away.

It was true enough that sometimes those same loves and hates started to weary her inexpressibly. At such times it all seemed so futile—a waste of time; waste motion that the people around her were all going through with such laughable passion. Couldn't they see that every motion, every word, was mandated by one before—a word of their own or of someone else's, uttered either immediately before, or days, weeks, earlier? Apparently they couldn't. At times like that there was nothing to do but up the dosage. Then things began to mean more deeply again, and the interest came back into watching the game, and the automatic part of her became so swift and sure at what it was doing that there was more and more time for her to spend observing the foibles of those around her.

Today, though, she had a headache, and that by itself was unusual. It had been a long time since she had last been sick; when she was interested in what was going on, she had no time for sickness and rode her body over and through whatever minor malaises it tried to inflict on her. The sweet seemed not to be helping particularly, either. Perhaps she should just take the day off, go home, have a little extra, and come back tomorrow when things were working correctly again.

"You all right, Joanna?" Carl said to her, from down by his desk. She looked at him, surprised that it seemed to take a slight effort—even more surprised that she actually had to make a conscious effort to do it. Usually the automatic part of her handled all her conversation with her fellow workers, while the rest of her sat back and enjoyed the deeper nuances of the interactions, reading their thoughts through their expressions, and being amused by them. But now she looked at Carl, and not only did no quick, witty answer come out without her needing to prompt it, but she couldn't even think of one—

"You okay?" he said. "You look kind of pale."

She opened her mouth, and nothing came out.

It was happening. It had happened once before, a flash of incompetence like this, but that had gone right away again—a horrible moment that had caused her to go straight home and increase the dosage considerably. But there was no way to do that right now. Or yes, there was; she could say she wasn't feeling well, she could just get up and head back to her flat, surely she could hold out for the half hour it would take her to get there—

Nothing would come out of her mouth, but that was the least of the horror beginning to run through her in time with her quickening pulse. The moment wasn't passing, wasn't getting better. What had happened before, was continuing this time. She was losing it. It was going. She could literally feel the clarity going out of the way she saw things, the enlightenment leaving her, seeping away like blood from a wound. She was losing it, once and for all. She was becoming as she had been before, before she had taken it even once—horrible thought. These days she hardly remembered that time before the division of herself, when she had no idea what someone was going to say before they said it, when work occupied her, even tired her out. When she was lonely and wanted something to take her mind off things, to keep her from thinking about herself. But now Carl was staring at her, was getting up from his seat and coming toward her, and she couldn't imagine what he was about to do or say—

It was draining out of her: all the omniscience, the power, the cool objectivity, the *knowing*. Her mind was snow in the sun, melting away under the office lights, thought and will sublimating off the way she had seen frost evaporate off the fiver's outside walls in vacuum. And not painlessly. She felt it going, felt every scruple of herself boiling off against the terrible growing heat inside her. Time sense going, memory, even recognition of the faces now crowding over her—she was on the floor: how had she gotten here?—everything was going but the horror. That grew worse and worse. Something was wrong, terribly wrong, and she couldn't tell what. Why couldn't she think of anything? What was the matter with her? Where was she? And who was that screaming, and why wouldn't they stop?

Why wouldn't they stop?

The screaming rose to a crescendo as she stared into

the lights. And then mercifully, an end to screaming, an end to the hammering in her ears, whatever it was—

Who was she? *What* was she?

Besides dead—

THEY CAME INTO FREEDOM FROM THE USUAL tourist-oriented angle: around from the nightside, so that the occulted Sun burst out from behind the glass of the L5's sky-window in diffracted rainbows, and searing-cool white light flooded out over everything, making the place look considerably newer than it really was. There was a slight patter of applause from some of the people further up in the cabin.

"Package tour, probably," Joss said under his breath.

Glyndower grunted. "They'll find out the rude truth soon enough," he said.

Docking took another ten minutes or so. Joss looked the place over from the outside, having more and more misgivings every minute. He remembered having come here at the start of college, all those years ago it seemed— only about seven, really—and being struck by how nice the place looked from space, how sleek it was, how it shone. Now he was none too sure about the validity of that impression. He could see outer panels that looked broken or burnt or seemed to be made of pieces of several panels welded together. Some of the window side of the L5 had been patched with opaque panels, making the place look something like pictures he had seen of the roofs of old-fashioned railway stations in poor repair. *Certainly it wasn't in* this *bad a shape when I was here last. Or was I just too starry-eyed to see it at all? It's hard to believe a place can get so run-down in seven years—*

The docking itself was a leisurely affair, as the shuttle aligned itself opposite to the zero-gee reception area at one end of the L5 and matched rotations with it, then eased into the docking clamps. Evan was levering himself up out of his seat well before the "unfasten your harnesses" announcement had been made. Joss went after him, saying under his breath, "You're not setting a good example for the passengers, you know."

"Ah," Evan said, "perhaps *you* should do that thing, and arrest me, eh?"

Joss followed Evan to the airlock, not quite certain for the moment just how hard his leg was being pulled, or whether humor had even been intended. The shuttle cabin crew who were undoing the pressure lock looked at Evan, or rather at his suit, and hurried rather faster with the undoing.

The lock swung open into the usual fiberglass and rubber transfer tunnel, the chase lights embedded in its floor and ceiling pointing the way down into the L5's reception area, as if there were anywhere else to go. Joss kicked himself over to one of the sets of handropes and began pulling himself along. Evan came after him. It was about a fifty yards' haul down to the other end. Behind them the chatter of tourists began to fill the tube.

"Somehow I never thought of this place as being somewhere one would go for entertainment," Evan said. "To live and work, perhaps—not that I would do such a thing myself. But for a holiday?" He shook his head.

"They're here for the casinos, mostly," Joss said. "No stranger than going to Las Vegas used to be. There was nothing else to do there, either."

"Where?"

"Las Vegas. It was out in the desert in western North America. The casinos did what the ones here do—they made it easy to get to and cheap to stay in, so that the gamblers were attracted there."

Evan lifted his eyebrows as they exited the tube into the large spherical room that housed the L5's immigrations control area. "Not for me," he said. "I can think of better places to holiday."

"Wales?" Joss said.

Evan glanced at him as they kicked themselves over toward one of the immigrations stations guywired across the center of the room. "Have you ever been there?" he said.

"No. London, yes, and Scotland."

Evan shook his head slightly. "Parts of Scotland are a little like. But north Wales—" He smiled, just slightly.

"Not as quiet as it was in the old days, I hear, but it's a nice place for peace, regardless. —Good morning, sir. Or whatever it is by you this time of day."

The immigrations officer, a young blond uniformed man with a large nose and a bored look, glanced at their badges, said, "Afternoon, actually, but it's nice to see you, too. Is this business or pleasure?"

"Business, I'm afraid," Joss said.

"Hope you find what you're looking for," said the man, coming up with something that at first sight looked like a large pen, but on closer examination turned out to be a chip-foil applicator. "This will give you unlimited exit and reentry privileges at the automatic gates and locks— you don't have to bother with us again till the next visit. Where do you want it?"

"On the badge, please," Joss said, and the man shoved the nose of the applicator gun up against Joss's badge, then removed it. The foil of the pinhead electronic visa flattened itself to the badge and clung by its electrostatic charge as if it were part of it. "And you, sir?"

"Is that bulletproof?" Evan inquired.

"Uh, I don't know," said the immigrations man. Joss thought to himself that it was probably the first time he had ever been asked such a question.

"Here, then," Evan said, and tapped the underside of his left upper arm. The immigrations officer tapped the pen there, looking slightly dubious.

"Thank you kindly," Evan said, and floated on past.

Joss smiled pleasantly at the young man, and then kicked off to sail through the air after Evan. "You did that on purpose," he said, not very loud, and trying to keep from laughing.

"One must encourage a proper respect for the law," Evan said, and made for the opposite airlock.

Just beyond it was another spherical room, smaller this time, with a schematic map of the station. They paused to examine it. "Here we are," Joss said, touching the scratched spot on the illuminated glass where thousands of others had done the same thing. "Take a lift down to the six o'clock slide level, then one of the high-speed slidewalks through the fields, then the escalator up to the administration level.''

They kicked off toward the lift. " 'The fields'?'' Evan said.

"Farmland," Joss said, touching the callpad for the lift. "You noticed how the cylinder of the fiver is divided up into slices, the short way. They're all separate pressures—this one was built while they were still seriously worried about the whole structure explosively decompressing. The outer slices are noisier, because of the closeness of the lifesupport plants and the engine assemblies, so they made them agricultural instead of residential.''

" 'The fields','' Evan said, not sounding too convinced, as they bounced into the lift. "Without gravity?''

"Light gravity, at least," Joss said. "Some things do a lot better at one-tenth gee. There are a few things they grow here that are really worth eating—you should see the tomatoes they grow in the uplevels. This big—''

Evan looked at Joss with an expression partaking as much of distaste as disbelief. "They probably taste like water balloons.''

"They do not. See, they get so much UV that it keeps them from taking up water the way they usually do—''

They began to sink to the floor as the lift settled out of the zero-gee core area and into those levels where the spin began to have some effect. Evan was still shaking his head. "You've got some convincing to do," he said. "A farm ought to have the sky over it.''

"These do—''

"But then again, you were raised on the Moon—this probably seems all right to you." Joss glanced up at the odd tone in the voice. Pity? Was that it? Difficult to believe in a man who came across so hard, so self-sufficient. *And I'm not sure I want his pity, regardless—*

Easy. Easy. "To each his own," Joss said as they got out of the lift and headed for the slidewalk. There weren't many people on the 'walk just now, but just about all of them were wearing either light skintight coveralls, to protect them from whatever work they had recently been doing, or else were dressed in the very light clothes that a permanently climate-controlled environment made practical—halfplants and singlets, or brief-body drapes, or short skintights in the alternating transparent/mirror metallics that were back in this year as part of the nostalgia craze. Those who passed them going the other way stared at Evan as if he was from Mars: which, Joss had to admit, was certainly a possibility.

"How do you get used to it?" he said.

"What?"

"The staring."

Evan glanced sideways at him, and after a moment, that grin spread over his face again. "You know something? Sometimes I don't. Sometimes I put the visor down and stare back, and never mind them twitching when I do it."

Joss chuckled. "I can see your point."

Evan nodded. After a moment he said, "They try to decondition you to it, in training. It never really works, I don't think. It never did for me, at any rate. And I'm not sure it's wise. Staring is a threat display, after all; even when it's innocuous like this. No use in purposely turning off one of your own warning systems . . ."

They changed slidewalks to an express lane and were whisked past more fields, all curving upward on both sides to a horizon several miles away: wheat, this time, actually waving in a huge fan-generated breeze, but wheat at about six different stages in its growing season, from seedlings barely a third of a meter high to golden stalks easily as tall as a man. Evan raised his eyebrows. "Wouldn't that have made them talk at home."

"It's the gravity again."

Evan nodded. "What do you think," he said, "killed my partner?"

Joss stared at him for a moment, thrown by the sudden leap of subject. "I think," he said, "that he got too close to the cause of the communications leaks. Maybe even the source of them. Or else that somehow—" he thought for a moment, since he wasn't too sure about this himself— "he stumbled onto something even more sensitive, more dangerous, than the leaks—"

"Something he wasn't expecting at all. Something that took him completely by surprise." Evan nodded slowly. "So that the people who killed him did so, perhaps, more

out of shock reaction than anything else. But they are
warned, now. And they know we're coming. They will
have had time to figure out what to do about us . . . or to
start figuring it out.''

Joss nodded. ''Looks that way to me.'' He glanced
around him and sighed as the slidewalk took them through
one of the major separation baffles between sections. The
next field was miles and miles of sweet corn, only the top
layer of fifty or sixty, Joss knew: the most intensively
farmed, as opposed to the lower, hydroponic levels for
less demanding cash crops. ''I'd be tempted,'' he said,
''to go off on a bit of a wild goose chase at first, so that
they can write us off as hopeless . . . before we start becoming busy with what we're really here for. Finding the
source of those leaks . . . but more to the point, finding
Lon's notes and records.''

''If they still exist,'' Evan said.

''If.''

They watched the green corn go by in silence for another mile or so. ''I'm with you,'' Evan said at last.
''Heaven knows, there have been dumb cops before. Let
it be so again.'

''For the moment.''

Evan grinned. It was not the usual grin. Joss took one
look at it and glanced away, hoping not to see it again too
soon.

They hit the slidewalk transfer at the end of the agricultural space and paused while Joss glanced around, trying to get his bearings. When he had been here in college,
the transfer area had been a sort of bare staging point for
six of the long multi-stage escalators used for transfer between levels in the center section. Now someone seemed
to have erected a sort of bazaar around and under the various escalator piers. Tents and awnings were everywhere,
sheltering small collections of tables where people were
selling jewelry, artwork, handmade clothing, food, drink,
old solids and tapes, all manner of junk. People with the
general newness of clothing that said *tourist* were moving
among the booths, buying, chatting, browsing.

''That one,'' Joss said finally, picking an escalator. They

got onto it, and Evan looked down as they rode up past the gaudy collection of tents. "Thieves' market," he said.

"Yes," Joss said, leaning over and looking down, too. "At least three pickpockets working down there."

Evan snorted. "Not what I meant. It used to be our old world at home for a market selling things no one would want to buy, only steal for a joke. They sell junk, play to the tourists . . . give them something picturesque and useless to take home with them." Evan frowned a bit. "But markets like that tend to be a symptom of places that aren't producing much that people really want, any more."

Joss thought about that for a moment. "Could be—"

"Is there a customs break for souvenirs here? You know, the kind of law that lets you bring home extra goods in excess of your allowance if you also bring back something that was manufactured here?"

"As a matter of fact," Joss said, "there is."

Evan leaned on the banister of the escalator as it flattened out briefly at one of the lower uplevels, to let people get on and off from the sides. 'Used to be something of the sort out in the Belts," he said. "A pitiful sight it was. Old men and women—miners, finders, pilots, you name it—had a market like that under an old beat-up dome on Eos. Selling the damndest worthless junk you ever saw. Or not selling it. Half the time, just sitting there, living in hope, waiting for the tourists." He frowned again. " 'Come see the wild rough-and-tumble world of the meteor-miner, the last frontier,' " he said, bitter mimicry of some voice Joss suspected he had heard and hated a long time ago. " 'Take home a memento of the untamed Outer Reaches, where men are men and'—aah, the hell with it anyway."

Joss nodded, looking upward and feeling uncomfortable. His memories of Freedom as clean and vital and lively kept jarring against the—admit it—*seediness* he kept seeing now, like the ends of a broken bone. He kept seeing stained and broken panels or floor sections, mostly poorly mended; dirt where dirt had never used to be; a faint bad smell in the air, as if the air conditioning was malfunctioning. He was becoming embarrassed. Granted, these were just the first few minutes of the visit. There had to be parts of the station that were in better repair. But first impressions were important, they had always said in training, more important than anyone ever suspected, and generally very much to be trusted, along with hunches. A sop had hunch training as well, though Joss had trouble trusting his. "You're too fond of logic for your own good," one of his instructors had told him. But now his logic was hiding behind embarrassment and a vague feeling of unease.

"Are you nervous?" he said suddenly to Evan.

"Pardon?"

Joss felt himself going red—the one tendency of his that he would have loved to be able to discipline out, and never could. "Do your hunches run in harness?" he said, using the phrase that his instructors used to use.

Evan looked at him for a long moment, and Joss was about to start going redder still when he said, "Sometimes they do. The *hywi,* they called it at home: not so much a hunch as a foreknowing."

"Is it ever any use to you?"

Evan breathed out, "Not at work, very much," he said. "Sometimes at the races. What's your hunch saying to you, then?"

Joss shook his head. "I'm not sure. But I don't like it a bit."

"Nor I," Evan said, "trapped in this great bloody orbiting tin like cat's meat waiting for the cat." Joss looked at him with a touch of surprise. "Well, think about it," Evan said. "If we have to run, we haven't a craft of our own to do it in, have we? There'd best be a shuttle in port when shooting starts . . . that's all I can say."

More people jostled onto the escalator with them, one level below the administrative offices. "I thought you could button that thing up and do just fine in vacuum," Joss said. "Attitude jets and all."

Evan leaned over toward him, leaned over him, actually, a great bulk of shining grey mass and weaponry, so that people standing near them edged away. "Joss, my lad," he said, whispering amiably, "you may be a low-gee-raised, bird-boned, weedy little wet of a baby rookie sop, but I wouldn't leave even you here with the people who did what they did to Lon. And even if I liked you much better than I do, I'd hesitate to try to fit you in here with me. Some bits would have to come off, probably bits you would want again later. So,'' he said, standing straight again, and speaking in a more normal tone of voice, ''keep the shuttle schedules in mind, eh?''

Joss nodded, externally smiling a bit, but internally starting to compose a very sharp note to Lucretia.

''Is this where we get off?'' Evan said innocently.

''Yes, indeed,'' Joss said, and led the way.

The administration level was the only place Joss had seen so far that did anything to tone down that feeling of seediness. It was plush: carpeting instead of tile or composite floor panels, wall hangings or textured wall coverings instead of extruded panelling with the color or pattern molded in. Big open-plan work areas were scattered across the level, which stood above all the other levels in the central area, an island in the sky, but an island a mile long and two miles wide, with little private office complexes built onto it like cottages. Over the curvature of it, eighty stories up, the black of space all lit with stars shone down through the huge sky-window.

Joss stopped a passing civil servant—the man had that bored, well-fed, job-guaranteed look about him—and got directions to the Station Administrator's office. Evan stared genially at the man, causing him to leave them at about three times the speed he had originally been travelling when Joss had stopped him. ''Now I must say,'' Evan said to Joss after a moment, ''that I would have gone to see the station police first.''

Joss shook his head. ''We start at the top,'' he said, ''and work down.'' He glanced sidewise at Evan. ''If you're right about—your conjecture—it seems to me that our friend might have come to grief amongst higher echelons than the police suspected—or would have been wise to. Me, I'd just as soon they had a chance to become nervous immediately, by seeing us right away.''

''You mean by seeing me,'' Evan said.

''And your grey flannel suit,'' Joss said. ''You betchum, Red Ryder.''

''Pardon?''

"Later."

They walked into the Station Administrator's office to find the place in a panic. The office, at least the ground floor of it, took up a whole one of those smaller "cottages" built on the administration island; and hardly a desk or console in the whole place was occupied by someone working. Well-dressed people stood around in little knots, talking in hushed voices, and looking fairly nervous already. Some of them turned when Joss and Evan came in the door, and the silence that fell over the closest groups spread to the farther ones until the whole place was quiet as a morgue. *And that's what's happened,* Joss thought. *Someone's dropped dead here. Within the last hour, I bet. Interesting—*

A subdued young red-headed secretary in conservatively dark business skintights came up to them. "You're here about Joanna Mallory?" he said.

"Among other things," Joss said. "O'Bannion, Glyndower, Solar Police."

"Yes, officers, please come this way. . . ."

The young man headed off toward a plush-looking cubicle with a door. Every head in the place turned as they walked toward it. The secretary was babbling something about the station police being here shortly, their full cooperation . . . Joss nodded absently, glancing around at people, trying to get first impressions of them. Mostly they turned away with the guilty looks of people who suspect they're about to be implicated in a crime which they did not commit, but which will serve to expose various things they *have* done wrong, and probably get them fired.

The glass door of the cubicle opened for them. It was a small office within the office, really, with two desks and a data console and some file storage cabinets; all depressingly clean and tidy to Joss's way of thinking. He hadn't seen the surface of his own desk for months. Three people were standing in the corner of the office, as far from one of the desks as they could get. One person was lying on the floor, staring sightlessly at the ceiling, limbs splayed out in positions that no human being holds for long without being dead. She was well dressed, well shaped, a handsome young woman, except when you took into the account the look on her face.

"I see," Joss said, though he didn't in the slightest. He had learned early on that confidence, or at least the appearance of it, produced better results in an investigation than careful repetitions of "I don't know." He bent down over the body and checked it rapidly for pulse—because you never could tell—and then for rigor, discoloration, temperature, and the other usual signs. "About twenty minutes ago," he said, glancing up at Evan. Then he looked up at the oldest and most conservatively dressed of the three people standing there, a woman in her middle forties, who would have been strikingly pretty with her long silver hair and her cool, almost sculptured-looking face, except that the face was distorted with anger.

"Drugs?" he said to her.

Her face got even angrier. Joss forestalled the outburst, getting up and holding out his hand to her. "I'm sorry," he said. "One mustn't forget the courtesies. Joss O'Bannion, Solar Police. This is my partner Evan Glyndower." All eyes flicked to the suit rather than to Evan's face, reacting immediately with the nervous tic Joss was coming to recognize, something about not liking the number and size of the guns on it. Joss thought to himself that if enough people reacted that way, the guns would never have to be fired. This struck him as a good thing, though he also had to wonder why Greater Britain had any criminals left in it at all, considering that the guns Evan *had* had were apparently three times bigger and more ferocious-looking than these.

"Yes, we were expecting you," the woman said, taking Joss's hand. *Firm grip,* Joss thought. *Assertive without being aggressive. Dry palms.* "I'm Dorren Orcieres," she said, "head of PR for Freedom."

"Ahh," Joss said. "Damage control."

She still looked irritated, but less so. "Yes, I'm afraid so. This is something of an embarrassment to us."

Yes, it would be, when someone in the equivalent of the corporate headquarters keels over and dies of a drug overdose in the middle of the workday.

"We're of course eager that this investigation should be conducted with as much discretion as possible—"

So as not to spook the tourists, Joss thought. "Of course—we'll want to work closely with you and your own police. I haven't seen anything that makes me think we would have to suspend local jurisdiction and invoke Solar."

The lady flinched just a bit, then calmed again. Joss noted the reaction for future consideration. "I take it your own medical services have been here," he said.

"They're on the way. So are the police."

Joss restrained himself from raising his eyebrows. Since when did it take a medical team twenty minutes to get anywhere inside an L5? Another bad sign.

"You mentioned you were expecting us—," Joss said to Ms. Orcieres.

"Yes," she said, "we heard from EssPat. I understand one of your people had an accident here. We'll do our best to be of help to you."

Joss nodded, keeping the look casual, even more casual than hers, while at the same time remembering the picture of Lon's body when it had been found, and wondering whether this woman had even seen it. Of course, she had to have, if she was PR. He wondered how someone could be so cool about a murder that had looked like that. But doubtless it was part of PR's business to keep the gang situation under wraps, too, or at least to minimize it for the benefit of the tourists. *Though how much benefit it'll be if some of them stray into places they shouldn't be, and get themselves killed—*

The door to the office opened and the medical people came in all in a rush: two women, one young, one middle-aged, with the six-pointed LifeStar flash on one sleeve, and a man apparently in his thirties, all wearing white skintights and aggrieved expressions. While one of her assistants opened a folded stretcher, the older woman knelt down by the body, checked pulse and mobility as Joss had, then peeled back an eyelid, and frowned. She pushed it back, peeled it open again. "Still reactive," she said to Orcieres, and then glanced at Joss, the frown deepening. "She was doing hyper," the doctor said.

"Hyper?" Evan said. The basso rumble of his voice caught in the helm of his suit, making it sound hollow and even more ominous than it did already when Evan pitched his voice that low.

Everybody stared at him, as if amazed that he could even speak, let alone say anything intelligent. *How does he stand it?* Joss thought. *Does everyone who sees a suit assume that there's a monkey inside it?*

The doctor looked at Evan and said, "2-hydro-6-propalo-methenpardrazine."

Joss's eyebrows went right up. Designer drugs had been around for hundreds of years, and both as chemist and sop he was familiar with most of the commoner ones. This was a new one to his police training. As a chemist, though, he had done the usual amount of receptor-site design, and the pardrazine group tended to insert into neural receptors in the brain in a rather permanent way, rendering them nonfunctional, over a longish period, without gradually increasing dosages of the drug. The problem, of course, would be with toxicity in the later stages of the addiction—

"Associative receptors, yes?" he said. "It would have to be almost exclusive. What do they call it?"

"Braindrain. Hyper. Blast, psycher, skosh, quick-think—those are the usual names." The doctor looked at Joss with a little less disapproval.

"Euphoric?"

"No, augmentative," the doctor said. "It causes the resistance in the myelin layer of the neural sheaths to drop. Not catastrophically, at first, but—"

"She was blasting, right?" said Orcieres, annoyed. "Fine. Do you mind terribly getting the body out of here and doing whatever you have to do with it?"

The doctor and her two aides picked the body up and lifted it onto the stretcher, having some trouble at first straightening the limbs out. "Nontypical rigor," Joss said.

The doctor nodded at him, reached into her pocket and took out a card. "You'll be wanting to talk to me later," she said, "after the autopsy. It'll take a few hours."

"Thank you," Joss said, glancing at the card, "we'll be in touch." LILA ORLOVSKY, RN, MD, FICM, it said. He was surprised. What was a Fellow of the Interplanetary

Medical College doing here? Normally they commanded higher salaries than this place was likely to be able to pay, from the way it was looking.

The two assistants took the body away. The doctor was the last one out, and ostentatiously failed to close the door behind her. One of the secretaries, as ostentatiously, went to shut it.

"Sorry," Orcieres said to Joss. "Death tends to upset me." She flicked a glance at Evan.

"Understandable," said Joss, "entirely."

"So what are your plans?" she said.

"Well, we'd like to get settled. I think EssPat has made arrangements for us at one of the hotels—"

"That would be the Hilton," Orcieres said. "One of my people will be glad to show you the way over. What then?"

"I think we'd like to take a couple of days to look around," Joss said, "and get a feel for the place, while we ask some preliminary questions, look over the dead man's quarters, and so forth. And we'd like to talk to your police, naturally—see what leads they might have turned up. Then we'll start to work a bit more intensively."

"Absolutely," Orcieres said. "I'm in the station directory: anything you need, please don't hesitate to call." She paused for a moment. "About this—," she said, nodding at the spot on the floor where the dead woman had lain.

Joss nodded. "You may rely on our discretion," he said. "We'll leave the PR to you, I think." He smiled at her, meaning it to be engaging.

She smiled back. "Thanks much."

At that point the door flew open again. More uniforms came through it—this time the dark skintights of the local police, all rank flashes and metallic appliques and insignia and heaven knew what else. Joss suppressed a smile. *The more ornate a uniform is,* one of his psych instructors had once told him, *the more the wearers of it tend to crave power, and the less sure they are of their right to use it, or their ability. And watch out for hats, too. Hats are very revealing.*

At least they don't have *hats,* Joss thought. But they *did* have more useless decoration on their uniforms than Joss had ever seen before except in old vids of the uniforms of South American dictators. Had these policemen held still for more than a few seconds, they could have been mistaken for Christmas trees. And they had guns which his psych instructor would certainly have described as "more than usually large, black, cylindrical, and generally penile in effect"—her standard amused and scornful indictment of weapons built more to look sexually aggressive than to be effective at stopping people, and meant to appeal more to the groin of the officer carrying them than to his brain.

The three officers who came in looked around them with mild confusion. The most-decorated of them (in both senses of the word), a greying man in his late fifties with little close-set eyes and a lined, downturned mouth, looked around him with an expression of deep disapproval that started with Orcieres and went on to everyone in the office, resting finally on Joss and then Evan with grand and serene opprobrium. "Where's the deceased?" he said.

"The body is on its way down to Medical," Orcieres said, glaring at the policeman. "The woman was blasting."

The policeman turned away with a look of disgust. "You called me up here for a blaster?"

"The blaster, as you call her," Orcieres said, "was one of our most valuable employees. The Head Office is beginning to become concerned, Chief Sorenson. Someone downstairs is not getting their job done, and the Head Office is beginning to notice."

"And so you've called the bloody sops in," he said, turning around to face Joss and Evan as if the whole thing was their fault somehow.

"Officers O'Bannion and Glyndower are here to investigate the death of their colleague Officer Salonikis last week," Orcieres said. "Their presence here is accidental . . . but I thought I might do you the courtesy of introducing them personally, rather than just leaving them to try finding their way down to your department. And by the way, Chief, we need to have another talk about response times by yourself and the other emergency services. We are in the center of the station, but somehow it seems to take people up to twenty minutes to get here from offices not more than ten minutes away—"

"This is a staffing problem," Sorenson said, deliberately, as if reciting a response to a question he had heard several hundred times before. "Before our budget was cut—"

"You yourself stated that you could maintain minimum staffing with the readjusted—"

"Excuse me," Evan said, "but perhaps we might be introduced?"

Everyone turned and stared at him again. Joss found himself thinking that the smart cop/dumb cop game had its advantages, but the way Evan was being treated was annoying him. Still, the three station police were staring at Evan's bulging forearms in a way that made it plain that they realized their own guns, no matter how big and impressive they looked, were no match for the sleek, discreet, faired-in cannons that Evan now folded casually over his chest. He smiled gently.

Orcieres had the grace to look embarrassed. "Please excuse me. Chief Edward Sorenson, head of the Freedom station police force. Officers O'Bannion and Glyndower."

"Pleased," said Sorenson, lying, and apparently not caring that it was obvious. "Any help we can give you, let me know. Delighted to see you down in my office any time you're ready. My people are all at your disposal. Meanwhile," he said, turning his angry attention back to Orcieres, "my complaint regarding your interference in police procedures will be up in the Head Office in the morning, and we'll see who has what to say about what. Good day."

And out he went, not closing the door behind him, either.

Joss breathed out. Things were already getting interesting. "Perhaps we had better get along," he said. "I think there's not much to be done at the moment. As soon as we're settled, Ms. Orcieres, we'd like a chance to sit down and talk to you about a few things. If you can work us in—"

"Any time," she said to Joss. "Just call. I'm sorry about that little unpleasantness, by the way—there has been some departmental reshuffling lately, and reapportioning of funds, and I'm afraid some toes were stepped on during the process.''

Joss made a nothing-important sort of shrug. ''We'll be as careful as we can not to make anything worse,'' he said.

''That's much appreciated, Officer O'Bannion. Stop by any time.''

They made their way out of the office block into the open air of the island and walked across it, slowly, back toward the escalators. ''Well, well,'' Joss said softly. ''What a little mare's nest we seem to have stumbled into here.''

Evan glanced about him and said softly, ''We really must do a surveillance check when we get to the hotel, by the way.''

Joss looked at him in surprise. ''Oh?''

''The place is loaded with cameras. Shouldn't be surprised if they were all equipped with directional sound as well.''

Joss nodded. Evan was being discreet. He himself was feeling unlike saying any of the things that were going through his mind at the moment. ''Where to first?'' he said. ''The doctor's office?''

''I think so. I should like to see how the autopsy's going.''

Joss pulled out the card, glanced at it for the address, and they went over to a directory and consulted it. ''Three levels down and half a pressure over,'' Joss said after a moment. ''It's a fairly nice area, about halfway down the atrium part of the central pressure.''

''Strange place for a morgue,'' Evan said, as they got onto the escalator.

''I'm beginning to suspect it's her own practice,'' said Joss.

And so it was. The area was residential, and its ''sky'' was an empty space between two islands higher up, below the Admin level. The houses were not plain windowless cubic, as they would be in the downlevels, but looked like a row of high-walled gardens with double doors set in them. Some were discreetly and expensively nameplated in brass; some had no names at all. The one at the coordinates they had been looking for had a plain silver metal plaque, anodized, that said MORGUE HOURS—MON-FRI 8-5.

"What if someone dies on Saturday?" Joss murmured.

"Waiting list?" Evan said. "Maybe they stack them up against the wall. Or the neighbors come and use them for fertilizer." He was looking down the wide corridor at the next property down. "Nice apple trees, there. You don't get apples trees that nice without some muck or manure or organic matter." He stretched the last word out, and Joss groaned.

"You hush," he said, and touched the annunciator pad.

"Yes, what?" said an annoyed voice.

"Glyndower and O'Bannion, Dr. Orlovsky."

"Oh—"

The door clicked open for them. They stepped inside the gateway and found themselves in an empty, stone-floored, stone-walled courtyard. At least it looked like stone. Joss suspected it was actually composite, though on touching it he found that someone had found a way to make it feel cold. He wondered about the composition. To one side was a wall with a door marked MORGUE; another unmarked one was off to the right. The branches of small trees hung over the wall, and some trailing vines.

"The lady, or the tiger?" Joss said.

"What? Man, you are the most obscure—"

"You haven't *seen* me try to be obscure yet," Joss said, going toward the door labeled morgue. "Wait for it. Hello?"

"Come on in," said the doctor's voice. Joss pushed the door open.

Inside was a large clean medical lab, all stainless steel and white tiled walls, with several large tables in the center. On one of them way lying the body of the woman who had died upstairs in Admin. Bent over the corpse was Dr. Orlovsky. She was wearing a rubber apron and a face mask, and she was busy with a scalpel.

"Didn't think it would spurt like *that*," she said idly, not looking up. "Do sit down, gentlemen. Just have to make sure of a few things."

Evan sat down on a bench at one side, looking with great interest at the framed antique print from *Gray's Anatomy.* "CNS dissection?" Joss said.

She glanced up at him for a moment. "Uh huh. You paramed or something?"

"Organic chemist," he said.

"A*ha.* What was it again? Joss?"

"Yes."

"Pleased. And your large friend?"

"Evan."

"Croeso," the doctor said. Evan looked up, startled. Orlovsky laughed. "My brother-in-law is Welsh. Have you run across this drug before?"

"No," they both said.

"You will," Orlovsky said, "and you'll wish you hadn't. This stuff makes old standbys like crack and long-lost look like baking soda."

"You did say 2-hydro-6-propalo-methenpardrazine," Joss said.

"Yup. That position makes all the difference to the molecule." She glanced up at Evan as she tossed a bit of something wet and purplish aside. "I won't bore you with the details. But after sufficient use, the drug renders some parts of the human nervous system useless for the usual neural receptor chemicals that govern things like cortical function—memory and logical thought. There's also an affinity for the corpus callosum, the place where left-brain and right-brain functions cross."

"Chemical receptors and their sites in the brain work like locks and keys," Joss said to Evan. "Some of them pick a given site and show such an affinity for it that they block out the chemical intended to fit into that particular lock. Some of them ruin the site, so that the chemical intended for it can never fit there again."

"I read *Scientific American,* for pity's sake," Evan grumbled. "You needn't preach to the choir. Just tell me this. Why do they take it?"

"It makes you hyperprocess," said the doctor.

"Come again?"

The doctor made an incision, looked with interest at a piece of tissue, lifted it out and put it to one side. "It increases the speed of transmission of neural impulses in 'white' neural tissue," she said, "and temporarily increases the apparent number of neural interconnections in the associative network. It's a software change rather than hardware," she added, looking up at Joss as he opened his mouth to say that that kind of thing ought to be impossible without actual additions of neural connections.

The doctor made another incision, then shook the knife clean and laid it aside. "It's a virtual change, and temporary," she said, "which is the problem. The drug itself isn't addictive, but the effects of it—"

She turned aside, reached into a stainless steel pan on a nearby rolling table, picked up a bone saw, and leaned over the corpse's skull. Evan flinched once at the grating sounds which followed. "The effect when you take a therapeutic dose," Orlovsky said, "is to suddenly have access to more of your brain, and to be able to use it more quickly, more efficiently, than you ever could before. Lost memories become accessible. Logical functions move more quickly. Any mental operation of which you were capable before, you can now perform at ten to a hundred times the usual speed, depending on how your personal affinity to the chemical works. Some people have a better match to the chemical than others." There was a loud crunch. "Did you two do anatomy work?" the doctor said.

"The usual required stuff," Joss said.

"Come here and look at this. —Emotion," she said, as she took the top of the corpse's skull off like removing a yarmulke, "isn't so much increased in speed as in detachment. Apparently there's some connection between the hardware and the experience of emotion: interesting scientifically—but this was a hell of a way to find it out. Would you mind picking up that suction? Thanks. The foot pedal is on your side."

"Where's your assistant?" Joss said.

"Haven't got one," the doctor said. "They cut my funds. Over there, please. That bit. Right." She picked up another knife and made a cut, then another, then lifted out a thin white wedge of tissue.

"There," she said. "There's the crossroads of the brain's associative network. That should be spongy and grey and white. Look at it.'' She poked a bit of the slice. ''Look at all the white glop there. That's residue from the overstimulated myelin sheathes. They're not meant to conduct as fast as the drug forces them to: the residue interferes with unaugmented conduction.''

''I would think there would be physical symptoms,'' Joss said. ''Muscle shakes and so forth.''

''The user,'' Orlovsky said, ''rarely lives that long. They might if they used the drug moderately. But no one does.''

Evan shook his head. ''Why should they?'' he said. ''If you can increase your intelligence ten or twenty times—what it must feel like to come down—''

''They don't call it braindrain for nothing,'' the doctor said, sliding the sample into a specimen jar. ''I've heard it described as feeling yourself trading the intelligence of a normal human being for that of a low-grade moron.''

''And so they never come down, if they can afford to—''

Orlovsky nodded and pulled another slice of white matter out of the brain. ''Most of them can't,'' she said. ''I think that may have been one of the few factors limiting the death rate so far. We rarely lose more than a few people per week. But this—'' She gestured at the corpse while she stepped away to a table on one side, where various instruments sat, among them an electron microscope and a dermatome. ''This woman is missing some clinical signs I'm used to seeing. Lesions in the motor neurons—'' She put the tissue in the dermatome and went about slicing off a bit thin enough to use as a sample, then put it in the microscope's freeze chamber preparatory to dehydrating it.

''Where is it coming from?'' Evan said.

Orlovsky turned and leaned against the counter with her arms folded. ''I would give a pretty to find out,'' she said. ''My guess is that it's locally made. We're not sure about the actual method of manufacture, but this place isn't exactly short of raw chemicals for the design of drugs. I *do* believe that someone professional, somewhere, designed the receptor-key part of the compound. Affinities like that don't happen by accident. But the rest of the design could have been amateur. There are some pretty talented amateurs scattered between here and Earth.''

''And you haven't found any 'factories'—,'' Joss said.

Orlovsky shook her head as the freezer chimed. She took the sample out of it on its slide, and slid it into the dehydrator chamber. ''Bearing in mind, of course,'' she said, ''that this place has more hideyholes in it than a termite's nest, and that the pursuit of those who might be responsible has not been, shall we say, terribly energetic.''

''Funding cuts?'' Evan said.

Orlovsky's eyes widened in irony. ''Whatever makes you think *that,*'' she said. ''Here, now.''

She turned the electron microscope on and fiddled with the field selector until a view full of spikes and holes made itself apparent. Joss looked at it with great interest, but could make out nothing at all.

Orlovsky *tsk*ed. ''Bad,'' she said. ''Very bad. Look at the receptors there. See the little cup-shaped structures? Normally in someone who had been taking the drug for a while, there would be lesions where the generator sites had been overstimulated into making more neurotransmitter chemical than was normal for them. But there aren't any lesions at all.''

''Meaning,'' Joss said, ''that this lady somehow got hold of a much higher than usual dose?''

''Yes. Not good. Usually there's not enough of the drug available at any one time, as far as we can tell, to *allow* a short-term overdose like this, even if the person can afford it.

''So that the supply has been increasing,'' Joss said.

''She's the fifth death this week,'' Orlovsky said, ''where usually I see maybe one. And the dosages have been increasing, to judge by the samples I've taken.''

''Could it be,'' said Evan, ''that the drug was being made somewhere else, and was being imported—and is *now* being made locally? Hence the increased supply?''

Orlovsky shrugged. ''It could be. But again, the police force seem more interested in other things.''

Joss leaned back against the wall. ''Like?''

Evan held up one finger and glanced at the ceiling, around the corners of the room.

Joss looked at him, understood, and had a sudden coughing fit. Orlovsky looked from one to another of them, briefly puzzled, then said. "Need a drink of water?"

"Yes, please—," Joss gasped.

She got him a glass, not glancing at the ceiling herself. "Well," she said, when Joss had had a drink or so and wasn't coughing any more, "I've got to get this lady in the cooler for the time being, until the inquest is over. Can I do anything else for you gents?"

"The main reason we were here," Evan said, "was to see if you might give us a copy of my old partner's autopsy report."

"No problem at all," Orlovsky said. "Would you prefer a solid or hardcopy?"

"Hard, please," Joss said. "Though you might route a copy to EssPat through the usual channels."

"I'll do that," Orlovsky said. "If there's anything else I can do for you, don't hesitate." And she did glance at the ceiling, this time, as she saw them to the door. "Where are you staying?"

"The Hilton."

"Some nice restaurants there," she said. "The Mexican one in the basement level, especially."

"We'll give it a try," Joss said. "You'll be hearing from us."

They headed out and made their way up toward the top level, where the hotel was. Joss was trying to digest what they had seen and heard. "Interesting drug, that," he said.

Evan snorted. "Not the word I would have chosen. Heaven above, how I hate drugs."

Joss nodded. "Especially the tailored ones. The trouble is, it's so easy to pick a site and build a molecule that'll fit into it better than whatever the body had originally intended to go there. And there are so damn many sites in the brain just sitting there waiting for someone unscrupulous to take advantage of them. . . ."

They came off the escalators at the top level and consulted a directory, then followed its directions to the Hilton, another building erected on an island by itself almost in the middle of the pressure. It had a huge central atrium down which green plants cascaded to a sort of central rain forest, in which the reception area and restaurants were hidden. Evan sneezed as they made their way toward the reception desk.

Joss glanced at him. "Hay fever," Evan said, and sneezed again.

"Oh, dear."

They presented their credentials at the desk, were duly gaped at (Joss found himself getting more and more annoyed by this), then had their keycards encoded with the EssPat credit information. "Your luggage is already in the room, gentlemen," said the desk clerk, handing the keycards over. "Fourth floor: the business level. Just put your card in the slot in the lift—it'll give you access."

"Thank you," Evan said, and sneezed again, several times in succession and very loudly.

They went up to the room, which was a double suite with a bedroom for each of them. The luggage was indeed there, and Evan hardly spared it a look. He began prowling around the room, opening the drapes, looking under first one bed, then the other, turning on the vid, poking into corners. Joss watched this with mild fascination, and said nothing. At one point Evan began sneezing again, picked up something from the corner of the floor that was partly hidden by the living-room drapes, and detached something from his suit—a microsolid, from the look of it, the kind that went into a portable recorder. Still sneezing, Evan went over to his own luggage, tapped the combination to open his case, pulled out a small black box, fitted the solid into it, and then held up the tiny object in his right hand for Joss to see. It was a microminiaturized sound recorder, of a kind that was often used for surveillance in the field. "Time I took an antihistamine and had a lie-down, I think," Evan said, while dropping the bug into the little black box. He shut the lid, and tossed it back into his luggage. From inside the box came the tiny sound of sneezing.

Joss raised his eyebrows in amusement. Evan grinned at him and went sneezing into the bathroom, then came out again after a couple of minutes. "I think there was just the one," he said. "My suit has an RF-based all-purpose jammer in it, anyway. It should take care of any bugs I missed. I'm afraid the video picture won't be very good while we're here."

Joss chuckled and sat down on a couch. "I've got my own player, and it's RF-shielded," he said. "Now I wonder whose that was?"

"I daresay we'll find out soon enough," Evan said, dry-voiced, "because as soon as they find out the one they're listening to has been fiddled, they'll be up to put another one in. I just wonder whether all the rooms on the 'executive' level are routinely bugged, or whether we're a special case."

"In any case," Joss said, "we'll have a day or two to investigate things before they realize that anything's wrong." He thought for a moment, then said, "Didn't Lon mention in one of his earlier notes that he had removed some bugs from his quarters?"

"Yes . . . and then there was no further mention of the fact. Perhaps because he thought his communications had been compromised at that point. . . ." Evan stared at the floor for a moment, then shook his head. "We should check out his old quarters tomorrow, I think."

Joss made a face. "The trail will probably be cold. Whoever was responsible will have had lots of time to remove anything that would have been useful to us . . . or that they *think* would have been useful to us." He looked over at Evan. "Well, we can only see what happens."

Evan picked up the room-service menu and glanced over it. "Sweet mother," he said, "look at these prices. Eight credits for orange juice!"

"Good thing we're on an expense account," Joss said, leaning back and gazing at the ceiling for a moment. "Did you notice," he said, "that Orcieres had the body taken away before the police arrived?"

"I did indeed."

"A bit odd, that."

"I was thinking so myself," Evan said. "But it didn't seem to be the time to be mentioning it."

Joss nodded. "You're pretty good at that strong-and-silent act," he said.

"It makes a fair protective coloration," Evan said, mildly, but not entirely without irony, as he tossed the menu aside. "At any rate, it struck me as an odd sort of understanding of the needs of police procedures on the part of Ms. Orcieres."

"Unless you don't intend the police to find out anything much. Power struggle, do you think?"

"Possibly. And not one I'm anxious to be caught up in the middle of. Not if we hope to get any help out of these poor clowns, at any rate."

Joss nodded, and allowed himself a grin. "Did you see those uniforms?" he said.

Evan broke out laughing. "Jesus Christ on a crutch, man, and their guns! You'd think they hadn't a John Thomas among them."

"What?"

"Later," Evan said, and grinned. "But we'll have to go down and beard them in their lair, tomorrow, before we look into Lon's room. They're the ones put the seal on it for us."

"Right enough." Joss glanced over at the little black box, which was still demurely sneezing to itself at random intervals. "I suppose you're going to have to sneeze at them all the time we're down there."

"Not unless their office is full of plants," Evan said, "which I somewhat doubt. But I'll continue as I've started, no matter how raw it makes my throat. The trick has served me well before."

He reached behind him and touched something. There was a soft clicking noise, and Joss saw Evan's armor suddenly develop joints, which it hadn't seemed to have a second before. Evan reached around under one arm to run one gauntleted finger along a seam. The other gauntlet split open along the seam from palm to elbow, so that Evan could lift it off. Piece by piece he shucked the armor off, revealing nothing underneath but shorts and a tight singlet as he piled the pieces up on the couch.

"How heavy is that?" Joss said, fascinated by the de-shelling.

"That information is covered by the Official Secrets

Act," Evan said, mock-severely, then chuckled. "About forty kilos. You get used to it."

"Not with my bones, I wouldn't," Joss said. "You're welcome to it, I'm sure. . . ." He put his feet up on the table in front of the couch and sighed. "This whole thing smells bad to me, somehow."

"You too, eh." Evan shook his head, sat down, and pulled off one of the two greaves as if it were a large and heavy boot. "No question about that. This place has a lot wrong with it. A lot of unanswered questions." He pulled off the other greave. "A lot of people hiding things. No one is going to be glad to see us, no one at all."

"Orlovsky was all right," Joss said.

"Yes," Evan said. "I wonder why. . . ." He put the second greave aside and leaned back luxuriously. "Well, well . . . all will be revealed in due time."

"You have a touching faith in the future," Joss said.

Evan cocked an eye at him. "Ah, then, anyone can predict things going wrong. It's predicting them going *right*, and then having it happen, that gets you noticed in this world."

Joss laughed. "And your *hywi* does that for you?"

Evan tapped his forehead knowledgeably. "Not that. Just this."

"I would appreciate it if you'd teach me how," Joss said, pulling his datapad over to him and unsealing it with the thumbpad contact.

"On this job," Evan said, sounding dubious, "there may not be much of a chance. . . ."

THE POLICE STATION FOR FREEDOM WAS A complex of offices buried in one of the islands jutting up into the central pressure; a place the size of a small apartment block, all filled with little cubicle offices. Many of them were windowless and smaller than Joss thought was at all in line with the modern idea of good working conditions, especially in an enclosed place like an L5, where space to spread out in was crucially important for the psychology of the people who lived and worked there. As he and Evan wound their way through the corridors of the place, on their way to the police chief's offices, Joss looked around him at the general dinginess of the place and reflected that the decreased efficiency of this force might very well have something to do with the fact that they didn't care for working in a rabbit warren.

The chief's office was a slightly larger warren than the other offices Joss and Evan peered into as they went, but it had the same ill-maintained look about it. As Joss sat in the office's waiting area, gazing around him, it occurred to him that Evan had been absolutely right about the plants. There were none. There were bare walls; a couple of plain plastic tables with chipped edges, with much-read hardcopies of *Police Procedural* magazine on them, issues from two years ago; and plastic chairs that in their design and general grubby looks verged dangerously on the antique. That was it. On the other side of the door Joss could hear one side of an argument being shouted into a hush circuit.

Evan said nothing for the first little while, just gazed at the young officer who had escorted them there. His visor was down, showing nothing but the blank grey shining stare. The officer began to fidget, then actively squirmed, and finally got up, muttered something unintelligible, and all but fled. Joss looked after him with mild amusement as Evan hit a chin switch inside the helm and pulled the visor up.

Evan rolled his eyes. "Nervous lad," he said.

Joss chuckled. "The Ray-Ban effect."

"You and your obscurities. Explain yourself for a change."

"Ray-Bans were an eyeshield the police favored on Earth some time ago," Joss said. "You see them quite a bit in the old vids. There was one called *ChIPS*—"

The door to the office opened, and the police chief looked out at them, his round face all one frown. "Where's Lewis?" he said.

"Looking for Clark?" said Joss innocently. The police chief stared at him as if he was from Mars, and ugly to boot.

"He was caught short, I think," Evan said, just as innocently. "Are you ready for us?"

"Come on in," said the chief, turning his back on them.

The office was much the same as its waiting room: plain beat-up furniture, chairs not meant for any human being to be comfortable in, and a desk that had only four pieces of paper and a data terminal on it. Joss eyed the desk with massive mistrust. No police chief should have so little on his plate, or appear to.

"Have you seen his place yet?" Sorenson said. "Your buddy."

Evan shook his head. "We thought we would come talk to you first."

"Waste of time," Sorenson said. "All the information is in the report, if you'd read it."

"We have," Joss said. "There are a few questions." He tapped his datapad and brought up a copy of the report, scrolling through it for bits he'd missed. "First of all, what success have you had with finding the people who did it? This report is dated eighteen-three and says there had been no arrests."

"Still none," said Sorenson, eyeing them both with an expression somewhere between wariness and distaste.

"Will there be?" Evan said.

"You gentlemen," Sorenson said, putting a sort of twist on the word that made it plain he didn't care much for gentlemen in general and the two of them in particular, "have to understand about this kind of thing. This isn't one of your nice clean-cut kinds of situations like they give you people out in space. A fiver's like a city with its head buried in the ground . . . and a lot of the people prefer to live that way themselves. The downlevels here are like rat tunnels. People can stay there for months and never have to come up into the light."

Joss thought of the places Evan had been recently, and "nice clean-cut situations," and kept his mouth firmly shut. "And of course one can't expect the police to go down into that themselves," Evan said gently.

"Of course not," the chief said, obviously a little surprised to have found someone who understood the situation. "Funding the way it is, we'd have to replace the whole force once every three months. We manage what we can. You know how it is."

"Yes, indeed," Joss said.

"Your friend," the chief said. "Sad kind of thing. Don't know what took him down that way—it was a bad place to be."

He reached into one drawer of his desk, came up with a sweet bar, offered it to Joss and to Evan. They shook their heads. "Inrunner gangs are everywhere down there. Every now and then we have to smoke some of them out when they get too close to the uplevel neighborhoods. But mostly they have their territories . . . they don't venture too far out of them. Unless uplevel people start snooping around." Sorenson munched meditatively on the sweet. "Your friend, I think he got mistaken for someone from the uplevels, someone gone down slumming for something he couldn't find elsewhere."

"Drugs?" Joss said.

"Yes, well, some cops like them, I suppose some sops might too," said Sorenson offhandedly, not meeting either man's eyes. Joss began to fume, very quietly, but kept his face quite still.

"That Mallory woman yesterday," Evan said into the brief silence that followed, "I suppose that kind of thing is fairly common."

"They drop like flies," Sorenson said, a look of disgust on his face. "The station says they want the trade stopped, but they won't give us the money or the people or the weaponry for enforcement. A few of *those*," he said, eyeing Evan's suit, "those we could use."

"I should imagine," Evan said mildly. "No matter. We'd like to examine my old partner's residence, and any effects you might have impounded, and so forth."

"Be my guest," Sorenson said, crumpling up the wrapper of his sweet. "The flat's still sealed. Any of his effects we picked up would be down in Properties, though I don't think there was much. His place was pretty well trashed."

"In addition," Joss said, "we're going to be continuing his investigation into the station's communications leaks. Can you think of anyone we should be talking to?"

"Orcieres," Sorenson said, with a look on his face that suggested just saying her name gave him a bad taste in his mouth. "Possibly Lassman, up in comms. He's one of the senior techs, helps us with electronic surveillance some-times.''

''Do a lot of that, do you?'' Joss said.

Sorenson shrugged. ''On court order.'' But there was a silence after he said it, a sort of thinking quiet.

''Right,'' he said then. ''Anything you need in the way of specifics, call me. Properties will have the keys to your partner's old flat.''

They said their goodbyes and got out of there in the minimum possible time. An officer outside directed them to Properties, which was several floors down, a glum little closet of a place managed by a sullen woman officer who chewed gum and popped it every few seconds, intermi-nably. Evan pulled up the station reference casenumber on the padlink inside his suit. He gave it to the woman, who went shuffling off among racks of shelves full of dingy bundles, and finally came back with a small packet of papers and solids.

She slammed the packet down on the counter, pushed a grimy, much fingerprinted datapad at Evan, and waited for his signature. Joss was trying to control his temper, while watching Evan and considering how it was possible for so well-educated a man to sign anything so slowly, as if he was trying to win a penmanship contest. Then again, the woman officer was getting more and more annoyed. In his present mood, this struck Joss as a good thing.

They took the packet and went out, heading for the lifts that would get them out of this place. Evan said nothing until they were out into the public ways of the uplevels again. Then he breathed out so hard that the sound of it rattled around in the helm.

''Idiots,'' Joss said to himself.

''Worse,'' Evan said. ''I was hoping we might at least see a little help from them. But what have we got? Cops on the take, cops on drugs themselves—to hear Sorenson tell it. And he didn't even bother trying to hide it.''

''Probably he knew we'd find out soon enough.''

''But what makes me want to punch his puny head,'' Evan said softly, ''is that he suggested it might be the same way with us. With Lon, particularly.'' His face was set and cold. "Lon's brother died of drugs," Evan said. "The likelihood of Lon—"

"Easy," Joss said.

Evan breathed out again. "Yes, well."

They paused a moment, and Joss reached out to take the plastic-wrapped packet so that Evan could go through it. There was the blood-stained shirt Lon had been found in, much ripped and torn; breeches, underwear, the same; the keycard to his flat, smudged with fingerprint fixative. A little station coinage, a bill or two, in one of the shirt pockets. Some papers with numbers and addresses scribbled on them.

"Not much to go on," Joss said.

"Not for what we're interested in," Evan said, "no." He held up the keycard, reading the address. "Deepdale Court—?"

"Dumb names," Joss said, "have followed mankind everywhere we've gone. Remind me to tell you about the development on the Moon called Dingly Dell."

Evan choked in a disbelieving manner. "Where are we headed?"

"Over half a pressure, down three levels. Not too bad a neighborhood, but not to flashy, either. A sort of up-and-coming professional's enclave, or at least it was when I was here. He wouldn't have attracted too much attention."

Evan nodded as they set off for it. For a while they made their way in silence. Joss was finding himself increasingly angry: at this place, at what it had become, at the attitude of almost everyone they'd met here so far, excepting perhaps Dr. Orlovsky. He had to wonder why she had been so forthcoming when everyone else seemed to consider sops in general, and them in particular, and what they were doing, a waste of time. But one thing was becoming increasingly certain: whatever they did here, they could count on little help, or none, or active resistance. Joss found himself very seriously wondering about that shuttle schedule Evan had mentioned.

"Is this the right level?" Evan said.

"Looks it. Now we just take the slidewalk."

The level was staggered with the other, higher levels

above it, rather like brickwork with gaps left in it so that the under levels could catch a glimpse of the roofed-in starry sky, and the bright artificially-lit air under the "roof." Joss glanced up and caught a sight of something he hadn't seen for some time: a shadow passing over, the glint of the low-hung central-pressure sun on mylar wings and long tail. A kiteflyer was going by overhead, one of the many people who kept an ultralight craft for pleasure, or sometimes for transportation, and used it in the middle airs above the highest levels, where the spin of the station was minimal and weight was at its least.

Evan saw it too, the shadow of wings going over somewhere high. "I've seen pictures of those," he said. "Looks like it might be fun."

Joss nodded, leaned on the armrail of the slidewalk. "They can be, if you know what you're doing. I was in one of the acro teams at college . . . we had competitions with the teams from the other L5's. It could get pretty rough sometimes." He smiled a bit, in memory. "We did some warkiting, when we could get away with it."

"I did mention your obscurities. . . ."

Joss chuckled. "No, this is a new one, not an antique. Instead of just doing aerobatics . . . we would get knife-edges made for our wing surfaces. Sharpened nylon, usually. Then you go up and try to slice the other guy's wingsurfaces and control surfaces while he's flying. If you're careful, no one gets hurt."

"And if you're not . . ."

Joss shook his head. "We were careful. But some people aren't. There used to be some kiting here, at nights, when they put the suns out and the airspace is, ah, harder to police."

Evan looked resigned. "These police won't even *walk* to dangerous places, from the sound of things," he said. "I much doubt they would fly. At least, not willingly."

"I also doubt," Joss said, "that they could get the funds, these days. . . ."

Evan snorted.

"No, seriously, though," Joss said. "If money for police equipment is really as scarce as they claim, ultralights would be few and far between. A good one is expensive.

Most of the kids who do it scratchbuild their own. If there are casualties, it's because the materials they can afford—or manage to steal—aren't of the best. Even a skilled flyer can die of bad workmanship.''

"I suppose," Evan said. "Is that the place?" He pointed.

"That's it. Let's get off."

Deepdale Court was a collection of little townhouses arranged around a central courtyard, with a wall around the entire complex. There was razor wire on top of the wall, and glass buried in not just the top of it, but the outside as well. Joss glanced at that with mild surprise. The neighborhood hadn't warranted *that* kind of security when he had been here . . . but this was obviously just one more of many things that had changed.

They walked down a little winding path to the place's main access, a gate set in the wall. It looked like many that Joss had seen in "garden" cubics on the Moon: mailboxes in the wall, a heavily barred iron gate with barbs on top, an annunciator box, a handpad and a card slot for getting in. Evan slid the card into the slot. The gate unlatched itself with a slightly rusty groan.

"Six-B," Evan said.

"Over there, I think. That ought to be 6."

There was a little stream running in a concrete bed among the entrances to the townhouses, and some water plants, though the water had more algae in it than anything else. There was even a duck floating in one little pool, its head under its wing, asleep. The place looked deserted, this time of day. Everyone seemed to be at work.

Six-B was done in fake facing-brick like all the other townhouses. There was a little hedged lawn in front of it, the grass plastic, the hedge real but withering from lack of water. The door to Six-B was badly scratched, as if someone had beaten on it with something, not to break it down, but to frighten the neighbors. There was a dent in the metal of it at one side, where it had been forced, probably with something simple like a crowbar. Evan slipped the card into the slot beside the door, waited: nothing happened. He tried the card again, pushing the door this time.

It leaned open with difficulty, having apparently been warped by the people who had forced it. Inside the front door was a hallway littered with broken furniture. Nothing expensive, Joss noticed, but all of recent make and of styles that would have been tasteful, before the stuff was smashed to smithereens.

They stepped in carefully, picking their way over the wreckage. Someone had indeed been through this place with a vengeance. The cushions on the chairs tossed into the hallway were all slit, back and sides. They went into the living room and found everything there well smashed too—the sofa and the murphy bed slit open, stuffing everywhere. Drawers from chests and bureaus were flung around their contents scattered every which way. Windows were broken—last, to judge from the way the broken glass lay over more things than under it.

Evan was standing in the middle of it all, shaking his head. "I can't believe this," he said. "The police have *been* here?"

"They were here," Joss said, "and then they left. Seeing what we're seeing now. This wasn't a search—not mostly. This was meant to scare whoever found it."

"Not hard, with this lot."

"No, but Evan, look. What need did they have to set things on fire? Look at the bed, the top of the table there— the drapes, for God's sake! This was meant to intimidate. Not to take the whole place out, either—they would have been a lot more careful. Our report said that nothing worthwhile was found here. Damn straight it wasn't, because nothing was *found!* This place is a gold mine. Let's get looking."

They began to sift through the wreckage, taking their time. Joss put his pad into visual record mode, never mind what it would do to the somewhat limited volatile memory, and let it look at everything he did, paying particular attention to which bits of the mess had actually been turned over or sifted and which had been left as they were. Very little seemed to have been touched by the police. There were some places where hardcopy paperwork had been set alight by the people who ransacked the place, then turned over absently by the police afterwards, completely removing any chance of forensics being able to do anything with the charred, broken material that remained. Here and there a storage datasolid of the kind you plugged into a datapad had been crunched underfoot, the splinters of silicon ground into the rug. Several of these had had paperwork dropped on top of them and burned. Joss shook his head at the destruction, but at the same time he carefully picked up the largest bits of one of the datasolids and peered at them. They were broken clean in large lumps, not shattered through.

"Tee?" he said to his pad.

"Mmm?" said the bored-sounding voice, instantly, as always.

"Remember when I asked you whether anything could be done about a broken solid?"

"Uh-huh, And I said I'd find out. Well, I did. Depends on the size of the pieces, and how much memory was stored in the solid to begin with. Over a certain size, the holographic storage quality of the solid cuts in, and you can restore the whole solid from a part. Under the threshold, or with a large-memory solid, nada. What have you got?"

"Bits and pieces. I'd send them home by courier . . . if I trusted the courier. Would you see if someone from Luna is scheduled out here in the next day or so?"

"Will do."

The carrier hum of her transmission cut out. "Is there a bag or bin or something in the kitchen?" Joss said to Evan, kneeling over another pile of burnt garbage.

"I'll look."

Joss went on around the room with his pad, recording, then took the bin Evan brought him and began carefully lifting papers and broken solids into it, trying to keep the layers together as much as possible. "Here," Evan said to him suddenly, "you're bleeding."

Joss looked at his hands in surprise: he had indeed run afoul of some slivers of glass. "You fool," Evan said, "let me." Together they went around the room, picking up the remains.

In the hall Joss paused, seeing nothing to pick up, but looking with sudden surprise at a place where someone had kicked a hole right in the wall, then dumped what appeared to be several rolls' worth of fiber toweling and toilet paper into it, and set them alight too. "What are you looking for?" Evan said, mocking, but not unkindly. "Lon did some strange things on occasion, but writing on loo roll wasn't one of them."

Joss shook his head. "Look at that hole," he said. "Front snap kick, yes?"

"I should think so."

"Small feet, though. And not too high up, either."

Evan gazed at it. "A child? A woman?"

"Child, probably. That hole looks too small for a woman's foot. But the one thing is that some of the inrunner gangs have always tended toward the younger kids—nine-to-twelves. They obey better before their hormones start acting up."

Evan frowned. "Filthy business, using children—"

Joss shook his head. "Some of those children know exactly what they're getting into—and like it better than a quiet home life. They make a lot more money than they would mowing lawns. . . ."

Evan glanced out the door at the plastic grass. "I daresay that wouldn't be hard."

They made one last sweep through the place, looking for anything of import that might have been missed. Joss stood in the doorway of the bedroom, looking around at the sorry tumble of bedclothes and furniture and clothes. Nothing. Some papers on a side table had been burned, as in the living room. He picked them up carefully, put them in the bin he had brought with him.

Then on a hunch he picked up one basket and tossed it aside. Nothing—He dropped it, picked up a sheet, tossed it aside. Nothing. Thought a moment, pushed the bed aside a little. The marks of its feet in the rug indicated that no one had done this for a long time.

He peered under. Nothing much but dust fuzzies. Not surprising; Lon would have had little time for housekeeping.

But there was a crumpled piece of paper under there. He reached under, picked it up, uncrumpled it.

Nothing. But faint indentations—as if a note had been

made on the piece of paper on top of this, once upon a time—

He put the paper in his pocket. "What're you at?" said Evan's voice from the next room.

"Nothing. Probably." But he was uncertain. "You see anything else worth noticing?"

"Nothing. Let's go."

They headed out the front door. As they passed, Evan glanced at the way it had been pried open and said, "Maybe not as professional a job as we were told, eh? You or I might have done as much with a credit card."

Joss snorted. "Might not have needed that much. But it makes me wonder how many other things we've been lied to about so far."

"I begin to suspect," Evan said, "almost everything."

THEY HEADED BACK TO THE HOTEL, RE-quested the largest size of sealable courier container, and carefully packed the bin and its contents into it, stuffing the bin with hotel towels to keep things from shifting too much. "You're going to get in trouble," Joss said, as Evan stuffed one last facecloth in.

"You're helping," Evan said, locking down the container lid and checking the pressure seal. "You're an accessory, you. Towelnapping." He snorted. "We'll leave them a note on the hotel net and ask them to add the charges to the bill. They'll be so amazed we bothered that I doubt they'll charge us a thing. But it *will* give us a reputation for probity and uprightness."

Now it was Joss's turn to snort. Evan looked suitably insulted. "*Some* of us," he said, "are raised right. Little things are important."

"Here especially," Joss said, picking up the container's little addressing datapad and starting to tap the forensic lab's address at Serenitatis into it. "This place has gotten *really* run down."

"In more ways than one." Evan shook his head. "Hard to believe those cops with their toy guns, and half of them on the take, I shouldn't wonder." He glanced at his inside wrist, where his chrono was faired into his armor. "They are going to be trouble to us, but on my word I shan't let it bother me. And I intend to be a bit of trouble to them yet. When is our appointment with the BurJohn folk?"

"Half fourteen."

"Good," he said, "there's time yet. I want to look at where Lon died."

Joss put his eyebrows up, then nodded. "Those all loaded?" he said.

Evan smiled a thin little smile at odds with the usual grin. "Are yours?"

Joss shrugged. His feelings about weaponry were sometimes mixed, veering between extreme fondness for its power and efficiency, and extreme unhappiness about the way people tended to look after you had been forced to use it on them. He liked to think of policing as something that only occasionally required so unsubtle a tool as the gun. But it occurred to him that this feeling might not necessarily be a valid one. It was one of the things that a sop was encouraged to think about on a regular basis.

"All charged up," he said, "and extra packs on hand." He paused a moment, then said, "We're not likely to be anywhere where loss of pressure is going to be a problem. I've loaded slugs, too."

Evan grinned, then, and glanced at his right wrist, where another faired-in aperture slipped open, then shut again. "We're of like mind," he said. "Sometimes I think people these days rely too much on 'light' weaponry. They forget what it's like to have something physical thrown at them, at high speed. I think a reminder may be necessary."

Joss looked at Evan and wondered for a moment what he was thinking about . . . then put the subject away. "Here," he said, picking up his datapad and bringing up one of the station schematic maps on it. "Here's where we are. Then, twenty levels down—"

"No islands down there," Evan said. "No view of the central zee-gee area at all."

"You might as well be living in an apartment block thirty stories high and eight miles long," Joss said. "No windows, except in the very outermost layer—but most of that cubic is taken up by industries that require close to one gee to produce whatever it is they're producing. Some hydroponics down there, for things that like to have their roots 'heavy.' But not many of the people who live here care for all that much gravity . . . or care to live away from the larger open spaces. And places in the high levels are rather more expensive. People who live down in the deep cubic tend to be there because they can't afford to be anywhere else."

"You're telling me that we're going to the projects," Evan said. "That I understand very well. Better than you, I suspect."

"There's no residential where we're going," Joss said. "It's further down than that—all converted or abandoned industrial. When the local force stopped policing it, the industries that were there moved out, or relocated to other stations." He stared at his pad for a moment, then said, "I have to find out *why* this place is being so cheap with its own utilities. It doesn't make good business sense to allow even a small part of a station to be abandoned. What's the matter with these people?"

Evan shook his head. "Heaven knows if we'll find any answers. Meanwhile, let's go give *them* some questions."

JOSS HAD SOMEWHAT GOTTEN OVER HIS DIS- turbance at what he had seen in the upper levels, he thought; or perhaps it was just that he didn't expect this part of the fiver to look any different from the way they found it. But there was no question that it was terrible.

The change didn't happen instantly, of course. For seven or eight levels down they passed through residential areas that seemed pleasant enough. But about the fifteenth level down, even the occasional staggering of accommodation that let a sight of the skyroof through suddenly ended. And for several more levels things were still all right, but at the same time there was a sense of uneasiness, a nervous feeling. There were no longer buildings with walled enclosures outside them, but plain walls that ran up to ceilings that grew increasingly lower. And the doors grew closer and closer together, implying that the flats behind them were much smaller than those further up in the fiver's structure. The walls began more and more to be marked with the various sigils of downrunner groups; daubed on in various paints, scratched into the walls, cut into the floors or sometimes the ceilings. They saw fewer and fewer people as they went. Those they saw had a furtive or worried look about them that Joss hadn't seen in the levels above.

There were fewer and fewer public escalators or slidewalks as they descended, and fewer of them were in any condition to run. The further down Evan and Joss headed, the more of the escalators and slides turned out to have been vandalized, either by having their controls wrecked, or pieces of meal jammed into the works, or (in one case) apparently by explosives. Evan looked at this last example with a sort of crooked admiration. "A talented amateur," he said. "They could have made use of that kind of talent in the Forces."

Joss looked wry as they stepped around the blasted part of the escalator and continued downward. "Concerned about the wasted potential, are you?"

Evan frowned slightly. "Wouldn't you be? Who would *want* to live like this? The anger has to go somewhere, and someone down here used a lot of ingenuity and went to a lot of care and trouble to make the kind of bomb that would do that. Someone's beer money, that was. Or bread money, and used for nothing but to let somebody, anybody, know how angry they were."

"I suppose," Joss said, "that if you had to blow things up, it would be better to do it as a job, and get paid for it, and be appreciated—as in the Forces. But on the other hand, this is exactly what some of the kids in the gangs are doing, I suspect. Someone's paying them well and appreciating what they do. Not the right someone, though."

"By our standards," Evan said. "But I doubt they care much about ours."

They kept walking down, down, always down, on staircases, on more shattered escalators that were little better than staircases now; in a couple of places down ladders through service ports, where the stairs were blocked from floor to ceiling with garbage and burnt furniture, all jammed together into impromptu, but effective, barricades. Some stairways had steel rods clumsily welded across them, so that Evan and Joss had to backtrack and find other ways. But all the ways were always down.

"Facilis decensus Averni," Evan said, *"sed revocare gradum superasque evadere ad auras,/Hoc opus, hic labor est—"*

"What?"

Evan looked at him in mild surprise. "Have you no education, man?" he said. And then grinned. "Or might it be that I can be as obscure as you when I set my mind to it?"

"Wouldn't surprise me. What does it mean?"

"Down is easy," Evan said. "Up is hard."

"I'm so glad I have you to tell me these things," Joss said.

They kept descending. There were no more residences down here—or at least, no cubic that had been built as residences. It was all industrial, some few factories hanging grimly on, all fronted with reinforced panelling and bristling with vandalized security systems, the panelling paint-daubed, gouged, ray-burnt, ripped half off in places. Other factories were long since closed, broken open and refortified by squatters, their outside panelling broken up with odd excrescences like sharpened spikes and homemade (or stolen and cannibalized) razor wire. Some doors had tripwires or hidden triggers in or near them that reminded Joss of crude terrorist traps invented during the old bush wars on Earth. Where there were no doors, there were only long bleak pale corridors that stretched on for hundreds of feet, or else blind alcoves that had been doorways once, but were now panelled over. The lighting was poor everywhere, and grew poorer. Light elements and plates had been stolen; those that couldn't be stolen had been vandalized, apparently out of spite.

"This is a war zone," Joss said, almost awestruck by the sheer wretchedness of it all.

"It is that," Evan said. "Think how many people we've seen in the last twenty minutes."

None, Joss thought. "But we've heard them. . . ." For

there had been shufflings, whispers, the occasional sound of something being dropped when there seemed to be no one there to drop it.

"Any minute now," Evan said calmly, gazing around them as they walked. "Something a bit more definite should happen."

Wonderful, Joss thought, resisting the urge to scratch the itch between his shoulder blades, the itch that he always got from being watched when he couldn't see who was doing the watching. His hand brushed his Remington as he walked, never doing more than brushing it, however. *No point in precipitating anything. But I'd be happier with head armor at least—*

The bolt went right past his ear and impacted the nearby wall, none too hard, but too hard for Joss's liking. It was a low-charge weapon from the sound of it, which meant the fire was moderately close. *Head armor would have been nice,* Joss thought, then looked around for the source. Whoever was shooting was well hidden—not too hard, in this dingy place. He dropped into crouch, which Evan had already done beside him, and looked around. Nothing—

"What do you—," he started to whisper to Evan, but found himself looking at a blank, shining grey mask, which had swiveled away from him. "About three point four meters," Evan said, "and around the corner. I can see his heat signature."

"Aha," Joss said. Evan lifted one arm, as if pointing— and there was a sudden terrific outburst of fire from the fairing under the arm. The slugs stitched a neat circle of smoking holes in the wall three meters away. *Point four,* Joss said to himself, as silence fell. There was no sound except what might have been a soft thump. Someone falling over?

Joss looked around in the dimness and listened hard. There was a soft scuffling sound. "Not leaving, I take it," he whispered.

"Oh, indeed not," said Evan, shifting a little in his crouch. "They're going to want to make sure that wasn't an accident. I daresay we'll have to do a couple more of them. You want the next one?"

"Not particularly," Joss said, "but I'll take him if I can see him."

"You needn't. About four o'clock low, on your left." Joss brought his Remington up, sighted along it. It too had a heat-sensitive sight, but in conditions like this it worked none too well. The wall panelling was a fairly effective insulator, diffusing the signature too much for it to be used for sighting, and the LED array on top showed nothing but a blur. "No," Evan said, "a little more to the left. Right, that's it. Up a touch. Hard burn now, that panel has been reinforced."

Joss fired. After about a second's burn there was a scream, another thump. "Good enough," Evan said. "That's two out of four. One of those two at least will survive to upset their friends. One more should do it."

"And they won't know how that last one was hit, seeing that I'm not wearing armor—"

When Evan answered, Joss was sure he could hear a grin in his voice. "No harm in you having a little protection, eh? Now, then. Here's my chance."

Joss watched Evan come up from the crouch, very slowly, the sound of the armor's assistance servos loud in the smoking silence. It was astounding how tall he suddenly looked in the dimness. Evan took several stalking steps forward, paused—*for effect?* Joss wondered—then reached out and simply put one arm through the wall, up to the armpit. There he stood, for a moment, unmoving; then pulled, and the panelling groaned and cracked and bowed and broke outward, and a human body fell out, pulled out by its shoulder.

It was a young woman, dressed in torn skintights with various bright rags tied about the arms and legs. She was dirty, and she stank, and her greasy blond hair was twisted into a plait and tied to the back of her head with a leather braid. Her sharp-featured young face was contorted into one snarl of fear, pain and defiance, but it turned mostly to fear as she looked up at Evan standing over her—the hard grey armor, the faceless helm, the still-smoking gun-port on one arm.

"One of them is dead," Evan said conversationally; "the one with the Heckler and Koch. Don't bother going back for it—my partner blew it up in your fat boyfriend's face. The other one should live, but his firing hand isn't going to be good for anything much any more. And what shall I do with you, now?"

He shook her a little in a goodnatured way, the way a terrier might shake a rat that was in no condition to get away. The girl's face went as far into the fear as Joss thought it could go, then into rage. " 'll bite your little thing off, if y've got one inside there," she screamed, flailing her arms and trying to find something about Evan that she could punch without hurting herself.

This was a futile attempt, though Evan let her wear herself out a bit. "Don't flatter yourself, then," he said finally. "I wouldn't care to bother with you even if you were ten years older and had the twelve baths you need, *and* bought yourself a brain. Get your ugly snotty little self out of here and tell your masters that my partner and I have business in these parts. Anyone messes with us, they're dead, that's all: no parleys in the act, no quarter given. Just dead and smoking, and if anyone wants their bacon after we're done with it, they're welcome. Now be off with you, and go wipe your nose. And give that bra back to whoever you stole it from—it'll be years before you need it." And with a casual gesture he flung her a third of the way down the corridor, so that she landed skidding and slid five or ten meters further still.

She scrabbled around to her feet, facing them, and backed several step down the corridor. Evan stood there silently, his arms folded, watching her. Joss hefted his Remington in a thoughtful sort of way. The girl dove around the corner and was gone.

Letting the Remington fall, Joss glanced over at Evan. "You have quite a way with women," he said in admiration.

"Ah, well," Evan said, "put it down to my misspent youth. But that should make things more interesting for the time being. Where are we headed?"

"Two more corridors down," Joss said, "and one over."

They started on their way again. "The dead one," Joss said after a moment, "that was mine?"

"It seemed wise," Evan said, speaking a bit more softly. "You don't have a suit, after all . . . but it seems wise to let them think that you're the meaner of the two of us."

Joss laughed. "And we're going to play Good Cop/Bad Cop with them?"

"Well, good sop, bad sop, anyway. No harm in that, considering that they have us a bit outnumbered. We must make the most of our advantages. . . ."

They turned the corner, looked down the corridor that led from it. There was a scuffle of movement down at the end—people getting hurriedly and belatedly out of sight.

"News travels fast," Joss said. "The next group should just watch to see what we do."

Evan was still for a moment, then said, "About five of them, I think. I can see where they've been. The heat trace is a little muddled together, but I don't think more than five people could have made what I'm seeing. They're not carrying anything too hot for us to handle, at least nothing I can read. How close are we?"

"Down to the end, forty meters, then around the corner again."

"Right."

They went softly down the corridor, looking from one side to another at the gang sigils scrawled there. The same one repeated again and again, a sort of spiral with a crooked line drawn through it. Then, about a hundred meters down, came the final corner. Around it was a little dead-end corridor, and to one side of it the panels were burned and scarred. On one panel was daubed the words: COPS DIE HEERE, and the spiral-and-zigzag sigil again. The bloodstains on the walls and floor had been carefully circled, just in case there should be any question.

Joss stood there for a moment. "Right," he said. "Shall we?"

"One must speak to people in their own language," Evan said mildly, reached out, and pulled the panel down off the wall—then broke it in two over his knee, doubled it and broke it again, and then crumbled up the remaining pieces in his hands, like crackers, and let them fall.

Joss nodded, pulled out his Remington, flicked it up to

high, and flamed the pieces of panel. It took only a moment to catch: a Remington's high setting can melt steel without too much trouble, though the thing needs frequent recharging and has other weaknesses. They stood there and watched the panelling burn, despite the fumes, which were bothering Joss fiercely—but he would rather have died than show it.

"That should make our initial position plain," Evan said. "Let's be out of here." And he glanced over at another of the spiral-and-zigzag glyphs, lifted his arm, and casually drew two lines of laser fire over it, so that a burning black x obliterated it in seconds. "Not that we won't be back," he said.

They turned their backs on the fire and began the long climb back.

"YOU'RE LATE," SAID THE SECRETARY IN THE BurJohn office.

"So is someone else," Evan said mildly. She stared at him.

"We were on business," Joss said just as mildly. "Unfortunately *our* business isn't usually the kind that can be conducted tidily from inside an office." He made a thin little smile, the "some-of-us-have-*real*-work-to-do" expression that had proved useful to him once or twice before. "Is Mr. Onaga ready for us?"

"Uh, yes," said the secretary, staring at Evan's helm. It was down, and the blank dark fore of it was staring at her impassively. "Go on in."

The inner office of the area chairman of BurJohn Freedom was as plush and prosperous-looking as Joss had expected. What he was not expecting was the rumpled-looking person sitting behind the desk. He was wearing skintights that appeared to have been sprayed on him sometime in the last century, before the technique was perfected, and the effect was inaesthetic to say the least. The style might have been the last century's too, with its sobersides stripes in "blood shades," but Joss was more occupied with the thought that there were some people who should not wear skintights, no matter how much they needed to stay in style. Mr. Onaga needed to drop about thirty kilos if he wanted to keep his health. On the other hand, Joss thought, there were always people who came to low-gravity environments specifically so that they *could* be fat and not have to do anything about it . . . at least, not for many years after they would have had to do something about it in a one-gee environment, or be dead of heart failure.

"Sit down," Onaga said to them, and they did, on matching fat loungers that had been set ready for them in front of his desk. At least the desk was messy, Joss thought: datasolids and hardcopy littered it, some of the copy bound. Some of it seemed to be slick product presentations, all glossy colors and bottles subtly lit from behind in pure blooms of light, masterpieces of the advertising photographer's art. Onaga was tapping at a terminal's data-input pad in his lap, less because it was comfortable that way than simply because he couldn't have gotten close enough to his desk to type if the pad had been there.

Evan glanced over at Joss, and the visor of the helm went up with a slight hydraulic sigh. Joss had had little enough experience reading Evan's expressions, but this one looked like humorous disapproval being strictly controlled. Joss waggled his eyebrows at his partner and sat back in the lounger, immediately wondering if that had been a good idea. It was one of those sensor loungers that listened to your heartbeat and EEG through any skin contact point and began broadcasting subtle soothing vibrations and pulses back to you on every wavelength presently legal. *Well, let it try,* Joss thought. *If it can manage to relax me after the last hour, it's welcome.*

The man finally finished what he was doing and looked up at them. His face had the pinched look that Joss had come to associate over time with people who were busier than was good for them. The gray hair was unusual, in a time when almost anyone could afford the course of medication that would re-energize the follicles. His eyes were almost buried in wrinkles, to a depth that was surprising in someone with as much Oriental blood as Onaga had.

Old, tired, annoyed, said the man's whole bearing. *Very* tired, said the eyes.

"You've seen the reports that brought your first associate here, I take it," Onaga said.

Joss nodded. "What we were able to. Several of them were written entirely in chemist talk." He did not mention that that posed no particular problem for him. "The rest . . . well, sir, if I may speak frankly, the rest didn't do us much good in terms of solving your initial problem with communications leaks. The parts that would have been of help to us—concerning the nature and uses of the drugs in question—were marked 'classified,' and edited out."

Onaga looked at Joss with an expression of profound suspicion. "Officer, I'm afraid you don't understand the problem here. The whole difficulty was in the fact that that information *was* being released. Our lawyers have advised us that it is extremely unlikely that possessing the—information—would do your investigation any good—"

"I'm sure they have," Joss said, "but I'm sure they also mentioned to you that we have the power to subpoena that information *ex judice* and on the spot, bypassing the jurisdiction of the local courts. I hate to resort to tactics that don't seem necessary among reasonable people—"

Joss held the old man's eyes with his own, waiting. Even a company with the status and connections of BurJohn would not want to antagonize the local judiciary by appealing against Solar Patrol prerogatives. Those prerogatives would be upheld, the courts would feel that their time had been wasted, there would be a lot of publicity about it, and the next time BurJohn came to them—say, with a lawsuit from some unhappy consumer—the results could be unfortunate. Joss watched all this go through Onaga's mind. The flickers of anger and indignation in his eyes were veiled, but still perceptible.

"Well," Onaga said. "I suppose I can see your point. But you understand that if I release this information to you, it's to go no further than you two officers until your investigation is complete. Our comms are still not secure here—all the most sensitive material has been passed Earthside by hand courier for some time now."

Joss and Evan nodded. Onaga turned with an aggrieved

sigh to his terminal, cleared whatever it was he had been doing, and started pulling up a different set of data. He waited for it to come up on the shielded screen, then scowled at that for a moment, as if the machinery were somehow to blame for everything. Finally he touched a control on the pad, and two collated sets of hardcopy slid silently out of one of the slots on his desk.

He handed the papers to Evan and Joss. Evan looked at his with the patented dumb-cop expression; Joss smiled slightly and paged through his own copy. It was a fuller version of all the original reports, with the chemical names and molecular diagrams of the chemicals involved filled in. Some of them were totally incomprehensible to Joss, but the precis accompanying them would explain enough about them—in "chemist talk"—that he could work out some of the details. One of them appeared to be a viral vaccine, the precis for which was so oblique that Joss suspected it must have to do with curing the common cold. Others were more forthcoming: one genuinely new antibacterial—in a field where penicillin was "rediscovered" approximately once a month, this was definitely an event— and a time-release topically applicable bone marrow stimulant. All interesting, but none of them particularly worth stealing, Joss thought; except maybe the antiviral. But that was so early on in its testing that no self-respecting drug company would bother stealing it just yet. *Much more sensible to let the people you're stealing it from spend the money to find out whether it really works. After all, they've been working on the cold for four hundred years now. . . .*

There was one precis buried in the middle of the set of reports, though, that stopped Joss the first time he saw it—then made him come back to it later. There was something wrong with its molecular diagram. There were hydroxyl rings where none should have been able to fit, no matter how you tinkered with the bonds, and other oddities— Joss looked at the diagram for a while, then shook his head and turned his attention to the precis proper. It became even more oblique than the antiviral had, which Joss thought should have been impossible. "This 'Substance 8188'—," he said.

"Yes?" Onaga said, and this time there was nothing veiled about his expression: it was pure panic.

Odd how much younger he looks when he's scared, Joss thought. "Where's the real diagram?" he said.

Onaga stared at him. Joss gave him the stare right back, but with just a slight edge of annoyance on it. "Mr. Onaga," he said, "when EssPat sends out someone to handle a case, they send someone *qualified.* I would very much dislike arresting you for obstructing a Solar officer in the pursuit of his duties. Not to mention the publicity—"

Onaga went ashen and began tapping at his pad again. "No offence, Officer," he said hurriedly as he typed, "but surely you understand how sensitive—millions and millions of credits—"

Joss just looked at him and said nothing. Let the man sweat, let him type. Obstruction of a Solar officer could put an entire *organization* behind bars, if the case was judged serious enough to merit . . . and the officer was the primary judge.

The printout slid out of the slot in the desk, and Onaga handed it to Joss with a shaking hand. Joss nodded, smiled—calculatedly, the thin smile again—and sat back to read the real precis. At least this time the diagram at the top of it looked normal. Not particularly complex, either: what in the Earth and Moon—

He looked a while at the chemical's name, its *real* name, and broke it down in his mind, making his own mental picture of the molecule, the way it would interact with skin—for it was another topical. After a moment Joss said, "Let me be clear about this. This is a skin preparation?"

Onaga nodded, calmer this time, but looking glum.

"And this collagen-protein complex here," Joss tapped the paper, "this is a live-derived fraction, isn't it? Something placental."

"Porcine," Onaga said, almost in a whisper.

Joss nodded, and took a long breath, and let it out. "A wrinkle cream," he said finally. "Or the active ingredient of one, rather."

Evan looked sharply at him, then back at Onaga again. Joss ignored him for the moment. "So this leaves us with two possibilities," he said, "and you'll pardon me if I'm frank with you again, but I dislike wasting your time as well as mine. This chemical is being presented, in the first precis you gave us, as a 'spinoff' drug, something that must be produced in orbit. Something that would doubtless drive up the cost of the final cream that Earth's wrinkly people buy. All well and good. But the second precis makes it plain that the colloid in question comes from the placentas of pigs. Doubtless they're pigs raised here on Freedom, to satisfy the requirements of the Trades Description Acts. Or are they?'' He glanced up at Onaga from the precis for a moment, but the man was already so flustered that it was impossible to tell anything at the moment.

"In any case," Joss said, "the second precis, which I certainly hope is the real one, seems to indicate that the colloid in question actually does some short-term good for wrinkles when applied topically. And the indications for long-term results for spray subdermal administration look very good, if this data is correct. That being the case, I have no particular concern whether you were going to pass this material on to your own cosmetics division, or sell it to a middleman, or another cosmetics concern on Earth, at a vastly inflated price. So no more needs to be said about that. —Now, the *other* possibility," Joss said, "is that this information—the first set of precis at least, possibly even both of them—is all part of a purposeful campaign of misinformation which you have been distributing to confuse eavesdroppers and spies from other companies in your industry. Mr. Onaga, the conclusion to which that leads me is that you people called in EssPat to make it look as if you were genuinely concerned about the loss of *real* information. Regardless of the good effect this would doubtless have on your competitors, wasting police time would barely even *begin* the list of charges we would bring against you were this the case. I encourage you to satisfy us otherwise."

Onaga was shaking his head so hard that his hair broke loose of the dressing that was holding it down, and began to flap like a flag. Joss had to restrain himself from chuckling at the sight of it, since that would probably break this very salutary mood. "Gentlemen, gentlemen," he said.

Aha, Joss thought, *he* is *desperate: we've been upgraded from mere policemen.* "You don't understand at all. The cosmetics branch of BurJohn supports all the others—we don't make half as much from our pure research as we do from—"

"Eight point eight billion credits from cosmetics last year, as against eleven point five million from medicines," Joss said, "but who's counting?"

Onaga gasped for air and kept going. "—a product like this one could increase that margin significantly—*more* than significantly—"

"Indeed," Joss said. *So if I was looking for something saleable, this is it. This wrinkle cream is something that he expects will turn the industry on its ear. But the person selling it would have to have some way of knowing what it was for . . . which argues an inside job. . . .*

"All right then," he said after a moment, and considered, while Onaga tried to recover his composure and his hairdo at the same time. "I'll expect you to send along solids of the substantiating documentation shortly. We're in the Hilton. Meanwhile, I want to know a little more about how you manage your communications Earthside."

Onaga nodded. "Everything usually goes through Freedom's main comm station," he said, "except the most sensitive material, which as I said we've been sending by courier. Our own communications people simply port their communications to the home office through the station net, almost always scrambled with the company ciphers."

"I take it you have the usual precautions," Joss said. "Frequent changes of cipher, different people using different codes—"

"Of course."

"How do the new codes come in?"

"Through station comms. Except recently. Our security people suggested that we courier the cipher material through until it was discovered where the leak was."

"Very wise," Joss said. "Who's your head of comms?"

"Trevor Litowinsky. I'll see to it that he's expecting you."

You're going to be glad to be rid of this *hot potato,*

aren't you? Joss thought. *Soon enough.* "Has he been with you long?"

"Two years now."

"All right. Later this afternoon will be soon enough for him. Thank you for your cooperation, sir. We hope to have some results for you shortly."

They took their leave and headed out through the office. Evan's armor drew the usual stares, but Joss was almost past caring about them at the moment. When they were well out into the concourse outside the office island on which BurJohn was built, under plane trees blowing in a breeze from artfully concealed fans, Evan said softly, "Wrinkle cream!"

"That was what brought Lon here," Joss said, "yes."

"And what killed him. . . ."

"Possibly. I'm keeping my options open. For one thing, what in the *world* that had anything to do with that cosmetic formula would have taken him into the down-levels?"

Evan's brow was thunderous. "I don't know. But I intend to find out, right enough. I'm going down there for a little visit later. Not all the way down, I think. Somewhere higher up, where the gangs are a little more accessible."

"Or bribable?"

"It's a tool, and we're allowed to use it. So I shall. Come with me?"

Joss breathed out softly, looking down into a little pool as they passed it, where small fish darted and hid in green weed. "I should say so. But this time I'm taking my armor."

"Might be more effective if you didn't. You'll have something of a rep from the last time, if word has traveled. And my guess is that it has."

"I might get a rep as a dead sop," Joss said, making a sour face. But it was a point. "I'll think about it."

Evan nodded, then said. "That was nicely done, that bit with the paperwork. It was all gibberish to me, I must admit."

Joss shrugged. "This is my specialty area. Nothing exciting about it. But *wrinkle cream?*"

Evan shook his head. "If Lon died because of this,"

he said, "I'd be tempted to stand Onaga on his head in a vat of it and see how long it takes the bubbles to stop rising, indeed I would."

"That makes two of us, partner," Joss said. "Late lunch? And then comms."

"A man's got to eat," Evan said.

"That's something I've been meaning to ask you about," Joss said. "When you're stuck in the armor for long periods, and you have to—"

"For pity's sake, not before lunch," said Evan.

THE BURJOHN COMMS CHIEF WAS SOMETHING of a surprise to them. Trevor Litowinsky was immensely intelligent, quick-witted, courteous, and glad to be helpful. He was also sixteen years old; a good-looking gangly kid with the fashionable shaved head of several years previous, and the trendy "baggy" clothing of someone raised Earthside who didn't believe anything that showed the actual shape of your body was decent.

"They didn't have any choice but to hire me," he told them cheerfully when his secretary had shown them into his office. The place was a cheerful clutter that aroused even Joss's admiration. Several of the chairs had to be examined before two could be found that could be cleaned off without completely ruining the "filing system" sitting three feet deep on them.

"My dad worked in comms here until he retired a couple of years ago," Trevor said. "I grew up with a house full of terminals that led into Master Comms. Dad preferred working from home when he could, you see—he was mostly a troubleshooter when he was older, came into the office only when there was something that needed laying on of hands. Or someone he wanted to embarrass in person." Trevor snickered. "But at home Dad had all kinds of back doors built into his access software, so he didn't have to deal with the comms security protocols. Toward the end, no one could tell at all whether he had actually accessed outward comms from the office, or from the bathroom."

"Your father had a terminal in the WC?" Evan said.

Trevor shrugged. "He used to say he got his best work done there."

"Used to say?" Joss said.

"Oh, he's all right," Trevor said. "He retired to Paradise. I might do the same in a few years."

Joss restrained the desire to whistle softly. No one retired to the Paradise L5 without a wad of considerable size. That a sixteen-year-old was thinking about retiring too, and even before he hit voting age, said something about the kind of money BurJohn paid people in this position. It also made the possibility that they would steal information for money rather more remote. But there might be other reasons—

"Anyway," Trevor said, "by the time I was twelve, I already knew more about the system than most people who were using it and getting paid to work on it. I'd made so many of my own accounts and crawled around so much of the system, even the secret parts, that they figured they'd better hire me before someone else did." He grinned. "It's just as well. I made improvements in comms that it would have taken them years to figure out how to use."

"Very civic-minded of you," Evan said.

Trevor caught the dryness of his tone, and laughed. "I never would have hurt anything . . . it would've broken my dad's heart. Nope, I'm an honest employee. Mostly." He grinned again. "And I really did improve the system drastically, especially the transmission algorithms. Saved them three-quarters of a million creds the first year. They were pretty impressed."

"It's the transmission protocols we went to talk to you about," Joss said. "If you were going to steal information and smuggle it out through the Freedom comms station, how would you manage it?"

"Oh, everybody does that," Trevor said, leaning back in his chair and looking meditative. "There are lots of ways."

"Everybody?"

"Sure. I told your friend so—" Trevor looked shocked. "Sorry, I forgot what happened. I meant to tell you I was sorry to hear about it. He was a really nice guy."

"Yes," Evan said, "we'd like to hear what you told him."

A little of Trevor's jauntiness went away at the cool sound of Evan's voice. "Nothing that should have got him killed. I took him over to comms, the same as I'll take you, and introduced him to George Alessandro over there—he's the Freedom comms coordinator—and after that, I didn't see him again. I was sorry to hear what happened."

"So were we," Joss said, and thought for a moment. "You were saying that 'everybody' smuggles information out—"

"Everybody *tries,*" Trevor said. A little of the self-assurance was coming back. "One of the reasons they hired me was to catch other people who were doing it."

"*Other* people—"

"Listen," Trevor said, "my girlfriend's still on Earth. You know how much a phone call to Des Moines costs from here? No, you guys have free comms everywhere you go. Well, I'm here to tell you that Freedom's comms department takes its position as a monopoly pretty seriously. A lot of the station revenue comes from there, of course. More than needs to! It's one of the most expensive comms systems in the whole Federation. You'd have to be crazy not to try to get the occasional free call, if you knew how."

"And how many people on the station know how?" Evan said.

"You'd be surprised. Most of the people in comms have the training to make it work—which is why they give almost everybody who works here, or in Freedom comms, free access accounts—to remove the temptation. The psych folks down in Accounting say anything is less attractive if you don't have to steal it." Trevor grinned again. "I suppose I understand their point. Anyway, there are lots of ways to manage getting info out, especially just voice calls. False phone account numbers, unlisted accounts—there are a lot of these, and some of us here know how to get at the lists of unlisted accounts, or how to manufacture new ones. Data calls are even easier. There are so many ways to add signal to an information packet that it's embarrassing. I keep having to find ways to stop the newer methods. In fact, one of the things I'm paid for is *inventing* new methods to beat the system, and then finding ways to defeat them."

Evan looked at Trevor from under his brows. "A statement like that," he said, "could make you a prime suspect."

Trevor smiled a little sadly. "That's what your friend said, too. I've got lots of opportunity; almost more than anyone but George over in station comms, and some of the other comms heads working for the big companies here. But you would have to prove motive. I don't have any. And you would also have to eliminate all the other people whose job description makes it plain that they know how to do this kind of thing—not to mention all the ones who've picked up the knowledge, but don't seem to be in any position to do anything about it."

Joss sat there thinking for a moment. "Let's put this aside for a moment," he said. "Tell us something about exactly how a phone call, for example, gets out of here to Earth."

"It's not too different from a ground-based voice or data link," Trevor said. "You pick up your phone and punch in a code. The local switching computer establishes the originating code, looks at the destination code and sets the charge rate, and sends the call—it's still really a request at that point—to the Freedom master switching computer. It confirms the origin, destination and charge, stores the information that the call was initiated, then crams the information into a little digital bundle, a packet, and routes it from the master switching computer to one of the three dish transmitters on the outer surface, depending on which one is best oriented for the Earth comms satellites at the moment. The dishes themselves are 'smart'—they look for the best-oriented satellite of the fifteen or twenty of them that are available at any given time, and they pick which satellite, and which transponder band on each, will give them both the strongest signal and the shortest transmission time. The information packet is then unloaded to the satellite, which routes it to the most convenient downlink center, and then to the local phone company, and so forth.

That process repeats every sixtieth of a second until the actual connection is made—then a packet is sent back here confirming the complete call, and each outgoing packet after that carries a little accounting tag with it, indicating how much the call has cost so far, how much this packet is going to cost, and so forth.''

Joss sat back and considered. ''So there are several different places where information could be added, if someone wanted to.''

Trevor laughed. ''Several? Hundreds. I've given you the easy version of what happens—the course I teach in intermediate practical comms takes four weeks to deal with the subject. Any given voice packet has tens, maybe *hundreds* of accompanying tags, with accounting information, info on signal strength, address changes, navigational data for the satellites, computers being referenced for copies and so forth. Data packets have much more, since they're already compressed when they come to the central transmission facility, and can carry more information in the same size bucket, as it were. The data address of the person sending the message or file, of the originating computer, of the network it belongs to, the Freedom data transmission computer's address, the destination computer's address, the system on that computer, the user address and ID number, you name it—'' Trevor waved his hands in the air. ''And a whole lot more. Information can be added to any of those.''

''Wonderful,'' Joss said under his breath.

''Ah,'' said Trevor, bouncing a little in his seat, ''but not without leaving a trace, you see. You can't fiddle with the size of a packet without leaving a trace of what you've done. The original numbers of the data bits in the packet will be different from the result that comes out at the other end after the packet's been tampered with. Sure, there are ways to cover your traces, but sometimes a person making one change will neglect to adjust everything else that needs adjusting in the packet to make that change look natural. And there are a *lot* of packets to change in a given transmission, even one that only lasts for a few seconds. There are as many ways to screw up a data adulteration as there are to commit one. *More* ways to screw it up, actually.''

"But if someone had found a new way to smuggle out data," Evan said, "you would have to know exactly what to look for to catch them.'

Trevor shook his head a little. "Not necessarily. It depends on what kinds of data are being smuggled, partly. If the info is being transmitted by voice, that makes the job that much easier."

"It seems to be mostly data, though," Joss said. "Illegal document and file transmission.''

"Graphics?" Trevor said.

"Yes."

"That makes it a little easier to trace," Trevor said. "Even now, graphic transmission has to be slower than other digital—noise is more of a problem, especially now, in sunstorm weather.''

He sat back and tapped his teeth with one thumbnail for a moment. "Tell you what," he said. "If you have a sample of what was smuggled out, one that's not too sensitive to give me, let me have it and I'll tell you what the best way to smuggle it looks like. It's about the best I can do for you at the moment, until you can give me a clearer idea of where it would be going.''

"We're a while away from that information, I think," Joss said. "But we can leave you at least one sample. I'll drop it in the station net for you, if you'll leave me an address.''

Trevor reached for a pull-pad, jotted a letter-and-number combination on it, and showed it to Joss. Joss pulled out his datapad and typed it in. "That's my private code," Trevor said. "To the best of my knowledge, not even the watchdog tech that Upstairs—" he jerked his thumb in the direction in which Onaga's offices lay "—has on me, knows where or what *that* account is." He grinned again as he pulled up the plastic of his pad and vanished the scribbled code. "It's pretty well camouflaged, so anything you leave me there should be secure.''

Joss smiled back, realizing that they had come across that most valuable of assets, the potential crook who has gone straight—in Trevor's case, before he ever went really crooked—and is now keener on catching crooks in his own field than any cop. "That's fine," he sad. "We can certainly use the help."

"I'll take you over to Freedom comms," Trevor said, getting up. "Once you get to know him, George will be a big help. Or rather, once he gets to know you. He's a little weird sometimes, but it's not a problem."

"Weird?" Evan said.

"Oh, you know, paranoid," Trevor said as they went out of his office and through the BurJohn main comms floor. "Always looking over his shoulder as if he's afraid someone's coming after him. It might take him a little while to get comfortable with you. I heard from my sources over there that he never did want the other sop hanging around much. I hope you do better with him. He can be a nuisance if you get on his wrong side."

Joss flicked a glance over at Evan. "We'll try not to do that," he said, "but we're going to need his help whether we're on his right side or not."

Trevor shook his head. "Wish you luck," he said.

Together they walked over to the Administration island. Leading away from it, over a railed bridge, was a high, stepped pathway to the next island over and up. The structure on it looked vaguely like a cluster of squarish medieval towers, all glass and chrome and steel; colored lights could be seen through some of the windows. "There it is," Trevor said, "phone city." He laughed a little bit under his breath. "They really ought to have put 'All hope abandon, ye who enter here' over the door."

Joss looked at Trevor for elucidation, but Trevor just shook his head and laughed again. "You'll find out soon enough," he said. "It's just that they're, well, not very organized. I hope it makes your job a little easier."

They walked in the door, which was devoid of any mottoes, and stood for a moment in a big barren reception area, while Trevor hung over the receptionist's desk and whispered with him for a moment. The receptionist, a middle-aged man with long, braided black hair and a scowl, lost the scowl after a moment and gazed over at Joss and Evan; particularly at Evan. Joss sighed.

"This way," Trevor said, gesturing them past the receptionist's desk to a lift. They stood together inside the airless little box and said nothing to one another. Evan's armor seemed to take up two-thirds of the place, and Joss smelled the peculiar steel-and-graphite smell of it very strongly, with a slight bitter overtone of smoke added—burning, the burning of panelling, from earlier in the day. Joss sneezed.

The lift doors opened on a big room with a glass ceiling, one that looked straight up to the glass of the L5's outer windowing, and to the hard clear light of the Sun and stars shining in. Various people moved about between workstations clustered around numerous brightly colored columnar structures—the associate nodes of the master management computer for the communications department. Here and there a head turned toward them as they walked through; then more and more heads. A silence began to fall in the place, not that it was any too noisy to begin with.

Trevor led them to one workstation that wrapped right around one of the node-columns, and had only one display unit and one datapad on it. Standing to one side of the datapad, glowering down at the display, was a tall slender dark-skinned man with tight-curled black hair and fierce, sharp features that might have been sculpted with a knife. His eyes had such a look of suppressed rage about them that Joss found himself wondering whether they were going to get any cooperation from this man at all. But as he looked at Evan, that expression settled itself into something more like speculation and surprise.

"Officers O'Bannion and Glyndower of the Solar Patrol," Trevor said cheerfully. "They're here about the data leaks from BurJohn, George."

"I suppose you're going to tell me somebody on my staff is dishonest," George Alessandro said, with the air of a man about to get into an argument he's going to enjoy. "Going to tell me I have thieves in my department. That I don't know how to pick my own staff—"

"Nothing of the kind, sir," Evan said, before Joss could get his mouth open. "We're just here to get a sense of how your system works up here, so that we know where to begin our investigations. Mr. Litowinsky here tells us that you're the one best qualified to explain it to us."

Joss kept his mouth closed, and smiled. Alessandro was favoring Evan's armor with that speculative look, and there was no fear about it; more fascination. *Techie syndrome*, Joss thought, and was more than pleased. Maybe this was going to go all right after all.

"Yes, well," Alessandro said, "been here longer than anyone else, designed half these systems myself, might as well show you around." He favored the display on his desk with one last disgusted look and stalked off toward the center of the room. "Come on, have a look at the guts of the place."

Evan went after Alessandro, his face fixed in an expression of polite interest. Trevor hung back for a moment. "How'd you do that?" he said. "That's a longer sentence without a curse in it than I've heard out of him in a couple of years."

Joss shrugged. "Be interesting to find out," he said. "Think we'll be all right from here?"

"Should be. Check with me later if he says anything you don't understand." And Trevor went off, whistling.

Joss tapped awake the remote sensor for his pad's memory and whispered, "Tee, you getting this?"

"No problem," said the tiny voice in his ear. "You go have a nice guided tour. This is going to be *very* interesting."

Joss strolled off after Evan. The next hour or so was spent looking at machines, around machines, and into machines, with Alessandro talking all the time in his growly voice, and Evan nodding and asking all the right questions at the right times. Once or twice Joss saw him surreptitiously tap a particular spot on his armor. Joss suspected that some part of the guts of the machine was being recorded in 3-d memory for later reference, though he was a little mystified about why Evan was singling out each particular piece of circuitboard or datasolid for attention. *Then again*, he thought, *possibly he's being 'eyes' for Tee too—*

This seemed to go on forever. Joss kept his mouth shut and followed his partner around, gazing with him at panel after panel and board after board, and all the while Evan nodded and smiled and asked questions about bandwidth and frequency and sine ratios, and all the while Alessandro got more and more voluble. The people around looked vaguely shocked at this, more so than at the sight of Evan's armor. *What must the man be like to work with* normally? Joss thought. When Evan got around to asking to talk to the people themselves, Alessandro cooled a touch: but not too severely.

"You want 'em all at once, or separately?" he said. "Can't have the place shut down by one sop, y'know."

Joss put his eyebrows up and didn't say anything. "One at a time will be fine," Evan said, "if you have somewhere quiet that we could use. I wouldn't want to disturb the other technicians' work."

"Didn't think you would," said Alessandro, with gruff satisfaction. "Got a little quiet-room over here, should be just what you need. Your assistant want some coffee?"

Evan blinked. "I daresay he might."

"Fine. You go on in there. I'll have it brought to you. Any particular order you want people in? Alphabetical?"

"That'll do."

The glass door of the plain little room closed behind them. Evan sat down at one of the four chairs around the stained plastic table and said, "Why don't *I* get coffee, then?"

"Maybe he thinks you take tea?"

Evan snorted. "Maybe he thinks I'm a robot, more like. We've a right techie here, my lad."

"So I gathered."

The coffee arrived: one cup, with sides of left-sugar and real cream. Joss looked at it, shrugged. "You take milk?"

"Usually. Sugar, too."

Joss doctored the coffee and passed it to Evan; they took turns handing it back and forth. " 'Your assistant,' " Evan said after a moment. "Sorry about not correcting him. I didn't want to rock the boat."

Joss chuckled. "No problem."

Shortly thereafter, people began coming in, starting with Ahrenses and Alsops and going on through Caicoses and Delacroixs and Faroukhs. Joss and Evan took turns asking them the usual questions, depending on which of them the person in question reacted to most strongly, either positively or negatively. They kept the questioning very calm, since at this point in the investigation the purpose was not to alarm, but to lull, if at all possible. They didn't want to disturb whatever was going on, but rather to keep it going that way. Questions were simple: name, address, how long have you worked for the company, what do you do here, do you like your work?—and so forth. But Joss had other things he was looking for, as he knew Evan did. Nervousness, a lack of eye contact, abrupt physical gesturing, on one level; personal appearance—did this person look like they were in need of money? Or as if he had more of it than his job provided him? Did the person seem overly smug or contemptuous of the job? And then the "bingo" question: did you know that data has been smuggled out through station comms? Almost everyone did—but their reactions to the question would differ, and that difference, from suddenly sweaty hands to an avoided glance, could make all the difference to Joss. He prided himself that the psychs who had taught him people-reading had done a good job. He suspected that Evan was as good as he, possibly better, and that knowledge relaxed him a bit. He could at least feel confident that his partner would be likely to catch anything he missed.

They went through the Hanrahans and the Lis and the Karpous before anything really interesting happened. A few bites, a few odd twitches in one female comms tech, name of Lowestoft, who seemed ill-dressed for such a well-paying job, and didn't like to talk about what she did with her money; another twitch from another very young tech named Malawi, who was belligerent and unresponsive to the questions, though it was hard to tell whether this was because of guilt or because he didn't like Evan's looks. Evan pressed him a little to find out why. But those were the only two, until Przno.

Joss's bells began to go off immediately he laid eyes on the man, and he couldn't tell why. This bothered him. He had as much training at "riding the hunch" as the next sop—never very much, actually, for the talent was a nebulous one and difficult to train even when strong—but he had never really been all that comfortable with it. Now here was the hunch standing up and telling him, *This one!*

This one right here!—and there was no possible reason for it. The man was perfectly normal-looking—even a little dull. Medium height, dressed no better or worse than he needed to be, well-spoken, a little bored with the whole thing, actually. And when the question of stolen data came up, he nodded as if it were the most common thing on the planet. "Oh, yes," he said, "it happens often enough. The security people are in and out all the time. There are so many ways to do it—"

Evan, who was doing the questioning, exhibited polite ignorance, and Przno began to talk about packet transmission to the satellites, the technology of the squirts, and how they were sent. "It's really the weakest link in the system," he said, leaning back in his chair. "It should have been designed out at the beginning, but no one ever thought it would be exploited this way—or could. You know how it is. People can add signal anywhere from the landline stage right up to the satellites or the shuttle, sometimes just by patching directly into a physical connection, a wire or solid, without even needing access to the system proper. It's full of holes."

"So," Evan said, "if you were going to try to catch someone who was doing this kind of thing, where would you recommend we look?"

"It would depend on the kind of data being sent, I suppose," Przno said. "Some kinds of link are better than others. It's a matter of transmission quality—"

It's him, it's him! Joss's hunch practically shouted at him. But there was no reason to suspect Przno—and Joss had had bad hunches before. He put this one aside, as he usually did when there was nothing concrete to back it up. Hunch was, after all, a secondary talent: logic was more useful in the day-to-day grind. . . .

Evan finished with Przno, thanked him, and sent him out. Another coffee suddenly appeared, brought in quickly by one of the employees they had interviewed earlier. Evan looked at it, amused, lightened and sweetened it, and passed it to Joss as the door closed.

"You too?" he said.

"Huh?"

"Don't grunt, man, for pity's sake. An educated sop

like you. I saw you twitching from here, though he didn't, thank heaven. That's our lad, I'm sure of it.''

''Why?''

Evan shook his head and sipped the coffee when Joss passed it back. ''Damned if I know. But now we will have to find out—quietly. Meanwhile let's see the rest of the crowd. How many more are there?''

''Thirteen.''

''Ah, well,'' Evan said, ''maybe he's got an accomplice somewhere. Hard to keep a secret in a place like this, I should think. I'd be tempted to date one or two of the ladies and see if anything could be found out that way.''

''Sexist,'' Joss said.

Evan eyed him humorously. ''Not having heard you make a statement about preference of lifestyle,'' he said, ''it seemed premature to suggest you date a few of the men to complete the coverage.''

Joss burst out laughing. ''You sonofabitch,'' he said. ''Never mind that. Let's get this over with.''

They spent the next hour and a half with the Rosenblums and Smiths and Untermeyers and Voonens and even one Zzy, a slightly embarrassed descendant of a man who had wanted to be the last proper name in the phone book. No one in the family had ever worked up the courage to change the name. And then the day shift began to fade away outside, and the floor of the comms room began to fill up with new faces.

''We're going to have to do all them tomorrow,'' Joss said, crunching up the empty coffee-cup and pitching it into a disposer. ''And the night shift, too.''

''Oh, surely,'' Evan said, ''but we've found our boy, I think. He's on the shift on which most of the communications run, from the opening of the Tokyo markets to the closing of New York. No accident, that. In all that traffic, you could lose almost anything. We shall see—I want to look at his work record. Meanwhile—''

''Dinner?'' Joss said hopefully. His stomach was going acid from all the coffee.

''I should think so. And then a little stroll.''

Joss realized that dinner was not going to help his indigestion.

TO HIS OWN HORROR, IT WAS JOSS HIMSELF who suggested where they should "stroll." Form his old college days, he knew which neighborhoods were safe to hang out in. Places like Little Italy and Nobrusk Under were very pleasant—long wide corridors, open to the sky of the spaceroof, where little cafes and shops lay ready and waiting for tourist and native fiver alike, all eager to remove one's creds as quickly and painlessly as possible. He had always preferred Little Italy himself, with its all-year-round food festival. In fact, he had had to stop himself from going there, in his second year. It was easy to put weight on in light gee, with the lowered metabolic rate that it tended to cause—and hard to get rid of the weight again.

But there were other places he had known about, places that the other kids in school whispered about; places where you could get different sorts of things than pastries and pasta. Places where you could get drugs, and gambling for bigger stakes than the fiver's laws permitted; places where you could get laid, or (if you were careless) mugged, or (if you were very careless indeed) killed. These places had all kinds of names that you rarely heard above a whisper in the student union: Gulag on Twelve, North by Northwest, Loose Plate Alley (for the number of bodies that were supposed to be buried under the deckplates there). Joss, with the extreme care of the adolescent prig, had made sure he knew exactly where those places were, so that he could avoid them. Now he told Evan about them, and Evan nodded thoughtfully, back at their rooms in the Hilton, and shucked off his armor piece by piece.

"You're out of your mind," Joss said.

Evan looked at him mildly. "Don't want to scare the babbies, do you?" he said. "This is an information run. Theirs, and ours." He chucked the second of his greaves onto the bed, got up from where he had been sitting, and stepped over to the closet to pull down his walkabout uniform. "The people who killed Lon," he said, "they know we're here. The people who run this place, *they* know we're here. Now it's time to let the ones in the middle know.''

Joss leaned back in his chair and steepled his fingers. ''You're thinking,'' he said, ''that whoever's doing the data-smuggling is using a middleman . . . from one of the gangs?''

Evan looked at him, surprised, as he slipped on his tunic. ''No, I was thinking of something else. Tell me, though.''

''Well,'' Joss said, ''let's pretend we're smuggling data from one of the drug companies to another. For money, yes?''

''Until we find another motive,'' Evan said, ''that'll do.''

''Right. So how are they going to pay you? Electronic funds transfer would leave a paper trail, or an electronic one. Almost *any* kind of paper transfer would be traceable, sooner or later. And if you're one of these drug companies, say, you would want desperately *not* to leave a trail of any kind. The possible penalties would be too high. But if you had a third party carry the money—and no one close to you, someone needing money, someone who wouldn't find it strange to keep his mouth shut about a transaction like this, someone used to laundering funds; and someone *you*, as the drug company, could get rid of without any problems, if there was trouble—''

''Stretching it a bit,'' Evan said, but he was frowning with thought as he pulled on his britches.

''But think about it. The gangs have been casual illegal labor on the fiver for a long time now . . . almost all of them, at one time or another. There's not always enough money to be made from drugs or prostitution—sometimes things dry up, and they come out and go briefly 'honest.' People use them for bouncers, bodyguards . . .'' Joss grinned a little. ''I heard of one lady who even got half a gang to come in and do the landscaping in her garden.''

Evan stood up and went into the bathroom. ''Were they any good?''

''They were terrific, from what I heard. Loved to dig and plant things. The police found six bodies there later.''

There was a spluttering noise from the bathroom. "Well then . . . I suppose this is something we should look into."

Joss looked after him. "What were *you* thinking of?" he said.

"Well, as I said, the upper crust knows we're here . . . and the gang who killed Lon knows. I think it's good time to let the group in the middle know . . . the ones who want to make a fast cred. The ones who want to find out what *we* want, and see if it's something they can use. There are always such about. And they might be able to tell us something useful."

Joss was still for a moment. He had been thinking that Evan was a bit more concerned about Lon than about any data leak, no matter if it was the size of a collapsed dike in Holland or a smashed-in pressure-suit helm. *But that's hardly strange,* he thought. *I just hope it doesn't start interfering. . . .*

"So where shall we go?" Evan said, coming out of the bathroom again. He was fastening his belt, from which hung an unprepossessing-looking little GE-Luger—a slim gun with a short stock which would almost certainly disappear entirely into Evan's hand if he drew it, and which would impress no one at all. Joss wasn't terribly impressed with it himself, considering where they were going.

"Saint-Pauli," he said. "It's about six levels down and over near the edge of the main pressure—where the top-level parkland turns to arable. Some of the kids like to go up top at night and scramble—it's good kite-fighting country. No one lives there, so no one calls the cops."

Evan snorted. "As if they would come."

"Well, they can get aircars out there, since there's mid-axis access. But they probably wouldn't come anyway; you're right. There are some bars and taverns out that way, but nothing residential." He thought for a moment. "Think of a country town, well away from the business districts. The farmers commute—they know there's nothing worth stealing: livestock are kept next pressure over, under better security. Not that there's not the occasional raid for roast pork."

"Pigs," Evan said, smiling slightly. Then the smile

went away. "And doubtless their placentas go to make that damn wrinkle cream."

"If the manufacturers are really using pigs reared up here," Joss said. "For the life of me I can't see what difference raising pigs in space should make."

"Just wanted to go whole hog, I suppose," Evan said, brushing himself off in the mirror.

"Oww!"

Evan looked at Joss with satisfaction. "Well, no matter. Let's go sit where we can be found, and see what we can find ourselves."

AND SO THEY WENT TO SAINT-PAULI, AND SAT outside a bar there in the "evening" light, gazing across the valley of air that lay between them and the same level on the far side of the fiver. About four levels down, the ground went "solid," ceasing to be a series of contoured, multi-level islands. The green of parkland stretched toward the big blank three-quarter-circular, "right-hand" wall of the main pressure. Closer to the wall, the ground below was yellow with a main crop of durum wheat coming towards harvest. There were high-intensity gro-lux lights strung along on wires over the curvature of the field, still burning even at this time of day, to hurry the wheat along, but they were shielded on top, so that their glare didn't bother the eyes of someone looking down from above. The field below looked like a huge, gently moving tapestry of burning gold against the evening dimness of everything else. Right next to the wall was a rich brown patch, unilluminated, waiting for the next crop.

Evan stretched in his seat, drank his beer, and sighed. "Pigs," he said.

"Hm?" Joss looked up from his own beer in surprise, having been deep in other thoughts, concerning the seediness of the place—it had been fairly tidy, the last time he had come here—the increase in the price of the beer, and the uncomfortable looks most of the clientele were giving them. If Evan was waiting for word to spread around that there were sops here, Joss was willing to bet that half the fiver knew by now. There had been a lot of use of pocket phones when they arrived, but it had now settled into looks wavering among hostility, nervousness, and greed. ''You said what?''

''I said pigs. Can't you smell it?''

''I smell *something*, and not even this beer can block it out.''

''Pig manure. They've been spraying that field down there.''

''You'd think they could use something artificial,'' Joss said, and drank again, rather desperately.

''You're mad, man. Nothing like the real thing. A whole century they tried artificial mucking, all that chemical stuff. No good, any of it. Real manure, that's what works.''

''Welcome to another episode of *International Harvester Magazine*,'' Joss muttered to himself.

''—brought to you by Longro Sheep Dip,'' Evan said cheerfully, '' 'and Harry's Fluke Remedy.' You think I didn't watch that when I was a lad? Joss, old son, food has to come from somewhere, and I grew up where it came from. Some of it, anyway.''

''Sheep mostly, I would have thought,'' Joss said. ''Can't have been much arable in north Wales.''

''No indeed, unless you were growing rocks,'' Evan said. ''But sheep there were, and some veg and fruit, and *those* I know about. Everyone did. That was all there was, after the coal went off for good, and before the aerospace people came in real force, thirty years ago, and turned the whole place into Iondrive Vale.'' Evan smiled.

''Must have made quite a difference.''

''Oh, ay,'' he said, ''people got rich in a hurry, and didn't quite know what to make of it. Some of them still say it doesn't feel quite right.'' Evan's face relaxed a little, into an expression Joss had never seen on it: wistfulness. ''One of my uncles was one of them. 'All this money,' he said to me once, 'all this, and for what? Because our da's land's half a granite mountain, and they want to store their wossname, their isotopes in it. Little load that one lorry wouldn't hold. They're madmen, boy,' he said to me, 'but if a madman comes down the street handing out gold pieces, by God you take them and thank Him for madness.' "

"Another one?" Joss said, for Evan had finished the beer after the last word, still smiling.

"This one's mine." He tapped the once-again control on the table's pad, then bent to rub at the table's surface for a moment. It was one of the touch-sensitive pads that were supposed to be vandal-proof, but someone had tried hard enough on this one. There were faint scratches where knives had mostly failed to score it, and slightly deeper ones where someone had taken a diamond pane-cutter to the thing, scratching a heart and RP + TD 4 EVER on it in a moment of premeditated affection, or probably just lust. All down the table, in more vandalizable spots, were kick marks, burns, knife chops, and numerous other traces of assault.

"Shy lot you've got here," Evan said under his breath, as the second lot of drinks arrived, carried out by a waitress the cut of whose skintight made it apparent that she might sell other things besides drinks, if asked nicely and given the proper incentive. Evan turned on her another expression which Joss had never before seen—not his usual infectious grin, but rather a smile that was almost gracious, as if the two of them were better-class people than anyone else there, and both understood that the waitress was just working there until a part opened up for her as Portia in the next available production of *Merchant of Venice*. She smiled back—actually it was just short of a simper—and went back into the tavern.

As the door slid shut behind her, Joss was gazing at the graffiti sprayed over the front of the place. Sprayed it had had to be, for the people who built the tavern had faced it in composite artificial stone meant to look like fieldstone, with artificial mortar in the joins. Various knives had been at work here too, and had mostly been defeated, by the look of the size and fewness of the missing chips. But paintsprayers had worked fine, and there was a good assortment of gang sigils of all kinds, sprayed in an impressive array of colors.

Evan followed Joss's gaze and nodded. "Not just one," he said.

"No . . . this is fairly neutral territory, from the looks of things."

"Good."

"Not the one we're looking for, though."

"Might be as well—"

"You looking for something?" said a soft voice over Joss's shoulder. He glanced up and saw Evan looking behind him, with his chin resting casually on his fist, and nowhere near reach of the GE-Luger. Joss looked up over his shoulder, not too quickly—that was always a mistake— and saw a face that might have come off a piece of classical sculpture, had it not been so completely and artfully tattooed and scarified. Scarification, with implants to make the building-up easier, had come in as a fashion about ten years ago. Most people settled for a small raised design on temple or cheekbone, on a shoulder or arm, or somewhere else. But some other people had become very attracted to the idea of human flesh as sculptor's medium, and had decided that moderation was cowardly. The owner of *this* face had obviously wanted no part of moderation. Forehead and cheekbones were scarified in swirled patterns of brilliant blue and metallic gold. There were small diamonds set into the centers of the cheek-whorls, and there were embedded LEDs scattered here and there, visible only as tiny bumps concealed in the pattern. The young man had apparently decided it was too early to turn them on, or perhaps he didn't want to attract attention in the dimness. His clothes were all dark—as much from grime as from the black-and-grey pattern of the foundation skintight and the black dagged tunic thrown over it—and his knife was black too, from blade to haft, a dull dark line where it was tied to his forearm. A show-knife, not a use-knife. But Joss particularly noticed the only bright thing about it, the single line of silver that was an edge sharpened almost to wire, but not quite.

"Depends," Evan said, "whatch' got. Sit?"

"Stand, thanks."

"Drink?" Joss said, not to be left out.

"Finger black death," said the young man, moving around a bit to gaze down at the order pad on the table.

He tapped it, then tapped it again for a double without looking at Evan.

Joss relaxed slightly at no longer having the kid behind him, then took a moment to look him over more carefully. He couldn't be more than eighteen; was raised here, to judge by his extreme tallness—six four easy—and the lightness of his bones and build. Tunnel-baby, they would have called him while Joss was in school here.

The drinks came. The waitress passed out their beers, and the boy's brennevin, and they all saluted one another and drank. The kid's brennevin was half gone when he lowered his glass, and Joss gave silent thanks that he didn't have this boy's liver, or for that matter, his tastes. Brennevin is not referred to in some circles as "panther sweat" for nothing.

"So," Joss said after the first swallow. "Got?"

The boy shrugged.

"Name 'change?" Joss said.

Another shrug.

"O'Bannion," Joss said. He gestured at Evan. "Glyndower."

"Huh," the kid said to Joss. "Don' look mickish."

Joss shrugged now. Most of downtalk, as he remembered hearing it from those friends who practiced it for their slumming adventures into "down," was gesture rather than speech. The shrug coupled with facial expression and stance could mean a hundred things, but the basic context of language and kinesics both was always "I don't particularly care." To care was to give someone potential power of threat over you. The deadpan delivery was everything, and one also dropped out of a sentence every word but those that were absolutely necessary. There was something similar in interviewing technique, when you let your "ears go unfocused" and tried to hear only the words on which the speaker put the most emphasis: those were the only ones that mattered. It wasn't that life was too short in the downlevels for long sentences, though certainly people died young. It was that almost everyone was too bored to be bothered talking, except for what was vital: food, sex, violence were the issues. There were only a handful of important verbs, and the majority of their uses were unpleasant.

A lot of the nouns were ethnic, and a lot of the adjectives, and this was one Joss hadn't heard in years. He laughed. " 'm mickish enough," he said.

"Glyndower," the kid said, jerking his chin at Evan. "Whassat?"

"Welsh," Evan aid. "Glyndower was a king."

"King, huh," the kid said, and his face began to screw itself into an amused sneer.

"King," Evan said, very calm, smiling slightly. "Old-time. People tried move in's territory. Killed 'em. A lot." He reached for his beer and drank. "Relative," he added, and drank again.

Most of the sneer went away. " 'kay," the kid said. "Cooch, 's me.'

They nodded at him. "Another?" Evan said, nodding at the brennevin.

"Mmmhhm."

"Right." Evan tapped the table for another double. "Sit?"

"Nah."

"Hurt m'neck looking at you," Evan said, with a wry look.

Cooch thought about this a moment, then pulled over a chair and sat down in a sprawl of arms and legs.

"You freelance?" Evan said.

Cooch shook his head. "Tied."

"With?"

Cooch shifted a little, uneasily, then said, "You know Squadron?"

Joss shook his head. "Strangers here."

"Not you," Cooch said.

"Now," Joss said. "Not years ago. But now. Never heard of Squadron."

Cooch nodded. "They did your other sop."

Evan nodded as if he had already known. "You?"

"I'm Lost Boys," Cooch said.

That was a name that Joss recognized, one that various gangs had carried over a number of years. There was no continuity implied. Usually all of a gang would die off, or disband, and another gang would adopt its name and "traditions," if anyone could remember anything about them. Names were much more liable to change than territories.

"So," Joss said again, as another round of drinks arrived. Evan had already finished his. Joss wondered whether Evan had taken an antimetabolic before leaving the hotel. *He* certainly had. Hangovers were one of his least favorite things, along with spacesickness and centrifuges.

"So," Cooch said. "Y'look'n for Squadron?"

"Found 'em already," Evan said in a tone of mild amusement. "You must've heard."

"No rush for them," Joss said, leaning back in his chair and gazing at Cooch as if he were something small and harmless. It took a little doing. "No rush't'all. Don't really need'em shopped. We've got other business." He took another drink.

Cooch looked faintly shocked at this piece of news. "Thought you were here't'do 'em," he said.

"Later," Evan said, and did not attempt to hide or control the small, satisfied smile on his face, as if the matter were already handled. It was another look that Joss decided he didn't want to see any more than necessary. "Looking for something else just now."

Cooch put his eyebrows up, and all the LEDs went off together, then sparkled down to darkness again in a quick random pattern.

"Runners," Joss said.

"Know where you can get some," Cooch said.

"Don't want fresh ones," Evan said. "Want ones that're working for other people just now."

Cooch looked suddenly suspicious. "This a buyout?"

"Could be. Depends on the runners."

There was a moment's silence, during which everyone drank. "Lot of groups," he said, "lot of freelance, running around out there. Hard t'tell who's doin' what. Some jobs, y'get killed y'tell."

"Don't want 'nybody killed," Joss said. "Just want some runners."

Cooch thought about that for a moment. "Could spread

some word around," he said. And then was still for a moment, looking at them.

"Kill fee, of course," Evan said. Joss wished he hadn't put it quite that way.

"And retainer."

Evan nodded. "Price."

"A hundred."

Evan shook his head. "Too much for no results yet."

"Fifty now. Fifty with the first runner. Ten a piece after."

"Ten each till the tenth one," Evan said, "and twenty each until twenty. And so forth."

Joss held his face still. Evan was a canny one. The first people they contacted would most likely be the least useful. It would be the latest ones who would probably have the most information. Evan's schedule of payment would make sure that his source kept potential runners coming for some time.

"Done," Cooch said, and put out a clenched fist. Evan matched the gesture: they banged them together lightly. "Where?"

"Here. Tomorrow night, late."

Cooch nodded, drank, then leaned back and looked at Evan and Joss speculatively. "What's it for?"

Evan smiled, turned his glass around and looked at it. "What d'y' think?"

"Someone else running something you want," said Cooch.

Joss nodded.

"Might be other ways to get it," Cooch said.

"Might," Evan agreed. And he smiled, and turned the drink around again, gazing into it.

Cooch was beginning to look almost twitchy with interest. "Want in," he said.

Evan raied his eyebrows. "You *are* in," he said, " 's far as you're gonna be at the moment."

"Is it creds?" Cooch said.

Joss glanced at Evan. Evan widened his eyes slightly at Joss in an expression that seemed to mean, *You take it.*

"Creds," Joss said, "yes."

"Running 'em?"

Joss said, "Might be. We're looking."

"Lot of that going on," Cooch said. And then paused, frowned with suspicion, and said, "See the color first."

It was Joss's turn to glance at Evan. Evan reached into a pocket full of discretionary and came up with two fifties. One of these he pushed toward Cooch. "For the runners," he said. "Now then."

Cooch grabbed the bill and stuffed it somewhere into the skintight layer of his clothes, then sat back again. "Some big runs going on, I hear."

"Recent?" Joss said.

"The last year or so."

"Other end?"

"Some guy," Cooch said. "Don' know much about it—it's a Teeker thing."

"Teeker?"

Cooch pointed at one of the sigils sprayed on the tavern well, a thing like a stylized stick-drawing of a cat with a leering face. "Them. Think they pass for some cooker down a few."

A cooker was a drugmaker, someone who ran a cookshop, one of the little workshops where raw materials were put together. "How big are the loads?" Joss said, meaning the money being passed.

Cooch held up a hand with fingers spread. Five-figure passes, then. That *was* pretty respectable. "What kinds of stuff?"

"Dunno," Cooch said. "Might be able to find out." And he stretched his hand out to the fifty on the table.

Evan drew it gently out of reach for the moment. "Frequent passes?" he said.

Cooch shrugged. "Every tenday or so."

A hundred fifty thousand credits a month . . . and regular. "Like to talk to them," Joss said. "Might be able to make them a better offer."

Cooch looked at him in astonishment. "Or someone else," Joss added, as an afterthought.

Astonishment started turning to greed. "Might make me a better one too," Cooch said. "Hundred each runner—"

Evan merely looked at Cooch. It was a very still, level

look, one that suggested the recipient might need a spanking . . . possibly with an axe. Cooch's mouth quirked as he changed his mind, and all the LEDs went off again.

" 'kay," he said. "Tomorrow. This time?"

"Good enough," Evan said. "Fly high."

Cooch ducked his head to each of them, then was away. Evan took another drink of his beer, then when Cooch was well out of sight, glanced over at Joss. Under his breath, he said, " 'A better offer'!"

"You mean they wouldn't give us that much?" Joss said innocently.

"Wish they would, by God," Evan said. "*I'd* be back home to find out if there was a welcome in the valleys, indeed I would!" He put his beer down. "You're a madman."

Joss shook his head. "You wanted to stir them up," he said. "We'll see some stirring now. Any crowd who wants to make a cred will be all over us. And I'll bet we'll have anyone who has something against the Squadron trying to climb into our pockets too, offering to do them for us."

"Not a bad idea to encourage," Evan said, gazing down at the wheatfield abstractedly. "A few weeks of that might soften them up for having to deal with me."

"With *us*," Joss said.

Evan looked sharply at him; then the look eased off a bit. "Yes," he said, "I forget."

Joss was quiet for the moment. *It's a new partnership,* he told himself, *there's no reason he should automatically include you in so soon. A de-partnered man always has some adjustments to make, and it takes time. . . .*

"Sorry," Evan said. But his eyes were still distant.

Joss's thoughts were uncomfortable. *This isn't exactly something I can press him on. He's been at this business a lot longer than I have. But a sop doesn't have time for revenge, or personal crusades . . . and the desire for them can get him killed if they blind him to other things that are going on. That kind of thing can get other people killed, too. . . .*

"Sorry," Evan said again. He stood up. "Shall we call it a day?"

"Seems like a good idea," Joss said.

I can get a head start worrying about tomorrow. . . .

THEY WERE UP EARLY THE NEXT DAY. IT BEGAN
with more interviews, this time of the exiting night shift
at Freedom comms. More people, by turns nervous, confused, unconcerned, annoyed, or interested, passed
through their little side room and answered their questions, and stared at Evan's suit. The reactions were beginning to amuse Joss now. Some people gazed at the suit in
horror, some in fascination; one annoyed employee cas-
tigated Evan as a tool of the military-industrial complex.
"Just the industrial, at the moment," he said mildly, and
confused the young woman into silence. There were a few
people who asked questions about the suit. Evan answered
them politely, and went back to his original line of questioning without any fuss, if he was asking the questions at
that point. But Joss noticed that no one, *no* one, ignored
that suit. It occurred to him that could well be considered
a weapon, in itself, without reference to any of its guns.
It was a symbol, and he found the symbol he wore, his
own uniform, paling a little in comparison to it.

Jealousy? he wondered. Not a good feeling to have
about your partner, if it *was* jealousy.

They finished their questioning and took a moment to
check over their notes. There were a couple of possibilities—people whose work records, and bank accounts, they
wanted to look at—but nothing more concrete than that.

Joss sat back and scowled at his pad. "Well," he said.
"I suppose we weren't exactly likely to see someone coming in wearing a sign that said I'M SMUGGLING DATA. I just
wish there were some more viable leads than the one we've
got."

"Which you don't care for," Evan said. He smiled
slightly.

"No," Joss said, "not at all. There's no solid evidence
to base it on. Nothing points to Przno at all."

"Yet," Evan said. He looked unconcerned. "Give it
some time. We haven't seen the night-shift people yet.

That strikes me as a possibility too, you know. Fewer people in the place to notice what you're doing—more time and leisure to work, if the smuggling takes much fiddling with the machinery at all.''

"We don't know that it does," said Joss. "Trevor made it sound like something that could have most of the dirty work done on a private terminal."

"Then we'll bug his private terminal," Evan said. "A good idea. We can get permission for that without any problem. In fact, this falls within our local action brief. We don't even have to ask. We can hit every terminal he touches."

"Without him noticing?" Joss said, and then added, "Though I daresay young Trevor could give us some suggestions about that."

"Right enough," Evan said. "What's next on the agenda?"

"Possibly we ought to split up for the moment," Joss sad. He tapped at his pad, idly bringing up the one double-tagged record. PRZNO, MICHAEL, it began, and went on for several inconsequential paragraphs. "I want to do some more research on our suspect. And I think you had some plans of your own. . . ."

Evan looked at him almost mischievously. "I was thinking that I might go slumming a bit more, if you wouldn't mind suggesting a few more places that seem good to hang out in."

"No problem," Joss aid, as he scrolled down through the interview with Przno, glancing over it. His pad, in transcription mode, had carefully taken down everything Przno had said, but every now and then its spelling still needed correction, or it would query some word that had been muttered. "You might try Eleven Down, over by—" And then he paused.

"By where?"

"Hold on a moment." He was comparing what he saw on the pad against what he remembered Przno having said, and they matched, to his surprise and great interest. "Evan, look at this."

He pushed the pad across to his partner. Evan scanned down it, looking for the passage that Joss had flagged. "People can add signal anywhere from the landline stage right up to the satellites or the shuttle, sometimes just by patching directly—''

Evan looked up. ''The shuttle?''

''I want to go talk to Trevor,'' Joss said.

''You do that, my lad,'' said Evan, with energy. ''Seems there's something he forgot to tell us.''

''Yes. I wonder why?''

''Do let me know. how about that list, now?''

''Here.'' He pulled over Evan's pad and tapped a few addresses into it, adding reference tags on the basic map of the fiver. ''Just watch out for this last one. It's a bit rough down there sometimes, but daytime should be all right.''

''I daresay I can manage it,'' Evan said.

Joss smiled a bit. ''I daresay you can. See you back at the hotel?''

''Right.''

TREVOR'S OFFICE, IF POSSIBLE, LOOKED EVEN worse than it had when they had been in there last. He looked up at Joss with a slightly unfocused expression, doubtless having something to do with the fact that he had been working on three different data input terminals at once. ''You again?'' he said. ''Where's your friend with the tin suit?''

Joss sat down and looked at him a touch coolly. ''Why didn't you tell us that data also gets routed out through the shuttle?''

Trevor zeroed out the terminal he was working on at the moment. ''Well, for one thing, not much goes that way,'' he said. ''Usually we fall back on it when there's sunstorm weather and none of the satellites are correctly positioned to punch through the interference. Corrupted data is expensive, after all. Times like that, it's cheaper to load the information into the shuttle's comms computers and have it squirt to the satellites from Earth orbit, as it passes them. More expensive than routing through the station, yes, but less expensive than having to resend defective data from here. . . .''

Joss sat back a little. Trevor looked a bit harried. He also looked, on closer examination, as if he'd been up all night. "It really is all about money here, isn't it?" he said.

"You have no idea." Trevor pushed a pile of hardcopy away from him so that he had a place to lean his elbows, and dropped his head into his hands, rubbing his eyes. "By the way," he said, looking up, "we had another leak last night. I was about to call you."

"Oh?"

"Yes. At least, I was told about it last night, and they hauled me out of—well, never mind. I just pulled the file, and there are no access records of any kind to indicate that anyone got at it between the time it came out of Research and the time it was encoded for sending."

"Nothing sensitive."

"Oh, no. They've been couriering everything. But Upstairs is frantic about it. They have a stockholders' meeting coming up, and if news got out—" Trevor grinned a little. "Did you know that even your presence here is classified information? Apparently Upstairs feels that just the news that there are sops on the BurJohn premises might do something bad. So people in the Earth offices know—a few—and the people who're here. But no one else."

"If anyone out there in the fiver decides to call home and tell Auntie Mame about the sop in the tin suit that they saw," Joss said, "the info might not be classified for long. —Well, we'll see what happens. Meantime, there are a few things I need to know. Is there any way that the crew of the shuttle can affect the information passed on to it?"

Trevor scowled with a moment's thought. "Not usually. The outgoing packets are arranged in a sealed squirt. It's dumped as a single file to the comm computers, and they use their normal navigational fixes on the comm satellites to determine when to onlink it. Then the comm satellite in question takes it apart. Normally the shuttle people consider it something of a nuisance, anyway."

"But if a shuttle pilot *wanted* to tamper with it—"

"Oh, a pilot or comms officer could mess with the packet, but I doubt any of them know how—or know how to cover their tracks. It's pretty delicate work. Also, they'd have to do it while actually flying the shuttle. You'd think someone would notice.''

"How?'' Joss said. "Come to think of it, how would you notice if it were taking place right here?''

Trevor sighed. "I guess you *would* have to be looking over the person's shoulder all the time,'' he said. "Which is what *I'm* going to have to start doing, it looks like. Upstairs is on a rampage.''

Joss thought of Onaga. "If necessary,'' he said, "I daresay I could get them off your back a little.''

"No,'' Trevor said. "If this leak really is happening in my department, I should be able to find it. I *have* to be able to find it. If it's not—'' He looked at Joss hopefully. "You have any ideas yet? Anybody who looks likely?''

He had to tell the truth. "No,'' he said. "Suspicions, nothing more. We're going with what we have. But it looks like it's going to take a while. This business with the shuttle is the most interesting thing I've heard so far.''

Trevor rubbed his eyes again. "It's a bit of a bottleneck . . . but if you think it's a real possibility, I'll help you any way I can.''

"Fair enough.'' Joss got up. "Call me if you hear anything useful.''

He headed out, noticing the interested glances of the people in the outer offices as he went. Joss met those glances until they dropped, considering that if he too wore a weapon, he was going to use it.

HE WENT TO FIND HIMSELF A PLACE OUT IN the open where he could sit and think through what to do next. Freedom had quite a few parks, its builders having been (correctly) terrified by studies regarding the effects of overcrowding and claustro syndrome on spacebound populations. Joss had had several favorite ones. Now he picked the best of them, the one "highest'' up in the fiver.

They had called it "Magic Mountain'' when he was in college. The park had an official name, that of some obscure Earth politician, but no one Joss knew had ever

known what it was. The place could be seen from anywhere in the main central pressure, rising above the business islands on its high stilts. Kitefighters, when they could
get at it by night, and more law-abiding ultralight fliers
during the day, loved to dodge among the stilts at high
speed. Occasionally someone came to grief against them.
Usually no one further down was killed, but almost always, the pilot was. The extreme lightness of the gravity
there, almost zero gee, was never enough to balance out
the effects of masses colliding with the usual inertia, and
of kinetic energy being expended.

The way up to the Mountain was via a lift in one of the
stilts, though some people insisted on flying in, and there
was a small facility off to one side of the park where they
could buy methane or alcohol for their flyers. There was
nothing particularly mountainish about the place. It covered about fifty acres, most of it flat and covered with
playing fields and large green areas. In the middle there
was a "wild" area, with a wildflower meadow, and some
small hills carefully covered with trees and undergrowth.
Joss suspected it didn't do to dig too deep in those hills.
The trees' roots probably had less to do with dirt than with
concealed hydroponics. But they looked reassuringly solid,
and even in the light of the nearest artificial sun, about a
mile away, they looked very Earthlike.

That was one of the things that had always made Joss
favor this spot: the fact that it looked like Earth, but without the miserable heavy gravity that always made him want
to go lie down and sleep for about a week. He could
bounce as lightly as during his childhood on the Moon—
considerably more lightly—and come to rest under a tree,
with a sky a reasonable distance above him, and the sound
of birdsong.

He picked a bench to sit on, and glanced up at the
skyroof, about a mile up, where the usual black starscape
looked through past the sun. Between him and that starscape, a lark skimmed by, singing. The kinds of birds that
had been brought here had been strictly regulated—no
pests like sparrows, for example—but birds that served as
predators on the insects that had smuggled themselves in
with the crops were always welcome. There were even a

few predators for the birds themselves. Somewhere near the left-hand side of the main pressure, on ledges of one of the higher office islands, peregrine falcons had been breeding for fifty years. Joss had seen one of them once, and had never quite forgotten the sight of the fastest bird on Earth, bred in space to have only a tenth of its normal weight to deal with, streaking by through the fiver's air at about three hundred kilometers an hour. A peregrine's stoop was short in Freedom, but inevitably fatal for whatever it was stooping at.

He pulled out his pad and pulled up Przno's records again, gazing at the readout . . . then woke up his comm implant and said, "Tee?"

"Right here," she said. "Got your package this morning."

"Was it all right?"

"Yes. I'm sending back the towels."

Joss laughed. "Always trying to keep me out of trouble. What about the solid?"

"I sent it down to Analysis with all the papers in that packet . . . we'll see what they can do. Marya didn't hold out much hope."

"Well, let me know what they find, if anything. Meanwhile, would you pull a file off my pad?"

"Which one?"

"It's labeled PRZNO."

"What's that? Some kind of cleaning fluid?"

"Tee. . . ."

"Got it." There was a brief silence. "Looks like a dull type."

"I think he's one of the links we're looking for."

"You want me to run a check on him."

"If you would, Tee. Don't miss anything. I want his whole history, right the way back; I want to know how often his diapers were changed."

"Kinky."

"Tee . . ."

"Consider it done. What else?"

Joss brooded for a moment. "Get me a listing, if you can, of how many times per week communications are routed through one of the L5 shuttles to the Earth communications satellites.''

"Shouldn't be hard."

"Also I want a list of shuttle pilots doing this run, and their schedules. Also information about all their bank accounts.''

There was a brief silence. "One or two bank accounts wouldn't provoke much interest," Tee said, "but a whole lot of such queries are going to raise questions. With Lucretia, if no one else.''

"Let her ask. . . . This is information we need."

"I'll tell her you said so."

"You do that."

Joss sat for a moment, scrolling through the file showing on his pad, and then shut it down.

"Something bothering you?" Tee said.

Joss sat, watching another bird go by, using only slight, quick, efficient flicks of its wings to move itself, rather than the steady beating that would have been required at one gee. "A bit," he said. "Tee, if I asked you to violate confidentiality—what would you say?''

"Probably something along the lines of, 'The color of my underwear is none of *your* business, you twerp.' Rather like the last time." Joss sighed. "Estimated three minutes on that shuttle list for you," she said. "What's clogging your jets?''

"How long have you known Evan?"

There was a silence. "Quite a while," she said.

"Did he ever strike you as . . . a little dangerous?''

Tee laughed at him. "Come on, Joss. That would require a value judgment, which we're not supposed to render to field operatives. As you know perfectly well."

"I'm worried about him, that's all.''

"The day I meet a sop who's not worried about her partner, that day I quit this job," Tee said. "The other list is coming, too."

"Stop changing the subject!"

"I never did any such thing." There was a pause, and a faraway sound of someone tapping at an input pad. "Tell me what your problem is. Not generalities.''

"I think he's riding the problem of his old partner's

murder so hard, he's likely to misstep somehow. Things
are not in good shape here. Large amounts of money are
changing hands for one thing and another . . . . and that
means real trouble. People are going to see that suit and
want to see it gone, away from the things they're up to."

"Here it comes," Tee said. Joss's pad went into reception and storage mode. Its transfer counter began to rack
up blocks of data. "Joss," Tee said then, "there never
was a suit that was welcome with *all* the people where it
showed up. Evan's used to *that* by now . . . and *anyone*,
even you, could have come by *that* value judgment, so it's
yours for free. You're just not used to leaning, that's all."

"Not when I'm not sure what I'm leaning against,
no. . . ."

Tee sighed audibly. "Look, you need shrink time, I'll
schedule you some. Any one of the online counselors
would talk to you in a second."

"No, no, I don't need them. . . ."

Tee snickered. "There've been times I had my doubts.
Never mind. Transfer's complete." She was quiet again
for a moment. "Some interesting correlations there," she
said. "Some six-sigma probabilities, in my machine at
least. Do a one-two plot on the schedules of the leaks and
the shuttle schedules."

Joss told his pad to plot the two lists against one another. Three of the leaks out of seven occurred when the
shuttle was in Earth orbit. . . .

"It looks a little too pat," he said, converting the universal-
time timestamps on the leaks into station time in his head.
"These leak timings, they're approximations at best. Plus-
one minute to plus-three hours . . . since upload time and
actual transfer time can be that long apart . . ."

"Possibly more?" Tee suggested.

"No, the station comms facility has a guarantee policy:
anything not going out within three hours has the transit
charge refunded. And those people hate to lose money, let
me tell you."

"From your report last night, I get that feeling," Tee
said drily. "Okay, I downgrade my projections from six-
sigma. Still, I find the correlations significant. I think you
ought to talk to the shuttle pilots."

"Noted." Joss scanned down the list of their names. There were about fifteen of them. They worked for the same Earth-government-owned company, and rotated occasionally to routes that served the other fivers, or the Moon. Joss did a little more work with his pad, trying to see whether any one or two pilots tended to be flying the shuttle when there had been a leak.

"No repeats, dammit," he said. "Separate pilots each time."

"That's not the only way they're doing it, then. Some has to be coming out of station comms . . . or some other way."

"But some of the leaks *are* shuttle-borne," Joss said. "So my hunch was good after all!"

Tee laughed. "Is this something surprising?"

"Just reassuring . . . I think."

"All right. Half a moment—"

"What?"

"Ssh!"

Joss was quiet, drumming his fingers on the pad. A robin alighted on the grass not far from him, hopped once, stood still, and cocked its head as if listening intently.

"That was Analysis," Tee said a moment later. "They have a message for you: 'Positive content in solid fragments. Beginning reconstruction and decode. Just wanted you to know.' "

"I'm going to take them all out to Selene's Place when I get back," Joss said, delighted. "You tell 'em that!"

"You're going to Selene's and you're buying?" Tee laughed sardonically. "You on the take or something?"

"You watch your mouth, lady. Some people *here* think so."

"Oh, lordy," Tee said. "Watch out for Evan."

Joss breathed out. "I have been."

"Good. Gotta go, Joss. I'll call when there's anything else interesting."

"You do that."

"Out."

Joss sat quiet for a moment. The robin took a few running steps, listened again, then bounced up in the air a little and on the downstroke drove its bill into the ground.

A second later it came up with one end of a worm. The worm was hanging on the best it could, but the robin had it outnumbered.

"You and me both, brother," Joss said to the robin, got up as quietly as he could, and went off to the shuttle facility to talk to some pilots.

THE SHUTTLE PORT AT THE RIGHT-HAND END of the cylinder was a bigger place than it had looked at the outset. This should have been no surprise to Joss, considering how much traffic passed through it, and how much cargo, every day. With a population of four hundred thousand, that meant a considerable import of food and other necessities, no matter how many of them could be produced here—and a huge tonnage of material and manufactured goods that *couldn't* be produced in space. The port facility itself took up something like half a mile of the entire cylinder, with other storage space scattered through the near-hull cubic right down the length of the fiver. There was mooring space for transient shuttles on the outside, close to the access ports for the customs and immigrations areas, but there were usually one or two shuttles inside for maintenance, floating tethered in the center of the zero-gee zone, surrounded by scaffolding and little tender craft, manned and unmanned.

Joss's business was in the office area, but he made it a point to stop in the "hangar" first for a look around. It was as much for the size of the place as anything else. He had hated to admit it to himself, but he had been finding the size of the cubic in the fiver a little restrictive. On the Moon, where one was digging rock rather than building an enclosed space, livable cubic had been less expensive to provide, and so bigger spaces, *much* bigger spaces like the UnderDome, were common. In Freedom, the roof always seemed a little too close to him, for some reason, even in the top levels where the sky was never closer than a mile away.

But the hangar refreshed him. Here no solid levels had been built. The whole space of the cylinder was empty, and you could see right across the radius of it, instead of just across a chord of it as everywhere else. The skyroof didn't extend this far down the cylinder—the whole curve, right around, was solid. Techs floated about on their business, in the center of the space; or out by the hull, they drove. You could look right above your head and just see people driving cargo-carriers along the far "wall"—the far floor, actually—three miles away, and seemingly upside down. Some few small offices jutted up into this space, on stilts, into areas where there was less gravity; some of them were mobile, and had little floater-craft to tow them around.

Joss made his way across to the very end of the pressurized part of the cylinder, where, around the huge airlock access doors, the offices and living quarters for the transient shuttle crews were arrayed. Most of them were mid-positioned, in the half-gee area, which relieved Joss a bit. He disliked sitting for long in more than about half a gee: it tended to give him hives.

The young woman behind the desk in the shuttle-line front offices seemed very glad to see him. Joss looked at her with interest, and mild regret. She was what his old vids would have called "jailbait," and though the laws were different on the fiver, she was still a bit young for his taste. She was a very tasty-looking lady of mixed African and Spanish descent, with a cloud of shining curly black hair, a model's cheekbones, and a red skintight that left Joss not knowing quite where to look, and she was willing to tell him absolutely anything he wanted to know, especially her commcode.

"Sorry," he said, suspecting that it was his uniform she wanted to date, more than him. "I think I need to see—" he checked his pad "—Mr. Poole?"

"I'll call him," the girl said, and tapped at her input pad. "Officer—"

"O'Bannion," Joss said. "Thank you."

He went and sat down where he wouldn't have to look at the young lady's skintight any more. Poole appeared shortly—a tall slender man, balding on top, with a friendly face. He was wearing what looked like a pilot's uniform, the usual sort of jumpsuit, but without any flight-crew insignia that Joss could recognize.

"Glad to see you, Officer," Poole said. "Come on into my office and you can tell me what you need."

Poole's office looked out on the hangar area through one wall that was entirely glass. He waved Joss to a seat and said, "How can we help you?"

"Forgive me," Joss said, "but you don't seem particularly surprised to see me."

"I'm not," he said. "When we heard that you'd arrived, everyone thought it was a fair bet that you'd be here shortly. The other officer was—the one who died. Sorry to hear about that."

"Yes," Joss said, "so were we."

"I take it that you're still looking into the same business—the data leak."

"Yes. I just want to eliminate the shuttle from our investigations. You understand we have to follow up all the possibilities."

"Of course," Poole said. "Who would you like to see?"

"The shuttle pilots and comm officers."

Poole pulled over a datapad and touched some of its keys. "Two pilots and two comm officers are in Freedom at the moment," he said after a minute or so. "A couple of them are based in the fiver, over in Residential; the other two are staying at the Hilton—they're based on the Moon. How would you like to work this?"

"I'll go to them, if it's convenient," Joss said. "No, don't call them; their addresses will do."

Mr. Poole pushed his pad over to Joss's and let his machine pass the information to Joss's via the physical-contact protocol port. "Anything else I can do for you, Officer?"

"No, that should do very nicely. Please let me know when any of the other pilots come in. I'll be wanting to talk to them, too." Then Joss paused. "One other thing. Would anyone other than the comms officer, or the pilot for a given flight, have access to the shuttle's comms computers before the flight?"

Poole thought for a moment. "You mean after data was loaded? Only the people in Freedom comms, by remote.

Our maintenance people only work with the onboard computers after their short-term memory has been flushed, and that happens after every flight.''

"But you do keep records of the in-flight transactions . . . of what was in the short-term memory."

"Oh, yes. All that goes into the archive solid. IAA and IASA regulations require that we keep all that information for a year, in case an accident or some irregularity needs to be investigated. Usually we try to keep two years' records, for safety's sake."

"I might like to look at those records," Joss said. "I'll let you know if it becomes necessary."

"Call if you need them, sir."

Joss thanked Poole kindly and headed out, winking at the young receptionist as he went. She rolled her eyes at him as he left.

Duty, Joss thought with only mild regret. *Duty . . .*

He spent the rest of the morning visiting the pilots and comm officers. Three of them—Captain Rouse, and comm officers O Dalaigh and Kung, were women, as might have been expected. Rouse and O Dalaigh were Moon-based; Kung and Captain Jensen, a man in his forties, were newly transferred up from one of the hyperplane services on Earth. They were all mildly surprised to see him, but all quite calm and helpful, even amiable. O Dalaigh in particular knew a lot of the same restaurants in Serentatis that Joss did, and suggested some new ones he might like to try. None of them gave Joss the slightest indication of guilt. He came away from his last meeting, with Jensen, feeling annoyed and slightly out of sorts. Heaven knew what Evan was up to, but Joss had wanted to have some useful lead to show him when they met again that evening.

There was nothing much to do but go back to the Hilton and sift through what he knew so far. There was already a lot of information to deal with, and too many different ways to attack it.

He settled himself in the downstairs bar in the Hilton, in a corner where he could keep an eye on things, and started tapping away at his pad. As the master menu came up, he saw the blink on the screen that meant Dispatch had something for him.

"Tee?" he said, turning his implant on.

"Just a note from Lucretia," she said in his ear. "It's in memory."

"Right. Anything more from Analysis?"

"Nothing yet. Anything exciting happen?"

"Not by a long shot.—You know a restaurant called Ipokratis?"

"Uh . . . isn't there one by that name down in Deep Serenity?"

"That's it. I hear the moussaka is good there."

Tee snickered. "You *have* been having an exciting day," she said. "Not as exciting as your partner, though."

"Oh? Where is he?"

"Somewhere in the Freedom downlevels, with some poor downers who're trying to drink him under the table. Futile exercise, if you ask *me*."

"Well, if he's full of antimetabolyte—"

"Evan? He's much too organic for that kind of thing."

Joss digested this. It was true that, among the bag full of vitamins and enzyme tablets in Evan's bath, he hadn't sen any containers of the usual sop-issue anti-alcohol metabolyte. "Is he busy at the moment?"

"Pretty much. When he has a spare moment, shall I have him call you?"

"If you would."

Joss was looking at the note from Lucretia. It said:

WILL BE WANTING TO SEE JUSTIFICATION FOR MASSIVE BANKING SURVEILLANCE IN YOUR NEXT REPORT. APPROVED, FOR THE TIME BEING, BUT THESE THINGS CAN CAUSE MORE PROBLEMS THAN THEY SOLVE. ALSO THEY COST MONEY. VERBUM SAP, OR IN THIS CASE, SOP. REPORT ON STATUS OF YOUR JOINT DISCRETIONARY FUNDS SOONEST. L.

"Wonderful," he said to himself, wondering how much of it Evan had spent so far, and whether Lucretia would approve. It was always hard to tell. Sometimes, if things were going well, she would let you be amazingly spendthrift with the Patrol's money. But if she felt things were moving too slowly, the purse strings would be pulled tight enough to leave you on bread and water. Joss wondered which it would be this time. . . .

The records of the bank accounts of the people at Freedom comms were now available to him. He started to go through them, looking for correlations to the data leaks—sudden deposits out of the usual pattern, for example, or account credits with incompletely documented sources.

He found only two. One of them was a comm tech's check for CR 1533.18, from the football pools, with all the correct verification codes attached, and its paper trail intact right back to Littlewood's PLC on Earth. The other was actually an inheritance, from a maiden aunt, referenced back to an attorney's office in Manitoba Province. There was nothing else out of the ordinary at all, certainly no sum large enough to be a decent payoff for the kind of info smuggling that was going on.

Joss sat and drummed his fingers, thinking. There was always the possibility, hell, the probability, that the account through which any given person was being paid off wasn't in the person's name. Well enough. If one could find out where the money was coming from, one could then do another cross-reference of Freedom's banking records and find the account it was going to.

Except that if I knew where the money was coming from, I probably wouldn't need to . . .

He paused, then tapped another control on the pad and brought up the note-memory, for Trevor's commcode. Joss touched the control to have his pad access the code, and waited.

YES? the screen said after a few minutes.

"Trevor?" Joss aid, watching the screen transcribe what he was saying.

CAUGHT ME AT MY DESK, said the screen. It was hard to tell whether Trevor was typing, or having his own pad or terminal transcribe. WHAT'S THE SCOOP?

Joss paused. "Do you watch old vids?" he said after a moment.

WHY?

"Your idiom is a little strange sometimes."

SO IS YOURS, KEMOSABE.

That Joss understood, and he grinned. "Never mind that just now. Questions for you."

SHOOT.—THEN AGAIN, MAYBE I'D BETTER RE-PHRASE THAT.

Joss laughed again. "If you wanted to get into the BurJohn accounting department's records," he said, "could you do it?"

THAT'S PART OF MY JOB.

"But without leaving any trace?"

A pause. PROBABLY. WHY?

"I want to make a comparison between some figures I've got here and those in the BurJohn computers. Date and time comparisons."

I THINK I COULD MANAGE THAT FOR YOU. IT MIGHT TAKE A LITTLE TIME.

"All right. Something else. Can you get into any of the banks' programs?"

ON FREEDOM? There was another pause. PEOPLE CAN THROW YOU IN JAIL FOR THAT KIND OF THING.

"Not if it's sop business."

I'D WANT IT IN WRITING, OFFICER. BANQUE SVIZZERA AND THEIR FRIENDS GET CRANKY ABOUT THAT KIND OF THING.

"Understood. I just want to run some other comparisons."

I HATE TO ADMIT IT, said Joss's screen after another pause, BUT IT'S DOABLE. I KNOW SOME OF THE PEOPLE OVER AT BS, AND IN THREADNEEDLE STREET. WE TRADE ROUTINES.

"All right. Pick your time. Not tonight, though, or tomorrow night. We've got some surveillance and questioning work at station comms."

NIGHT AFTER, THEN. THEY DOWNLINK TO THE EARTH OFFICES THEN ... THAT'S WHEN THEY'RE LEAST LIKELY TO NOTICE A COMPROMISE. DROP ME A NOTE ON THIS CODE.

"Thanks."

The screen blanked itself.

Joss got up and went off to look for Evan.

HE FOUND HIM BACK AT THE TAVERN, INSIDE
this time. Afternoon light, Joss suspected, was too broad
and open for some of the people Evan was talking to.
When he first walked in the glass door of the place, and
paused in it, things got abruptly about twenty decibels
quieter than they had been, and faces turned to look at
him from all over the tavern, most of them scowling. It
was a touristy-looking place, or had been once, with beams
and ''stone'' floor and scratched ''wooden'' tables, trying
hard to look like an Olde Englishe Pubbe, and only partly
succeeding—the speakers and terminals of the information
systems hanging here and there rather ruined the effect.
They were presently showing a baseball game, at top vol-
ume, and for some moments the roar of some crowd in
Cincinnati, and the voice of a commentator stalling over
a pitcher's balk, were the loudest sounds in the place.

Joss stood there for a moment wishing that he had a hat
to take off—the cops' traditional signal that he was not
''after'' anybody in the place, but there on more informal
business, or possibly just to drink. After a few seconds
the hostile faces started to turn away from him, and he
stepped further in to the bar. It at least looked to be a
genuine antique, all real wood fifteen feet long, carved in
elaborate first-Victorian patterns, with brass rails held on
by ornate and brightly polished elephant's heads. The barman was leaning over the bar talking to another client, a
shaven-scalped young woman dressed in what appeared to
Joss to be bits of a rag rug, tied around her at appropriate
intervals. She looked Joss up and down as he leaned
against the bar, then audibly sniffed and moved away.

The barman shifted his gaze to Joss. He was a slim
man, his head shaved in narrow strips, and braids hanging
down from each strip at back. His face bore old burn scars,
as did both his arms—difficult to tell whether from an industrial accident, or one involving firearms. He jerked his
head over to one side, wiping his hands on his sleeveless
tunic, and indicating an area around the bar and to the
back. ''Your friend's over there,'' he said. ''Drink?''

''Beer,'' Joss said. ''Mild, please.''

The man turned away without any further words. Joss went around the bar and found Evan.

He was sitting at the back of a booth, surrounded by five of the least likely-looking people Joss had seen in a while. Their clothes—they varied between the trendy and purposely damaged, and the simply outlandish—leathers, kilts, tights with the most outrageous codpieces Joss had seen in a while. And *those* were just the women. Scarified faces and painted ones eyed him with cool interest.

"My partner," Evan said, as Joss pulled over a dented wooden chair to sit down.

Joss swept the group with his eyes, nodded to them *en passant,* and looked over at Evan.

"We're discussing rates," Evan said.

"Ah. Yes," Joss said. "Lucretia was interested in that very subject."

Evan rolled his eyes slightly. "And why wouldn't she be," he murmured. "Well, we'll make our peace with her later on, shall we? Right now we're discussing the transfer of information in the downlevels. And its redistribution."

There ensued one of the most subdued but cutthroat bidding sessions Joss had seen since he was last in Christie's auction rooms in Serenity. It went on for three-quarters of an hour, six pints of beer, five glasses of assorted spirits, and three plates of something claiming to be nachos, though Joss strongly suspected that the Monterey Jack had more to do with soybeans than with any cow, and that the scotch had never been any closer to Earth than geosynchronous orbit. At the end of it nearly two thousand credits changed hands, all in cash, and the variegated young people went away seeming well pleased. One of them actually shook Joss's hand and told him it was a pleasure doing business with him. Joss smiled and thanked her politely, ducking a bit as she left so as to avoid being hit in the head by her codpiece, while wishing he had known more about exactly what the business entailed.

It got quiet, then, as approximately half the people in the tavern left. Joss realized they must have been mostly audience—observers from gangs not taking part in Evan's "business," just curious about what was going on. He waited while they headed out, and when the noise had settled and his drink came, said, "Well, then."

Evan drank the last swallow of his present beer and put down the glass. "There appear to be about six really prominent gangs here at the moment," he said, "and about another eight tributary ones that support one of the major ones. All six of the majors and several of the minors are doing running for various companies and other interests in the station—including the one that claims to have killed Lon."

Joss sat still for a moment, then said, "Claims?"

Evan shook his head. "I'm not sure they did. There's a possibility one of the other gangs staged it to look like Squadron's doing—to produce the exact result they've got now: angry sops out to kill them."

"Or that they think they've got now."

"Well," Evan said, "yesterday's little demonstration didn't leave them in much doubt."

"Which 'them'?"

"Both Squadron itself, and the various other gangs that would like to see it taken down a peg. I've had visits from representatives of all of them today." The smile Evan made was crooked and amused. "Every one of them is trying to find some way to use us against their rivals. I've heard every kind of accusation and counteraccusation you can think of. And some rather substantial bribes."

Joss smiled at that.

"At least they *thought* they were substantial," Evan said. "They were a little shocked to find that our price was so much higher than the cops'."

Our price? "So you were right, then," Joss said.

"Oh, aye. Our friend Sorenson . . ." Evan's mouth worked as if he was thinking about spitting, then decided not to bother. "He's comfortable, I'll tell you. The gangs pay him well to stay out of their sensitive areas."

Joss breathed out. It was no fun to find that this suspicion was true. But it certainly explained why any murder that seemed gang-related was as poorly investigated as Lon's had been.

"Any road," Evan said, "I've done a bit of discreet purchasing myself. I've bought a few runners whose business is to keep making their runs for their usual employers, but also to be carrying seeing-eyes when they do it. We shall have some faces to work with; we'll see who's paying who what, and how much.''

"Right. Meanwhile—'' Joss pushed his pad over to Evan. He tapped it, looked at the files Joss had flagged for him. "You *have* been busy.''

"A bit. Evan, we have some problems.''

"Oh?''

"Yes. All this looks just fine . . . but I'm not sure the files that Tee got for me haven't been compromised themselves. Someone with the knowhow to cause the initial data leaks could very well subvert the data files that are coming through comms to us.'

"You mean break the Patrol encryption on the signal—''

"Remember that Lon suspected something like that was happening. . . .''

Evan looked a little nervous at that. "So he did,'' he said softly. "Heaven knows what's being overheard.''

"Yes. We're going to have to be a little careful about what we say, even to Tee. Meanwhile . . .'' He told Evan his thought about Trevor and the banks.

"That's not awfully legal, my son,'' Evan said. "Not without auth from the Patrol . . . and I doubt we're going to get that.''

"Can you think of any other way we're going to get at the truth here? We might as well be working with bags over our heads. And the people we're up against aren't bothered by the little scruple that what *they're* doing isn't strictly legal.''

Evan was scowling. Joss's beer came. He drank it and looked at his partner.

"Let's wait a while,'' Evan said. "I'd like to find another way. It bothers my oaths.''

"Mine too,'' Joss said. And after a little while, added, "How long is a while?''

"At least a couple of days. We should finish with the station comms people, and look at our primary suspect for a bit, before we do anything like this. Especially since if we get caught—''

Joss thought of how Lucretia's face was likely to look in such a case. "Yes. . . ."

Evan shook his head and got up as Joss finished his beer. "I wish things here *were* the way Sorenson thinks they usually are for us," he said, "simple and straightforward. I'd give a lot at the moment just to have something to shoot at."

"That makes two of us,' Joss said.

THEY WENT TO AN EARLY DINNER, AND THEN back to their rooms to try to catch some sleep. Any sop who found himself or herself on night work had several different kinds of drugs to fall back on if necessary, but neither Joss nor Evan cared much for these. No matter what claims the medics made for the fewness of their side effects, they always left a person feeling as if there was something missing from his performing edge, a lack of acumen or alertness. Joss found simply changing schedules preferable, and like other sops had been taught the necessary autosuggestion techniques to make the change fairly painless.

One thing cheered Joss a bit before he went to sleep; the note he found waiting in his pad's memory that said: HAVE AN IDEA. STOP BY MY OFFICE BEFORE SHIFT TONIGHT. T. *That boy has a devious mind,* he thought as he lay down. *I wonder what he's thinking of?*

Something more devious than our boy Przno, I hope. . . .

EVAN GOT INTO HIS SUIT FOR THE LAST BOUT of questioning. "Are you really sure you want to do that?" Joss said to him, while they were suiting up. "After we finish with the questions, we're just going to be watching the comms people all night. . . ."

"I'll be fine," Evan said. "It's not as if it's uncomfortable, you know." He laughed a little as he checked the seals and contacts on the suit's southern half, before starting on the breastplate and the rest of the upper part. "At least," he added, "not if I don't overeat."

Joss was a little amused at that. He checked his gun in its holster and said, "Do you have to diet on purpose, or can you just maintain your weight?"

Evan groaned softly, shouldering into the breastplate. "Ah, heavens, man, I can't look at a pudding or a tart or a chocolate ice, or anything with cream. It's hard cruel, it is, a man with my upbringing reduced to lean meat and veg." He snapped open one of the sleeves and slipped his left arm into the foam and neural-contact padding, then closed the sleeve carefully. "But you get used to it, I suppose. I can't think when I last had a proper scone with clotted cream on it." He picked up the second sleeve. "What I give up to see justice done. . . ."

Joss looked curiously at the inside of the second sleeve. "Funny," he said, "I thought there would have been more wiring and such in there."

"No," Evan said, "that's the comfort of it. All that is buried right under the outer shell. The circuitry needs the cooling coils, you see—that next layer. And then come the negative feedback pads—they have to be quite soft, to work. They read the pressure of your muscles directly, you see, and try to 'jump' away from any movement you make. That's the movement that the circuitry reads and uses to drive the suit proper. And for the suit to work right, the neural foam has to be fairly thick. If it compresses after heavy use, I have to get it replaced." He sealed up the second sleeve. "At least I don't get cold inside here," he said.

"I'd think you would sweat like a pig," Joss said.

Evan reached over for the helm. "I do," he said, "and what it smells like when the foam is getting old . . ." He trailed off.

The thought had occurred to Joss that it was getting a bit old right now, but he didn't say anything. "Ready?" he said.

"Just about." Evan looked around the living room of the suite for his pad; then his eye fell on the little black box where he had left the police bug and his countermeasure. Evan stood in a listening attitude for a moment. Curious,

Joss went over to the box, bent close to it. The sound of sneezing had stopped.

He looked up at Evan and cupped one hand to his ear in a "someone's-listening" gesture. Evan grinned—a look of mild surprise—and waved Joss toward the door.

When they were out, and a good way down the hall, near the soft rumble of the lifts, Evan said, "I was wondering when they'd get up the courage. Mark my word, they'll be in here tonight, rummaging our things. You haven't left anything in there you don't mind them seeing, I hope."

Joss shook his head. "My laundry isn't *that* harrowing. Let them paw over it. Everything important pertaining to this case is in here." He shook his pad gently.

Evan looked at his own pad thoughtfully. "I remember from Lon's notes," he said, "how reluctant he was getting to pass information on about his case, even through the Patrol comms net. How have you been storing your files?"

"On solids," Joss said, "in my locked luggage."

"That lock secure enough for you?"

Joss thought about it for a moment. "Now that you mention it," he said, "I suppose someone with enough time and intention could get it open—"

"I think maybe we'd better send out another courier container," Evan said as the lift came for them. "I'd hate to see something happen to *our* reports."

"Agreed." Though the thought occurred to Joss that he would also hate to see something happen to *them* shortly thereafter, as it had to Lon. All Lon's records, and all the history about him that Joss had from Evan, pointed to Lon being a most cautious and thorough man, careful with his research and his materials. Where had he gone wrong?

More to the point, where had he gone wrong that Joss and Evan were possibly going wrong, right this moment? *Damn,* he thought.

IT BEGAN TO BE ONE OF THOSE NIGHTS RIGHT away, because when they got to BurJohn and went up to Trevor's office, they found him gone—and no one there could tell them anything about where he had gone, or what he was doing, or when he would be back. There was nothing in that office for them but furtive, hostile looks. Evan stood looking grim but calm while Joss scribbled a quick "we-were-here" note on the peel-pad on Trevor's desk. When they were out the door again, Evan said softly, "Bets that there's been another leak?"

Joss thought about it. "A bit early," he said. "At least according to what pattern we've been able to detect so far."

Evan sighed as they headed over to the slidewalk that led toward the station comms island. "It occurs to me," he said, "that the whole business of the information leaks could well be automated . . . and set up to distribute the blame so that any investigator would be confused."

"It would make sense," Joss said. "There's one thing that's been bothering me, though . . ."

Evan made a politely interested look as they stepped onto the slidewalk.

"Are you expert enough," Joss said, "to catch our young friend in the act if he actually *does* anything to-night?"

"Hard to say." Evan looked around him as if trying to find something to distract himself with, and failing. "I was just thinking of making him nervous, actually. That's a healthy state of mind to inculcate in an evildoer."

Joss had to laugh out loud at the turn of phrase. "Meaning you wouldn't know what he was up to if he wore a sign."

"We'll see," Evan said. And he would say nothing more until they got to the comms center.

Joss had to admit that there was really little more they could do but be there, and reinforce the knowledge that the place was being watched by interested eyes. They checked in with the evening duty comms supervisor—a plump young woman named Meier—and then simply started to wander around, looking over a shoulder here, watching a screen there as a load of data came in or was sent out. Joss was a little amused to find that the comms staff talked as if they literally considered data a physical thing, like a load of bricks or a tanker of milk; a malleable material to be labeled, molded, pooled or subdivided, routed and rerouted, tossed into electronic mailboxes or waiting host computers the way an old-fashioned newspaper might be thrown onto someone's front lawn. Their conversation was interesting, on that account, but Joss went from station to station in growing frustration, knowing that he had very little understanding of what was going on. And Evan, who seemed to understand this kind of thing, had not much more, and no clue as to what might be happening right under their noses.

Przno was working this shift, and Joss was making an effort to stay away from him most of the time. There was no use in so frightening the man that he would refrain from doing what they so very much wanted to catch him at. But Joss was not above passing him by every now and then, on his way to the toilet—he was not above drinking more tea than necessary, as a handy excuse to move around—and asking artless questions about what was going on. Przno answered a little nervously at first, then more calmly. Indeed he seemed to calm down quite a bit after the first hour they were there; he went purposefully from terminal to dataport to pad in a very organized and easy kind of way, slotting in a datasolid here, changing a timing there, like a man who has had enough practice to make a complicated job look as casual as a dance. Przno was also (Joss observed ruefully) one of the fastest typists Joss had ever seen. Joss was a hunt-and-peck man himself. He had flunked the EssPat touchtyping course four times in a row now, and Lucretia kept making him take it, he thought, out of sheer astonishment that someone so otherwise talented could be so thumbfingered. (Naturally she typed like the wind herself, and compassion for thumbfingeredness was not in her.)

Joss sighed and put his feet up, about halfway through the shift, and leaned back to gaze out one of the comms center's windows. They had long since turned the sun off for the night—or rather, turned it down to a bare firefly glow. Station environmental research had long since discovered that it was unwise to let any section of an orbital habitat go completely dark. It bred madness.

He lounged there with his back turned for a while, certain that Evan was missing nothing. Besides, if Joss acquired a rep among these people for being the careless one, some night when he was here alone, someone might do something careless . . . and they would have their man, or woman. No harm in seeming a bit leisurely.

The comms center windows had a good view of the skyroof, and the stars. They burned brightly in the darkness, here and there obscured by one of those opaque patching-panels that Joss had noticed on the way in. *Odd,* he thought. *It's not as if reinforced glaspanel was that expensive. . . .* It was that seediness calling itself to his attention again, that lapse in the way Freedom looked and felt. *Very strange. Why is this place going to pieces? Why doesn't anyone act as if they care?*

Behind him he heard the soft whisper of Evan's armor servos as he went by, moving from one data terminal to the next. *And where was Trevor?* Joss wondered. Supposing there had been another leak. If someone as clever as Trevor hadn't been able to find it, what hope did *they* have?

Defeatist thinking, Joss thought, and promptly threw the thought out, as he had been taught. Giving up early produced no solutions. He got up and went to look over the shoulders of some of the comms staff beside Przno.

Three hours later, when the shift ended, it seemed to Joss that they might as well not have bothered. He had seen nothing even remotely suspicious, which was doubtless what any perpetrator would have wanted. As he and Evan headed toward the doors, to check with the incoming morning comms supervisor before leaving, he threw Evan a glance that said, *I told you so.*

Evan shrugged, said "Cheerie-bye," to the comms supervisor, and shouldered out through the door. "Breakfast?" he said.

"Do you ever think about anything but food?"

Evan laughed at Joss. "Better than sitting here all night souring my stomach with that tea they make in there," he said, "and having bad thoughts because of it. You should have seen your face. They're terrified of you."

"What?"

"Oh, aye. I think word has started to get around among

the upper echelons about our little foray into the downlevels. A suit, they expect to perform miracles, but that little potshot of *yours—*" Evan laughed softly. "They have you set up as some kind of obsessed gunman. I near wet myself not laughing."

"Well, thanks loads," Joss said, a little nettled. "I'd hate to cause a crisis in your plumbing."

Evan roared with laughter. "You need breakfast," he said. "Be still and come on."

They made their way back to the Hilton as the sun began to come on again, and slipped into a corner of the coffee bar in the lobby. Joss was trying to resist Evan's disgusting good humor after a night shift, and succeeding, until after the first couple of poached eggs. After that things seemed slightly better. In the middle of the third egg, a voice from behind him said, "You're hard people to find, you know that?"

He looked over his shoulder. It was Trevor, looking even more haggard and run-down than he had the last time Joss had seen him. Evan waved a fork at him. "Sit down, lad, for pity's sake," he said. "You look like a rainy day and the washing caught out on the line. Here, take that chair. So. Have my tea. They don't make it properly here. More trouble last night?"

Trevor sank into the offered chair and nodded, rubbing his eyes for a moment and then drinking Evan's cup of tea right down. "They had me Upstairs all night," he said, pouring another cup. "Sorry I missed you. How was your first night?"

"Dead," Joss said.

Trevor nodded. "Might have known. I have a present for you, though. Might make it easier."

"Aha," Evan said. "Good. But a moment. Was this leak like the others?"

Trevor nodded wearily and drank the second cup of tea. "Promotional material, this time. Not crucial, but—" He shook his head. "The Earth offices are getting *really* paranoid about the leakages. They're talking about shutting down the Freedom branch of the operation entirely if it can't get its house in order, security-wise."

Joss was surprised. "Could they afford to do that?"

"Probably. They have three other orbital facilities . . . and this is the oldest of their group. They probably wouldn't mind an excuse to kill it. I've seen some reports. . . ." Trevor sighed. "I shouldn't have, but what the hell. Profits at this branch of the company have been slipping from their usual disgustingly fat levels."

Evan nodded slowly. "So there is panic Upstairs, I take it."

Trevor rolled his eyes in a way that made it plain that panic was a poor word for it.

"Right. So what have you brought us?"

Trevor reached into his pocket and came up with something small and dark-colored, flat and round, about a centimeter in diameter. Joss looked at it and shook his head. "A bug?"

"Not your usual one. This one is RF-sensitive."

"Aha," Evan said softly.

Trevor handed the little thing to Joss. "Put it away. It's not legal."

"Oh?"

"It sucks signal," Trevor said softly. "Listen, do you know how much radiation in one frequency or another our comms equipment gives off?"

"I thought it was all shielded," Joss said.

"Oh, the dangerous stuff is. And machinery that gives off high radio-frequency stuff is shielded enough to keep it from interfering with other machinery close by. Especially the high-security or high-accuracy instruments. Otherwise if you put them close enough together, you could read one data terminal's output on the next terminal over."

"But if they're shielded—"

"Oh, they are," Evan said, with a conspiratorial smile, "but you can never shield *completely*. There's always a little leakage. And if you have a sensitive enough receiver—"

Joss smiled slightly. "Aha, then. What is this hooked up to?"

"Nothing, if you mean by microwave link or the usual cordless methods. Those would alert anyone in the area. This one has a molecular memory in it."

Joss's eyebrows went up. Molecular memory was incredibly effective and compact, but not at all cheap. "So," he said, "we put this on a person we're interested in . . . and it 'reads' everything they do on a computer or other piece of electronic equipment. Eh?"

Trevor nodded and poured a third cup of tea. "When you're done with your next surveillance shift, you recover it and play it back. Your pads would have the protocols you'd need."

Evan sat for a moment, considering his toast and marmalade. "Why haven't you used this before to solve your own problem?" he said.

Trevor started at that, then sighed and said, "I just had it smuggled up a week ago. I was going to use it . . . but—"

"—but penalties for illegal use start at five years—yes, I know," Evan said. He picked up a piece of toast and started buttering it. "Just as well," he said. "Heaven knows whether I would have thought of it, and if I had, I would have had Hell's merry time convincing our supervisor that we needed it."

"Amen," Joss said. "I think I get to spend another night shift or two up in comms, and then I plant this thing on—" he didn't mention the name aloud "—and see what we find."

"Should be most enlightening," Evan said. "Clever lad, Trevor. Clever indeed."

Trevor actually blushed at the compliment. "I have to go," he said, starting to get up. "I'm just on a break."

"You eat this," Evan said, and gave Trevor the toast, and turned such a grim look on him when he tried to protest that Trevor finally just smiled weakly and ate it.

"Good for you," Evan said. "Marmalade cures everything. Now scoot."

Trevor scooted.

"Nice lad, that," Evan said. "Glad he's on our side."

"Seems to be, at least," said Joss.

Evan nodded, thoughtful. "True. It's early to be taking anything for granted. What are your plans for today?"

"Sleep first. And then some more interviews with pilots."

"Think you've got something there, eh?" There was something curious about Evan's voice, a dry sound.

"Think I do." Joss thought a moment, then said, "Having second thoughts about Przno?"

"No indeed. My hunch remains in harness." Evan leaned back and took another piece of toast. "But I have a feeling that your hunch and mine may be tied to the same cart."

"You mean you think that the data could be being smuggled out *both* ways?"

"One must keep an open mind."

Joss rubbed his hands over his face. "Then," he said, "after the pilots, I want to talk to Customs about how they search flight crews coming in and out. If they do."

"Hmm," Evan said. It was his turn to look thoughtful. "Plug-in components, you're thinking. Add a little bit of machinery to the in-flight computers, have the right program running—and no one notices the little private message you send."

"I want to discuss it with Trevor. But, yes, that had crossed my mind."

"Devious," Evan said, with great satisfaction. "Devious, you are, and you have an evil mind." He looked at a third piece of toast, then pushed it away. "A man after my own heart."

"Oh? And what are *you* thinking of?"

"Using some of my hired labor," Evan said, "to do a little surveillance."

"Przno?"

Evan blinked. "Nothing *illegal*, of course. But I should like to see what he does with his off-shift time."

Joss smiled. "I should be most interested in finding out, Officer Glyndower."

Evan made a wry expression. "Glun*door,*" he said.

"What happens to the *w?*"

"That's the *oo* bit."

"But the *y*—"

"It's a *u.* Or a *schwa,* actually."

"A *what?*"

Evan leaned back in his chair and went for the last piece

of toast after all. "What do they teach them in these schools," he murmured.

THE FIVE HOURS' SLEEP LEFT JOSS FEELING LESS than wonderful, as was usually the case when he had just begun to throw his system out of whack when working on a case. When he finally woke up and had a long hot shower, he knocked on the door of Evan's suite: nothing. He poked his head in and looked around: no signs. There were no notes. Evan was too cautious an officer to leave notes around in a situation like this, where any communication might be vulnerable.

He went back into his own room, checked it over as thoroughly as he could for listening or viewing devices— there was always the chance that one might have been slipped in recently—but the pad's bug detector showed him nothing. Not that that was always an accurate indicator. No matter. He touched the pad and said, subvocalizing, "Tee?"

"On the spot, as usual," she said through his implant.

"Any word from Evan?"

"He says he's gone off to find you a Welsh grammar. Something about a boiled tongue having better pronunciation than yours."

"Truly, I need this," Joss said. "How are the people down in Analysis doing?"

"Not too well. That solid was badly shattered, they say. Parts of it can't be reclaimed. But others can."

"All right. Anything from Lucretia?"

"Peace and quiet."

"So there's something to be thankful for, at least. No more trouble about the expense account?"

"You haven't submitted it yet."

Joss sighed. Evan had said *he* was going to. "Never mind. Look, if he wants me, tell him I'm going down to the shuttle offices again, and then to Customs, and then station Admin. I want to ask the people there a few more questions. And see if I can get them to help me with something."

"Any details?"

"Not yet."

"You just don't want to look dumb," she said, "in case what you're thinking about doesn't pan out."

"No comment."

She made one, a rude one.

"You be quiet. How are you doing with those bank accounts?"

Joss sighed. "I have to get back to those. It's slow work. The computer may be smart, but sometimes I can't find ways to tell it exactly what I want."

"You need more programming training. You need—"

Joss stopped Telya before she got started on Favorite Lecture Number Six in a series of several hundred. "But what are you *after?*" she said after a moment.

"A needle in a haystack, I think."

"A what? I swear, somebody should marry you and buy you a brain transplant. You've got cobwebs or something in this one. Antiques."

Joss laughed and switched her off.

THE NEXT GROUP OF SHUTTLE FLIGHT PERSON-nel was as dull and colorless as the first lot had been interesting. There were three pilots and four passenger service people: two Moon-based, four living on Freedom or the next nearest fiver, Farflung. Joss asked them all the most provocative questions he could think of, and got nary a rise out of any of them.

That left him only three more sets of flight crew to talk to, but they wouldn't be in until later in the week, so Joss took himself off down to Customs. They were a cheerful lot of people, considering that their work consisted of long periods of boredom interspersed with moments of hectic excitement, and then more boredom while the paperwork got written up. Their chief, a big friendly-faced man named Pat Higgins, took Joss all around their facility—the examination areas for arriving passengers, the questioning rooms, their own database center—and was as helpful as he could be; which wasn't very.

"We don't search the flight crews at all," he said, "past the usual passive means. It's traditional; a courtesy. Besides, the passive sniffing equipment would catch anything contraband, unless it was so well shielded that a sniffer couldn't catch anything. And anything wrapped like that is so bulky, the scan or X-ray catches it before the sniffer has a chance."

Joss sighed as he sat in Higgins's office, gazing out through the one-way mirror at the examination stage, where another shuttle-load of tourists was being examined. "Would your scans catch something like small electronics, if they weren't wrapped like that?" he said.

"Probably not. We have 'hound-dog' listeners built to catch electronics with low latent power signatures; it's standard anti-terrorist stuff. But a little chip or board—" Higgins looked thoughtful. "Probably not. Not much to be made in smuggling electronics into this place, considering how much of it is manufactured here. And we don't search people outgoing. Just the usual sniffs."

Joss shook his head. "What would happen if you *were* asked to search outgoing?"

Higgins laughed. "Are you crazy? We'd do it, and collect the overtime. But station Admin wouldn't like it. Bad for publicity, they'd say."

"Tough," Joss said softly. Higgins grinned.

"I think I like you," he said. "Officer, these people are down on us every time something illicit makes its way in here. But they won't give us the money, the staff, or the equipment to do what we need to do to *keep* the place clean. Truly, I wouldn't mind seeing a little trouble in their ivory tower."

"I suspect there may be some," Joss said. "I'll keep you posted." He mused a moment, then said, "There *is* a lot of illicit, I take it."

Higgins was still smiling, but the smile had acquired a grim edge to it. "It gets in," he said. "Much of it gets in through freight . . . in a lot of different ways. We figure out one and stop it, and some bright person comes up with another." He breathed out and said, "This sounds blasphemous, but I think the station encourages it to some degree. There are a lot of people here who have no way out but drugs . . . and the drugs keep them quiet. Very convenient for everyone involved. Also, the station tax base doesn't lose numbers through mass immigration . . . the percentage of tax the companies pay to support the place stays high. . . .''

"Ahh," Joss said. "Money raises its ugly head again."

"As usual," Higgins said. "Look, Officer, do you think we *are* going to have to do outgoing searches?"

"I think I may ask you," Joss said, "if the line of investigation I'm following at the moment doesn't turn anything up."

"Just try to give me some warning, all right?" Higgins said. "I have people with vacations coming up. I'd like to get rid of them early, so they won't be disappointed, and then give the rest of the troops a little warning so I can distribute the overtime equally."

Joss nodded. "No problem. But it's just the flight crews that will need investigating."

"Oh, but surely a fair proportion of the passengers, as well," Higgins said. "And container cargo, both pressurized and dry. That way they won't complain to their unions that they're being singled out unfairly, or that their civil rights are being violated in some strange way. Thus ruining your investigation."

"Well, yes," Joss said. "And that way your people get more overtime."

Higgins smiled at him. "What a pleasure to do business with you, Officer O'Bannion."

"My pleasure, I'm sure, Inspector Higgins."

HE MADE HIS WAY TO STATION ADMINISTRAtion wondering how he was going to find a polite way to tell them that he was about to seriously disrupt their tourist trade, on a hunch. *Not my problem, though,* he thought, strolling along the walkway to the Admin island. *They called for help. They get to deal with being helped whether they like the form it arrives in or not. . . .*

"Ah, Officer O'Bannion," said a voice from behind him. "Come to tell us the bad news, no doubt."

Joss turned, surprised. It was Dorren Orcieres, the PR lady. "Not that bad," he said, "yet. But what makes you think—"

"Your face," she said. "It could curdle plastic. I take it you're not finding much that's of help to you."

"Bits and pieces," Joss said, "but I'm not sure whether they're ever going to make a picture." He fell into step beside her as they walked up toward the Admin building.

"I was going to say that you seemed to be casting your net pretty wide. All these computer searches."

Joss raised his eyebrows, a look of mild surprise. "Noticed those, did you?"

"Oh, yes. Accounting got a fat wad from EssPat in the morning reckoning, for database access and so forth. Having you gentlemen around could be very profitable." She laughed, a cheerful sound. "Do all the searches you like."

"I'll make a note of that," Joss said. They went in through the dilating doors, and strolled across the office floor toward Orcieres's glass cubicle in the back. "Do you usually hear about things like this from Accounting?"

"Oh, yes. But it's more in the nature of gossip than actually as part of my job description. Really big bills, or billings—" She chuckled as they stepped into her cubicle, and she tossed the document envelope she was carrying onto her desk.

"Bills for what?"

"Oh, all kinds of things. Staples, air, comms, transport—We had one guy a few weeks ago who went back and forth to the Moon *twelve* times in one—"

"Comms?" Joss said. He sat down in the chair that Orcieres offered him. "Private people's comms bills?"

She blushed a little. "I know it's supposed to be confidential," she said, "but people do talk, inside the office at least. It's harmless, really. I'm sure they don't repeat—"

"Heavens, I'm sure they don't, too. Ms. Orcieres, if I should requisition—"

"Dorren."

Joss smiled at her. "Dorren, then. If I should requisition personal comms records for—for people who lived here, looking for bills of unusual size—"

She looked up from behind her desk, where she was going through a drawer in search of something. Her expression was bemused. "You'd have a lot of looking to do. We have quite a few subscribers."

"That may be, but all I need is to have my computer go through the lists, do a little correlating."

She leaned back in her chair. "Officer, you really think that the info-smuggling is simply being done using the regular phone network?"

"Joss," he said, "please."

"Joss, then. Thank you. Are you serious?"

He shrugged. "It's a possibility that needs to be investigated. I'd like to investigate it, before getting all fouled up in the intricacies of the comms department proper."

She frowned. "You would need to subpoena the comms accounting department," she said. "They tend to be a little protective at the best of times."

"Entirely within their rights," Joss said. "Consider it done."

Orcieres stared at him, then laughed. "I keep forgetting," she said, "you sops can do that kind of thing. It's kind of refreshing, after our own police—"

"Yes," Joss said, "well. Never mind that. I'll take care of the subpoena later on. Dorren, you're a great help to me."

She smiled, shook all that silver hair. "Any time."

"Dinner, perhaps?" Joss heard himself say.

Another smile, this one a little subtler. "Perhaps. I'll need to check my schedule. Not tonight, I think—work is going to keep me."

"I'll call," Joss said.

He strolled out of the office. *If Evan can cultivate his punks,* he thought, *I can do a little cultivating of my own.*

He went off feeling entirely pleased with himself, and headed for comms, and their accounting department.

"YOU ARE GOING TO GET *HIT,*" TELYA SAID TO him some time later, as he sat in a quiet corner of a restaurant some levels down from comms. The place was trying very hard to be a Russian restaurant, and failing. It had an odd but pervasive smell of cat pee, which Joss couldn't account for, there seeming to be no cats in the area. And the stroganoff had been uninspired, to put it mildly. But he wasn't paying any further attention to that. His pad was in the middle of the table, next to a mostly demolished plate of blini, and he was hammering data-search parameters into it as fast as he could.

"Lucretia," Telya said to him, "is going to hit the ceiling when she sees *this* bill. Not to mention the process fees for the subpoenas."

"Lose it in the system for a day or so," Joss said as he typed. "Tee, I beg you. By all that's holy."

"What's going to be holey will be my pension plan," she said, "because they'll fire me."

"Honest, they won't. If this turns up something useful, we'll have saved ourselves weeks. It's completely justifiable."

"And if not—" Telya sighed. "Then again, I suppose if Evan can pay out six thousand three hundred creds in bribes in one day, I guess you can spend—"

"*WHAT?*"

"Ssh. It's all right. Will you do what this is supposed to do, already, so I can capture it? Since you're so antsy about your own pad's memory. . . ."

"Here," Joss said, and told the correlation program to run. The screen blanked, and stayed that way for some seconds.

"There should be something showing by now." Joss said, concerned.

Telya snorted inside his ear. "With the lump of data you just fed it? Better order dinner."

Joss had another drink of tea-with-jam and stared at the screen. Nothing. "Did I break it?" he muttered.

"Serve you right if you did. Only so much crunch *in* that poor little creature—"

And a little list of names came up on the pad's screen. Joss read them twice . . . and his eyes went wide.

"*Bozhe moi,*" he said.

"Downlink it, for pity's sake!" Telya said.

He hit the proper control, and sat there looking at the screen.

"Is this what you needed?" Telya said. "Joss, wake up! Moon to Joss!"

"Cecil T. Jensen," he said softly. *"Look* at that bill."

"And who might *he* be?" There was a brief silence. "Sheesh! He must have a girlfriend on Mars."

"He's a shuttle pilot," Joss said happily. "He's one of the shuttle pilots I interviewed the other day. A nicer man you couldn't imagine."

"But if he was smuggling data, why would be be doing it *this* way instead of using the secure link through the shuttle?"

"Hide-in-plain-sight," Joss said. "Or maybe he really *doesn't* know how to manage a secure transfer from the shuttle without it showing. At least, using the usual comm circuits—"

Joss tagged the man's name, hit another combination of keys. The pad's machine went blank again, for a shorter period this time, and then came up with a fuller record of Jensen's comms usage.

"Look at all those calls to the Moon," Telya said.

"And look at the end of his account information," Joss said. "His account was cut off. *Very* interesting."

Joss took another slug of the tea. "I want to look at his bank account information, in this light," he said. "It should be interesting. And with his comms account dead for the moment, if he tries to smuggle anything else out, we stand a pretty good chance of catching him at it. He's either got to use somebody else's phone, or computer—"

"Or the shuttle," Telya said. "And, Joss look *who* cut that account off. Mr. Disinfectant."

Joss scanned down to the bottom of the page. "Account suspended," it said. "Last payment bounced—" and the account number of a station comms employee, and finally the name: M. PRZNO.

Joss smiled thoughtfully. "Could be a coincidence," he said.

"Bets?" Tee said.

Joss shook his head, dumped the pad's contents to Telya again, then cleared it. "You got all that?"

"Written in perms," she said. "Shall I send copies to Lucretia?"

"Oh, do, please," Joss said, rubbing his hands together. "Where's Evan?"

"Somewhere in the downlevels again. He left me a map."

It came up on Joss's pad. The spot was another neutral area of the sort the tavern had been; a place where gangs met to socialize. "Right," Joss said. "Tell him to expect me, if you would."

"Don't you just sound smug," Telya said reproachfully.

Joss grinned and called for the check.

HE FOUND EVAN LEANING AGAINST THE OUT-side wall of a bar six levels down and not too far from farm country—a place fronting on a beat-up corridor with a low ceiling. Someone had painted that ceiling black and then added fluorescent stars, producing an effect seedy beyond belief, especially where the "sky" was peeling. Inside the bar might have looked the same. It was impossible to tell, being as dark as Joss imagined the inside of a coal mine. *Maybe that's why he likes it,* Joss thought.

Evan was leaning against that wall with a drink in one hand. Leaning against the same wall, two on one side of him and three on the other, were five downlevel people, any one of whom made Cooch from the day before look like an advertisement for rampant normality. One of them, a person of indeterminate gender, appeared to be made up as a sort of humanoid tiger, complete with fur and scars, and a fur loincloth. Another was black, not by descent, but sprayed that color, even inside the mouth. The other three were more or less in Cooch's mold—bright rags of clothing woven together or just wrapped around, and scarification even more emphatic. On one of them, a female to judge by her body, it was almost impossible to make out any facial features. Her eyes were buried in conical swellings of tissue that made her look vaguely like a monitor lizard; her skull was shaven and swirled with raised and colored patterns.

"Afternoon," was all Joss could think to say. Evan saluted him with his glass.

"My partner," Evan said. "What's yours, Joss?"

"Beer—"

One of the five nodded, went into the blackness of the bar. Joss looked over at Evan and said, "Heard from Tee lately?"

"Yes, indeed." There was an interested gleam in his eye. "More about that later. These are Lala—Krakow—Tun—Morrie. Sivney's inside."

"Pleased," Joss said to them all, and leaned against the wall between Krakow, the tiger-person, and Tun, the lady with the lizard eyes.

Evan said, "These ladies and gentlemen came in answer to our . . . uh, advertisement."

Joss nodded. "Runners?"

"We run," Tun said, in a soft throaty voice very much at odds with her looks. "When the money's good enough." And she glanced over at Evan with an expression of interest.

He looked back mildly. "Are we still haggling? Thought we were settled about that."

"Not sure," Tun said. Sivney came out with Joss's drink. All paused, with a curious courtesy, while he had his first drink. Then Tun said, "Not sure what you want . . . and what it'll get us into."

Evan took a drink of his drink, and said, "My business, I think. Especially at these prices."

"Just don't want to get done after you're through with us," said Krakow, in a surprising, light soprano.

"My guarantees have already gone in to EssPat," Evan said mildly. "Not even the police here will try to violate *those*. You get me the information I want—or the people—and you won't regret it."

There was a silence, possibly of acquiescence. "How long?" Evan said then.

"Day," Tun said. "Maybe two. Bonus for early delivery?"

Evan nodded. "You manage that, you'll deserve it."

"All right," Tun said. The five of them nodded at Evan, at Joss, and then faded off down the dingy corridor.

Evan looked after them with almost an expression of affection. "Twitchy lot," he said.

"Not half as twitchy as I am," Joss said. "How much did Tee tell you?"

"Everything you'd found." Evan took a drink of his beer, smiled into it. "Partner, you know your business, you do indeed."

Joss froze with surprise at the praise, then breathed out and said, "What have you been up to that's been so expensive?"

"More recruitment. I think we're getting closer to some interesting business. This crowd belong to that group that Cooch mentioned—Teekers. There are quite a few of these people being used as underground cash carriers. In fact, we should pass most of this information on to the local police when we're done with our work—sparing our sources, of course. Half the organized crime in this place would come apart if you organized a couple nights' worth of hits on the cash runs. Meanwhile—" Evan smiled again. "I've taken the widget that Trevor gave us, and arranged for it to be planted on Przno. Which, in light of what you've found out, should be very interesting indeed when we get it back."

"Shame he doesn't have another one," Joss said, "for Jensen."

"Where is he?"

"On Earth at the moment, on layover for the night. He has a flight back in tomorrow."

"Good enough." Evan finished his drink, and put the glass down beside the others lined up against the wall. "Nothing we can do but wait, now. Our snooper will be reclaimed tomorrow morning. And then—"

"We'll see," Joss said. "But this waiting. . . . There are times when I wish there were something I could just *shoot* at."

Evan laughed at him. "And I thought you were the one who wanted to reason everything out? Heavens. Want to borrow my armor?"

Joss chuckled gently and said, "Let's go get some supper."

JOSS WENT TO STATION COMMS THAT NIGHT, to do his stint of surveillance, as he had planned to. Przno was on shift again, as he had been scheduled to be. The man looked quite cool this time, as if he had gotten over his nervousness about Joss being there. Joss, for his own part, pottered around comms peering over his shoulder or that, making friendly conversation with the other night staff, but never getting any closer to Przno than he had to, except when the man was obviously doing nothing in particular. Joss soured his stomach on the tea again, but he had come prepared this time: he was carrying enough antacid to last him for several days. He sat with his feet up, for most of the second part of the shift, doing his damndest to look like a bored policeman, and doing crossword puzzles on his pad.

Morning came without incident. Joss said his goodbyes and went back to the Hilton. Evan was still in bed. Joss shrugged at that—the man was surely entitled to sleep in every once in a while—and went downstairs to breakfast.

When he was finished, as he walked by the front desk, one of the clerks said, "Officer?"

"Yes?"

"Someone left a message for you, sir." The clerk slipped through a door into the office behind the desk, then came out and handed Joss a little brown plastic envelope, padded. Joss thanked the man and went away, smiling slightly, without opening it. There was a small hard round bump inside.

Joss took himself back upstairs and pounded genially on Evan's door. "Come on, get moving," he said, and went into his own room, tapping his pad into its countermeasures mode and running over the common living room with it, checking every corner.

Evan came staggering in after a few minutes, wearing an astonishing plaid cashmere bathrobe that Joss had seen and secretly admired. "Ah, your posh frock," he said as Evan flopped into a chair.

"Away with your noise," Evan said. "Do you know how late I was up last night?"

"No, and I don't care. Look here."

Joss put his pad down, broke the seal on the envelope and tipped out the little RF bug. "Let's see," he said, unclipping one of the panels on its side. "Just a plain-surface contact be enough, you think?"

"Should be."

The bug limpeted onto the little silicon-and-metal plate. "Now, then," Joss said, and started tapping at his pad, telling it to sort out which protocol the bug wanted to use to dump its contents, and then uplinking to the computers at EssPat. Tee didn't answer when he called her; but that was all right. He would catch her later, and meantime one of her offshift people, a gentleman called Ivar, came on.

"How's it going?" he said to Joss.

"Better and better. Ivar, I can't guarantee that we'll be able to store this dump on this end—"

"Problem with your pad?"

"Other troubles. Tee'll fill you in. Just copy what we send and tuck it away somewhere safe. Ready?"

"Got a file open now."

Joss tapped at the pad, told it to display any signal the bug sent it, and then typed the order to start the dump.

For a while nothing happened, and Evan looked over his shoulder dubiously. "Is it broken?"

Joss stared at the blank screen. "Or did Przno find some way to jam it?"

"Run ahead a little."

Joss thought about that, then tried something else. He told the pad to accelerate the speed of the dump. For a few more seconds nothing kept happening, then suddenly the pad's screen went crazy in screenful after screenful of dump. "Whoa, whoa," Joss said, and slowed it down again. "Realtime recording, that was the problem," he said over his shoulder to Evan. "I'll just tell it to edit out the blank parts."

It took another few seconds' worth of tapping. Then the pad began displaying its screenfuls of data again. Joss hit the pause control to hold up the first few of them as they passed, and found that they were typical comms log-on procedures. He let the pad continue.

More screenfuls came up. They were menus from the

station comms computer, asking the operator—Przno—for decisions about routing, priorities, the amount of data to be packed into one bundle. They watched the words spill across the screen as Przno instructed the machine in what to do. And the spill grew faster and faster. "Look at that," Joss said. "He really gets into the swing of his typing after a while. Has to be a hundred twenty words a minute."

"It's pure envy, that's what it is," Evan said.

"Oh, shut up."

Screenful after screenful of data came and went. Some of it was more garbled than other screenfuls, being the random radiation picked up from other terminals in use in the comms center, as Przno moved around. Then he would come back to his own station again—or work at another one—and the signal would come clean and strong again. It was innocent stuff. Then, without warning, something not so innocent. In the middle of a data dump to one of the Earth communications satellites, they saw a long spurt of what seemed to be nonsense characters, garbage. The screen filled with it. A second later it was gone. The screen went back to showing the master comms menu and its list of options for the comms controller. More commands were typed in, and data transfer went on as it had been doing.

Joss and Evan looked at one another. "You make anything of that?" Evan said.

"Not a bit. But I bet Tee'll be able to . . . or one of her friends down in Analysis or Crypto." Joss smiled a bit. "lvar," he said, "make sure that that burst, and any others like it, get tagged in your records for Telya's attention. She knows what to look for."

"Right you are, boss. Anything else?"

"Just stay with us till this dump is done. This is hot stuff; I'd hate to lose any of it because I hit the wrong button on this thing."

There was a subdued chuckle on the other end, but no further comment. Evan looked curious. "Telya," Joss said, "thinks of me as hopelessly useless with any machine more involved than a bicycle. She calls me a 'techno turnip.' "

Evan laughed. "Not just you," he said.

More data came and went. Then there was a break, a

longish one, the pad indicated. "Lunch break," Joss said.
It was interrupted only once or twice by more bursts of
garbage. "Hmm," Joss said. But Evan looked closely at
them and said, "No. . . . I've worked with these once or
twice before, and misinterpreting *that* got us in trouble.
You see how that character repeats? And there's a pattern.
Sine-curve, you'd get, if you asked for a graphic rendering
of the signal. It's a microwave oven."

Joss laughed. "Learn something new every day. . . ."

"Had one of those almost bugger up a beautiful surveillance once," Evan said. "We were in the Bogside—"

Another screenful of data appeared, another logon, and
then a different request—access to the public comms network rather than to the station comms system. "Checking
his mailbox?" Evan said.

"Probably."

They watched Przno tap in the number of his electronic
mailbox and its password. There were several messages:
routine stuff—tag messages for bills, one from a local gro-
cery, another for some rented entertainment solids—and a
message that from its routing code seemed to come from
a public terminal, a cash box, rather than a private one.
Przno ignored the other two messages, told the machine
to display the third one.

It said, simply: TURN IT BACK ON OR ELSE.

Joss and Evan glanced at one another again. The words
remained for some time, as if Przno was staring at them.
Then he issued a command to the machine to delete the
message. There was no way for him to reply.

Another pause. Then Przno exited the mailbox and went
back into the station comms system again, this time starting to execute what seemed a standard menu of checks on
the system itself. And that was all that happened for a
good while.

The playback was coming to the end of the shift when
the room phone blipped. Evan whistled at it and then said,
"Yes?"

"There's a package for you downstairs, Officer. The,
ah, person who brought it is waiting for a reply."

"Have someone bring the package up, if you'd be so

kind," Evan said. "I won't keep the 'person' waiting too long."

"Laundry?" Joss said.

"Indeed not. I do my own. I took the liberty," Evan said, "of having some of our young friends from the downlevels do me another favor. They've got some fine small vid equipment, they have. Stole it from someone, I suspect, but we have other business at the moment, and in any case the statute of limitations may have expired. But I thought it might be wise to have a visual record as well as an electronic one of the evening's doings. We'll keep doing it as long as we need."

"That was a good idea!"

"I do try," Evan said. "A very interesting message, that last one."

"You said a mouthful—"

There was a knock at the door. "Come," Evan said, and one of the hotel desk staff entered, with another package—a bit more peculiar, this one, being wrapped in a cheap towel from a public washroom. The hotel employee was carrying it as if afraid it would either blow up or infect him with something dubious. "Thank you," Evan said. "Please give this to the courier who brought the package." He handed the man a fifty. "And this for yourself," he said, and handed him another.

The gentleman from the front desk thanked Evan effusively and hurried out. "Being a little free with it, aren't we?" Joss said.

Evan smiled gently as he undid the towel. "Lucretia's lucre is going to a good cause," he said. The towel contained a small vidcassette, the kind used in the cameras favored by tourists. He glanced down at the pad. "Almost done there?"

"Almost." Joss waited for the dump to complete itself; more screenfuls of data, the check on the comms computer run through. Everything was in working order, apparently. Then Przno's logoff, and a few more ghosts of other screens as he walked past functioning terminals on the way out.

"That's it," Joss said. "Got it, Ivar?"

"All canned."

"Wait for this," Evan said then. "Video follows. It's a PDRC format, lvar."

There was a soft sound of tapping keys through the implants. "Ready for it."

Evan took the RF bug off the pad and touched the vidcassette to it, and poked a couple of the pad's controls. The pad came alive with a vid image: not very good—the color saturation on pads was never of the best—and grainy with signal degeneration, as if the solid had been used over and over. There was sound over, the sound of someone muttering at a machine that they weren't quite sure how to work. Whoever was using the vidshooter had shaky hands, but not so shaky as to interfere much with the image, of a window in a towerblock set on one of the higher-up islands. The window was a lower-story one, floor-to-ceiling, and there were no curtains. The place was well-furnished in a modern style, though a little messy. A shape was sitting on a lounger near the window, hunched over a coffee table littered with books. Abruptly it straightened up, held something to its face: a little inhaler, such as asthmatics used.

The figure put the inhaler down after a second, stood up and headed out of shot of the camera. It was Przno.

"Anything in his medical records about respiratory trouble?" Evan said softly.

"Not a word. Not a single word," Joss said. His mind was racing. If this meant what he thought it did—

The camera wobbled, there was a scuffling noise as someone put it out of sight; the padscreen went dark, but not totally so. After a second the camera's lens recovered enough to show an exciting view of the inside of a shabby jacket. This it continued to show for some time. "Good long-distance lens on that thing," Joss said.

"Let's just hope it stays that way after being in this lad's coat," Evan said.

Several minutes more of coat-interior passed. Then suddenly the camera was dragged out and brought to bear on two men, one of whom had just left the towerblock and was halfway across the little garden terrace leading to the nearest slidewalk. There was another man taking the last few steps toward him, talking hurriedly, in a low voice.

The camera wasn't close enough to hear it. The person carrying it seemed unwilling to get any closer. An occasional word was loud enough to make it to the camera's sound input over the hurried breathing of the person carrying it. "—damned . . . can't do a . . . need this now, I don't . . ." The voice began to escalate. The first man, Przno, tried to walk away from the second; the second man followed him, grabbed his arm. Przno shook it off. "—mess this whole thing up," the second man nearly shouted, then made an apparent effort to quiet himself, and grabbed for Przno again, pulled him close. This time Przno wasn't able to shake him off. The second man said something very soft, too soft for the camera to catch it. Przno spoke. Not more than a few words, also inaudible. Then the second man let Przno go, not violently, but as if he had changed his mind about something—

The camera turned to follow Przno, as the second man walked off out of shot. "Damn," Joss said softly, "damn, *damn—*"

"What's the matter?" Evan said.

"That," Joss said, "was our friend Cecil. The shuttle pilot. Oh, for a second camera—"

Evan's eyes brightened. "Indeed," he said, as they watched the pad, watched Przno walk away, heading for the slidewalk. "Ah, well; can't be helped at the moment."

They watched Przno make his way to the comms building, tailed by Evan's "young friend." Przno never looked to right or left. When he went into the building, the camera went into the coat again. Evan stared at the weave of it thoughtfully. "I hope," he said, "that my lad uses a little of that fifty to get himself something new to wear. That weave's in a bad way."

"That *is* new," Joss said. "Distressed fabrics are back in again this year."

Evan sighed. "Heaven save me from worrying about fashion."

"Yes," Joss said, "the suit *is* a classic. . . ."

Evan snorted, and turned his attention back to the pad. There was more rustling and the thud of footsteps. Then the camera came out again, having been taken some distance away, to the island next to the comms buildings, where there was a park. It was trained on the comms level where Przno worked, and showed through the windows only his stooped shape as he worked at a terminal, with his back turned, typing faster and faster and faster. . . .

Then the vid ran out, and the screen went black.

Joss looked over at Evan. "So much for envy," he said. "How much do you want to bet that man was blasting?"

Evan nodded slowly. "Question now is," he said, "is it casual use? Is it coincidental? Or is it something a bit more—loaded?"

"Something important enough to get Lon killed?" Joss said. "I think you're right. But *what,* exactly . . ."

He trailed off.

"We've gone a bit further than Lon did in his investigations," Evan said. "He had been to see the shuttle pilots, as you have. He had been up to comms. The question is, did he see what we're seeing? Are we on the right track?"

"If we are," Joss said, his voice a bit grim, "then we're as ripe to be killed as he was. I'm going to start wearing *my* body armor. And if I were you, I'd start wearing yours. Good impressions or not."

Evan nodded. His face was thoughtful. "There's an idea for you, then," he said. "Could it be that our man is smuggling information not for its own sake . . . but to pay for his drug habit?"

"Did you hear me about your armor?"

"Yes, Mother," Evan said, with just a flicker of annoyance. "What I want to know is, how does your pilot fit into this? Was that garbage we saw a blind? Is the real information smuggling happening through the shuttle after all?"

"Or," Joss said after rolling the thought around in his mind for a moment, "is it secondary to something different? Drug smuggling, perhaps?"

Evan unclipped the vidcassette from the pad, turned it over in his hands. "One would need to know which way it was being smuggled," he said. "The drug's not very prevalent on Earth. Therefore one would think that it was being manufactured somewhere else."

"The Moon? Or in orbit?"

Evan nodded. "So we should look for it being smuggled *out*, I would think, to one of those places. It has been noticed on the Moon, I believe. Doubtless it's intended to start coming to Earth in larger amounts, if it's successful. And if Lon was getting close to information about people who were doing *that*—the kinds of money involved could definitely have caused them to become bold enough to kill even a sop." He frowned. "Much bigger money than anything from industrial espionage."

"I think," Joss said, "that we'd best go have a talk with the Customs people. Very discreetly, you understand."

"I'd sooner not end up in a crema-pak either," said Evan. "My mother gave me strict instructions to die in bed."

"The only problem is," Joss said, "what if some of the *Customs* people are in on this? It's happened before."

"Nasty thought," Evan said. "No matter for that at the moment. We oughtn't manufacture troubles that aren't there. Unless—What's your feeling about it, anyway?"

"It's not Pat Higgins," Joss said, absolutely certain. "But he has a lot of people working for him. And not on wonderful pay, either."

Evan stood up, wrapping the cashmere bathrobe more tightly around him. "Never you mind that just now. It's your lactic acid and your low blood sugar making you paranoid again. You go off and get some sleep."

"And what are you going to do?" Joss said.

"Make some courtesy calls. Nothing dangerous, I promise."

"I've heard *that* before," Joss said, but he wasn't up to arguing at the moment. Having seen what he'd just seen, at the end of a long night, he was suddenly very tired. He went into his own room, whistled the door shut, lay down, and immediately fell asleep.

IT WAS THE SCREAM OF THE PHONE THAT woke him up, some hours later. Joss squinted at his chrono, found that it was about the time he should have been getting up anyway, swore softly, and rolled over to stare at the ceiling. "Yes," he said. "O'Bannion."

"Time you were moving about," Evan's voice said.

"I was getting up anyway," Joss said, rolling to a sitting position and rubbing his eyes. "It's still my turn to do the night shift."

"Not any more."

"What?"

"Better get over here. Island fourteen."

It was the island on which Przno's towerblock stood. "Holy alarm call, Batman," Joss said softly. "On my way."

"What?" Evan said, and then sighed and closed the connection down.

Joss got into his uniform, looked at his body armor, and then sighed and decided against it. *Damn public relations anyway,* he thought, but there was nothing for it. A cop who looks threatened is working at a lower level of efficiency than one who does not, no matter what he likes to think about it. He grabbed his pad and headed out.

Or started to. For shoved in a crack of the door, from the outside, he found a small dirty piece of paper. It fell down at his feet when the door opened. Joss unfolded it carefully. TALK, it said, in an unsteady childish scrape of block letters. There was a hatchmark under the word. Joss recognized it as a tattoo that Cooch had been wearing on the inside of his wrist. Carefully he pocketed the message and went off down the corridor.

The forecourt of the island was buzzing with people—curious spectators, and the station police with their silly guns, all standing around and trying to look useful. Among them Evan towered in his armor, making them look less than useful no matter what they did. They were crowded at the door of the towerblock, keeping people out. (Or in: through the glass walls of the lower level, numerous annoyed tenants were visible, being kept away from the door by ropes and more station police.)

Joss strolled up to the group outside the door. The station police, to a man, glared at him. Joss smiled kindly at them, nodding, and said to Evan, "I take it something untimely has happened."

"Oh, aye," Evan said, and turned toward the doors. Together they went in.

About twenty feet away from the doors, inside the building, Przno lay twisted on the terazzo floor. He had been needled. Not just once, but several times: at least a hundred of the inch-long metal needles, twice the thickness of a hair, were buried in his face and upper torso. The neurotoxin with which they were usually treated had done its job. No cobra could have killed Przno more quickly, though no cobra would have made him spend his last few seconds feeling the aqueous humor spraying out of his eyeballs through pinholes, the causes of which were then buried retina-deep.

There were no other wounds, at least none immediately apparent. The man's leisure coverall seemed intact. Near him on the floor lay his wallet, empty, and a little bag of groceries; evidently he had been out doing some shopping.

Joss looked down at the man and shook his head. "Did anyone see it happen?" he asked, looking around him at the various station police.

The four officers nearest him all began talking at once. Eventually, after some confusion, Joss got them to tell him that there were four or five witnesses. None of them agreed on a description of the attacker, but the witnesses—people either going into the building or coming out—had seen Przno coming in through the doors toward the elevator banks in the center of the building. The assailant had leaped out from behind a small refreshment kiosk near the elevators—the kiosk being closed at the time—and demanded Przno's money. The attacker was wearing a black hood and dark clothes: that was all the witnesses could agree on. They also all agreed that Przno had dropped his groceries, understandably shaken, then had fumbled out his wallet and given the assailant his money, no more than a few creds. And the robber had then shot him, several times, as Joss had thought, and threatened the witnesses as well. They had dropped to the floor, or run screaming to hide behind the bank of elevators. No one had seen which way the murderer had gone.

"Where are they now?" Joss said to the nearest policeman.

"Downstairs being questioned."

"We'd like to talk to them, too," he said, "after you're done. Please let us know when you're ready." And he nodded politely to the various officers, and walked out of the building with Evan.

Evan had his helm's visor down; the blank face of it turned to Joss as they went. "I have a feeling," he said, "that things are going to start getting lively."

"I think you're right," Joss said, reaching into his pocket for the piece of paper. "Here."

Evan took it. The blind helm stared down at the bit of scribble for a moment. "Our young friend Cooch," he said.

"I thought so."

They headed down toward the slidewalk. "Meanwhile," Joss said, "we'd better go have a talk with Cecil the shuttle pilot."

There was soft laughter inside Evan's helm. "You're thinking he had something to do with this?"

"Maybe not directly. But it ought to be looked at. He could have hired someone to do it without too much trouble."

Evan nodded as he strolled along. "Granted, it certainly looks like a robbery. Meaning one of two things: someone wanted it to *look* like a robbery . . . or it really was one."

"Would you care to bet on the odds of that?" Joss said. "Just after we start doing a surveillance on the guy?"

As they got on the slidewalk Evan tossed his head. The visor went up, revealing a slightly puzzled expression. "Maybe not," he said. "But Joss, what would the motive be? Just being investigated isn't enough to get a man killed, as a rule."

"Unless someone thinks he might be arrested, and tell what he knows."

"Some other person involved in the data smuggling, you mean."

"Or in the drug connection."

Evan stood there with his arms folded, considering. "The latter seems more likely, I have to say."

"I was going to say that, too." Joss stood quiet for a moment as the slidewalk took them through one of the pressure barriers, into the beginnings of farm country. He looked out at the yellow of the wheat, rippling in its fan-produced wind. "I mean, consider the weapon," he said eventually. "That's not the kind of thing a petty crook can usually get his or her hands on."

"Not that often, anyway." Evan looked out at the wheatfield, which gave way shortly to a vineyard, with extra sunlites strung over the vines to hurry their grapes along. "So, then. Who might it have been? A supplier? Someone sent by someone *above* a supplier?"

Joss shook his head. "I should hope we'll find out."

They changed slidewalks a couple of times, making their way toward the tavern where they had met Cooch the first time, and where Evan had done his first recruiting. They found the place very quiet—no one about outside. "Early yet for a crowd, I suppose," Joss said.

"Probably," Evan said as they walked into the dark tavern building proper. There were only a few people sitting in booths; they looked with the usual astonishment or near-panic at Evan. A couple of them tried to make themselves small, hunching up where they sat.

"Beer, twice," Joss said, after glancing at Evan. The bartender kept his face expressionless as he served them, but as Joss turned away, he noticed a worried scowl settling into place.

They walked outside and sat at the table near the door, again, with their backs against the wall. "I think the *patron* is a little nervous about us," Joss said, sipping at his lager.

"Can't blame him," Evan said. "If somebody walked into my bar wearing a tank, I'd be relieved when they left. If they came back again, later, I'd be extremely glad to see the back of them as soon as possible. Tanks attract things that—"

Evan's glass of beer blew apart as he was putting it down.

Joss rolled and dove under a nearby table, pulling out the Remington, as Evan kicked aside the table they had been sitting at. The helm slammed down and Evan's arms came up as he turned quickly in a circle. There were more shots: the unmistakeable sharp crack!s of a slug-throwing weapon. *Wonderful,* Joss thought, cursing himself thoroughly and swearing not to pay any more attention to public relations, no matter what his conscience said. He wriggled around as best he could and tried to get a clearer idea of where the shots were coming from.

It was hard to tell. The tavern fronted on a long terrace area and it was a long drop down from the terrace, so there was definitely no one shooting from *that* direction. To the left or right, then: possibly both. His view to the right was clearer—at least there were fewer tables there. Joss peered between the table legs, thought he caught a glimpse of motion, fired at it—

Off to his left Evan had found a target. Apparently he had decided to reply in kind. Joss heard the sound of twin rotaries coming up to speed, a soft phased whine that suddenly went quiet. Then there was a sound more like a rainstorm on a tin roof than anything else—though Joss had heard precious few rainstorms in his time, and fewer tin roofs, except in old vids. The paired machine guns uttered a long roar of metal that tore a nearby wall into shreds. Something broke from behind the wall, a running shape, but its dive and roll didn't save it. The rotaries were eccentrics, and their line of fire was not a line but an ellipse, a probability field. The attacker stumbled into that field and simply exploded, as Evan's beerglass had, into shreds and liquid. A few parts that had not come fully into the fire-ellipse fell down whole instead of as ground meat: a foot, a bit of head.

Evan swerved, looked around for another target. Joss saw it first, off to the right: someone crouching low, trying to move. More cracks, closer together this time. The person on the right had a semi-automatic, or an auto being fired in short bursts. *Right,* Joss thought, *he may have perfect aim and electronics and all that*—and he picked his spot and squeezed the bolt off. It went right through the dark shape's elbow. The shape lurched, the gun spun away, the other arm flung out,—*but how about this,* Joss thought, and the next bolt went through the other elbow, as neat as neat. The dark figure screamed and staggered back into cover.

Silence fell. Evan stood there in his armor, looking around, as if daring anything to break it again. There was the slightest sound of someone making a painful and bloody escape down the corridor that led away from the tavern. The sobbing dwindled, died away after a while.

Joss came out from under his table, brushing himself off. It was largely useless. He had been rolling in the beer, and now smelled like a brewery. There was a sting in his thigh, too: he looked down in surprise and saw a large shard of broken glass sticking out of it. Not deeply, thank heaven. Gingerly he pulled it out and tossed it away with a faint *tink* as Evan came back and started picking up the tables.

"You were saying?" Joss said, making one or two more futile attempts to brush the worst of the floor-dirt and grunge off him. "That places where tanks congregate, attract things that shoot at tanks?"

"I must watch what I say," Evan said, the visor sliding up. He righted another table and the bench that had been near it, checked it to make sure that it too wasn't covered with beer. Then he put his head in the door and called out, in a cheerful voice, "Two more of the same, please."

Joss sat down, breathing hard. Evan sat down next to him, seemingly unruffled. Joss glanced at him, piqued. "Do you ever break a sweat?" he said.

"In this suit I try to avoid it," Evan said. To do him justice, he was slightly breathless. "But my pulse's up a bit, I'll reckon." He swallowed. "That was nice shooting."

"He spilled your pint," Joss said. "Or his friend did. I was annoyed."

"Remind me not to spill yours."

"Right."

The second round arrived with unseemly haste. "Noisy neighbors," Evan said calmly to the bartender as he came out.

The bartender grunted and went away, but not without a glance at the shattered wall a hundred yards off. The end of the wall, what remained of it, had been newly spatter-painted red. Mostly red, at least, except where bits of other colors, grey and white mostly, were sticking to it.

Evan shook his head, looking at it, and lifted his beer glass again, this time waiting a second before he drank. Nothing happened. He took a long pull off it and said, " 'He that diggeth a pit shall fall into it; and whoso breaketh a hedge, a serpent shall bite him.' "

"What?" Joss said.

Evan smiled a little. "Ah," he said, "one for me. Now tell me: what the devil is a 'batman'? Besides a servant in the old RAF. Which I assume is not what you meant."

Joss laughed a little and told him as they drank. Every now and then someone came to the door of the tavern, peered out, saw Evan and Joss still there, and ducked hurriedly back in. "It's all right," Joss said once, "go ahead." But no one came out.

"Nervous," Evan said after another long drink of beer. "I wonder if they know something we don't." Then he lifted his head. "Footsteps," he said.

"I don't hear anything."

"I've got my plugs in. It seemed wise. . . ."

The footsteps approached from around the corner. No hesitation, no caution. It was Cooch, dressed much as he had been before. *Does he even have any other clothes?* Joss wondered, and then noticed with some surprise that his hand was on his Remington again.

Evan's arms were resting on the table in front of him, in a gesture that might have looked peaceable, if one didn't have a clear idea of what he had up his sleeves. Cooch came over to them and sat down, but not without first taking a long look at the ruined wall and its decoration of ruined human being. His sitting down was a slow, tentative matter, and he looked at Evan nervously.

"I should hate to think," Evan said, very quietly, "that we had been set up."

Cooch went dead pale under his scarification. "No, no, no way," he said.

"Take some convincing," Evan said. "Never mind now. You wanted talk? Talk."

"I, uh," Cooch said, totally flustered. Joss shook his head and leaned around into the open doorway. "Another beer, please," he called, then said to Cooch, "Or bren-nevin?"

"Beer, sweat, whatever—"

The drink came. Cooch put half the beer down him in a second and sat there, staring at it, shaking. "Come on," Evan said. "Their ears aren't that long, in there. They're scared to hear too much. I can hear them saying so. Just keep your voice down. What's the problem?"

Cooch muttered something. "Come on," Joss said quietly. "Mr. Radar Ears here may be able to make this out, but I can't."

"Didn't tell you everything the other day," Cooch said, not looking up.

"No surprise there," Evan said, leaning back against the wall. "Thought you were skimming extra."

Cooch started, then said, "No, not that."

"You *weren't* skimming?"

"No. Mean, not that much. Not that, man!"

"What, then?" Joss said.

"This dead guy."

"Oh, that," Evan said, gazing through half-closed eyes at the wall. "Target practice, we were. It's happened before."

"Not that dead guy. The other one."

Evan's eyebrows went up.

"At island fourteen, you mean," Joss said.

Cooch nodded. "Knew him."

"Indeed," Evan said.

There was a pause while Cooch drank more beer. Then suddenly he stood up. "Said too much," he said. "Word gets around."

Evan reached up and pushed Cooch back down into the seat. "Too late for that," he said. "You're here. Word's going to get around about that as it is. Might as well tell us why you came. No use getting killed for nothing."

"That's it," Cooch said miserably, slumping down into the chair again, his voice dropping to a whisper. "They don't care. Lotsa downs get killed for nothing."

"Or for something," Joss said. "The drug."

When Cooch raised his head and stared at Joss, the terror in his eyes was awful to see. Suddenly there was a frightened young boy behind the scarred fright mask. "They crazy, man," he said. "You do wrong thing, say wrong thing, that's it, all of a sudden. You're meat."

"Sometimes the meatgrinder gets ground," Joss said, glancing over at the shattered wall. " 's why we're here. Talk."

"You knew the guy," Evan said quietly. "Przno."

Cooch held still a moment, then nodded very slightly. "Handed to him," he said. "Didn't know names. Just faces."

"Collected from him, too. And paid someone else," Joss said.

Cooch nodded again.

"No names," Evan said. "Just faces."

Another nod.

"Must be a lot of people you hand to," Joss said. He was keeping his voice as steady as he would have when talking a suicide in off a ledge. He could have trembled with excitement at their first real break, except that it would have ruined everything.

"Some. Never too many to one runner." Cooch smiled, not a happy look. "They say it gives you ideas."

" 'They,' " Evan said. "The suppliers."

Nod.

"And Przno—you handed him a little? a lot?"

"A lot. He wholesale."

Joss found himself wondering whether Mallory in the comm offices had been one of the people Przno wholesaled to. He would have a look at their comms records; they might give some confirmation. "Then he would hand you the cash back—"

"Then I pass."

"To another courier," Joss said. He glanced at Evan, wondering if any of the people he had been "interviewing" were Cooch's connection to the supplier.

Cooch stared into the beer again. "Don' like it any more," he said softly. "Was good to start with. Nice money, lotsa booze, the Teeks look up to you. But now—" He looked around him nervously, then down again. "He—Przno?—he got dead. Maybe means *I* get dead next." There was a long pause. "Don' wanna get dead. . . ."

"Understandable," Evan said, a bit drily. "We'll see what we can do. Who drops to you?"

Cooch shook his head.

"Come on," Joss said.

"No, can't tell," Cooch said. "Guy's all dressed like a sump—" that meant a janitor, so Joss supposed Cooch meant a coverall such as the station janitorial staff used "—'clava on top—no face, gauze on the eyes. Nothing. Passes to cover orders, and a little. Seed supply.' "

"Freebies," Joss said, "for the potential users."

"You blast yourself?" Evan said.

Cooch looked first outraged, then sank down into a kind of dull anger. "Once," he said. "No more. Stuff kills you too fast. And you come down. You come *down,* sop. You wanna be a genius, then be stupid? And know stupid is how you *really* are?" There was a bitter look on Cooch's face. "Better to stay stupid and be alive. Easier."

"Where's your supplier come from?" Joss said. "Any word in the holes?"

"No word. No one knows. Not the stuff either. It just comes."

"Would be nice," Joss said, "to know where it *does* come from. Might make things simpler for us. We know where it comes from, we find who's sending it, we take them home with us." He shrugged. "No one else gets killed."

Cooch looked dubious. "Only two of you," he said.

"Lots of your friends," Evan said. "You tell them the word. They come to me, they give me the word about where this stuff comes from, it's big creds. *Big.* I'll ten-times-over their supplier's best offer for a month of runs."

Oh, dear heaven, what is Lucretia going to say, Joss thought. But he had to admit it was wise. The runners in question would know that if they brought Evan the word he wanted, they would be effectively putting themselves out of work. It would take a mighty incentive to push them toward it, and Evan was offering them one.

"*Ten* times," Cooch said.

Evan held up both hands. "Count 'em."

Cooch stood up. This time Evan made no attempt to stop him. " 'll see," he said, and went off the way he had come, a little more calmly.

Joss leaned back and watched him go. "So," he said.

"You were right," Evan said. "I bow to the Master." He did, and his armor creaked.

Joss laughed softly. "Thanks," he said, "but I'm not nearly right enough, yet. We're missing a lot of information. And I want to talk to that shuttle pilot."

"Let's go do that," Evan said, rising from his seat. He glanced over at the wall with the long hole in it. "And I suppose we'd better call the police."

"You think they'll come down here?" Joss said, as they made their way toward the slidewalk.

"If they won't," Evan said mildly, "maybe the street-cleaners will."

THEY WENT OVER TO THE SHUTTLE FACILITY, and the shuttle-line offices. Miss Jailbait in the front office looked in fascination at Evan and was very demure and polite with him; at least, she offered him her commcode as quickly as she had offered it to Joss. Joss had the mild satisfaction of seeing Evan blush.

"Is Mr. Poole around?" Joss said.

"Just inside. I'll call him for you."

"Thanks."

Poole emerged a few seconds later, greeted Joss cordially, and shook hands with Evan as if he wasn't wearing a suit at all—a refreshing attitude, Joss thought. "We're looking for Captain Jensen," he said. "Just a few extra questions."

"He's not here, I'm afraid," Poole said. "We had to send him out about two hours ago. The tourist crush is going to be particularly bad this weekend—half Europe is having a bank holiday—and the downside office insisted we run several extra services. With the usual turnaround, he should be back tomorrow night or the morning after."

"But he was here until two hours ago?" Evan said.

"Oh, yes. We had to rout him out of bed. He didn't like it much. But then neither would I."

"You went and got him up?" Joss said. "Or called?"

Poole looked at him a little oddly. "I called him. Unfortunately my office is busy enough that I can't manage these things personally."

"No, of course not," Evan said. "Well, when he gets back, we'd appreciate it if you'd let us know. Please don't mention it to him beforehand, though."

"Tends to confuse the questioning."

"Of course," Poole said. "No problem, gentlemen."

They went off around the edge of the shuttle facility, which was empty of shuttles now, and almost empty of people, there being nothing to work on. "What now?" Joss said.

Evan sighed. "We work what leads we have until Jensen gets back, I suppose. Though I think you may be following a false trail on this one."

Joss was quiet for a moment. That thought kept coming up for him too. Worse, this had been nothing more than a hunch on his part, and his hunches made him uncomfortable. "Well," he said, "we'll see. I suppose we should go tell the local cops about that little dustup down by the tavern."

Evan grinned at the thought. "Yes," he said, "a little harmless entertainment would come in nice around now."

AND UNTIL TWO MORNINGS LATER, THAT WAS all they had to amuse them. Evan continued recruiting his runners, and trying to find out who had engineered the attack on the tavern. Rumor said it was Teekers, the gang who had murdered Lon, but Evan was not prepared to jump to any conclusions yet. Instead he sat quietly with his contacts, collecting every shred of information they were willing to give him, lies and truth together. Joss kept up his surveillance on station comms, for appearance's sake, though he did change over to day shift. He wasn't sure what real good it would do, except that it might make anyone watching them think that the sops were confused.

No mastery there, he thought, more than once. *We* are *confused.*

There was one bright spot when he got a note on his pad from Trevor. BEEN BUSY, it said, BUT FOUND EVIDENCE OF FAIRLY EXTENSIVE TAMPERING WITH BANKING SOFTWARE OVER THE PAST FEW MONTHS. MANY FILES DO NOT CHECK AGAINST THEIR BACKUPS AS TO TIMESTAMPS. CAN'T GET AT CONTENTS AT THIS POINT, TOO MUCH SECURITY.

Joss smiled to himself when he read it. If he knew Trevor, the problem wouldn't last long. He just hoped the boy could find some way to come up with the information that wouldn't reveal to anyone running this operation that they were in the process of being found out.

Nothing else of interest happened until Joss's pad went off at breakfast. "O'Bannion," he said, swallowing hurriedly.

"Pat Higgins in Customs," said the pad. "Officer, can you or your partner come down here? We have something here that I think is going to interest you."

"On our way," Joss said, as Evan took a last bite out of his toast and dropped the crust.

Out in Customs' semispherical processing hall, a great crowd of passengers were jostling amiably against one another as they were processed. Higgins met them at the doorway to the offices, looking both satisfied and angry.

"You got some," Joss said immediately.

"More than that. Jensen was carrying it."

"What?"

Higgins led them inside, past the reception desk and into a small debriefing room, its walls lined with the polished steel sanitary fittings of a place used to examine the excreta of someone suspected of "body carrying." There was a hand-scrawled sign over the toilet with the built-in sieve, reading: PLEASE!!! LEAVE THIS AREA CLEAN FOR THE NEXT PERSON. At a steel table in the middle of the room, several uniformed Customs people were turning over the contents of what looked like a cellophane bag of sweets. Joss looked at it in dawning surprise.

"Oh, no," he said.

"Oh, yes," Higgins replied. From a sink nearby he picked up a plate and handed it to Evan. The plate contained a hard candy cut in half. Inside, the candy was filled with something white and powdery.

"Haven't seen *this* one in ages," Higgins said. "They give the drug a dip in something heat-resistant, and then dunk the pieces in boiling sugar syrup until they'll pass for hardballs." He put the plate down. "The crew manifest record shows that Jensen only left the shuttle while on Earth."

"Where is he?"

"One of the interrogation rooms, down the hall. The stuff was found in his grip. He says he never saw it before, and it must have been planted on him. He's been maintaining that pretty strongly." Higgins shrugged. "We'll see if he maintains that during the body search."

"Ultrasound hasn't shown you anything?"

"No," Higgins said, "but sometimes it doesn't. We want to be sure. And it's wonderful what a good enema, or the prospect of one, can do for your memory sometimes." His smile was very mild. Joss made a mental note never to get near this man if he was holding an enema bag.

Evan went over to the table and picked up one of the sweets. It was wrapped in a little twist of cellophane, and the bag from which it had come was a recognized Earth brand. "Supposing some kiddie had gotten hold of one of these?" he said, turning it over in his fingers.

Higgins looked grim. "It would have been the smartest kid on Earth for about half an hour. And then it would have been dead. That's a massive overdose for about fifty people, in that one candy. Blast is pretty concentrated to start with, because it's tailored to the receptor site. Usually it *has* to be cut with some conveyancing medium, otherwise the effective dosages are just too tiny to physically handle. But this stuff is pure. I've never seen purer. I don't want to, either."

Joss agreed. "Can we take a sample?" he said.

"Be my guest," Pat said, and looked at the bag with disgust. "There's plenty of it."

"When do you think you'll be done with Jensen?" Evan said.

"Oh, tonight sometime. We want to give anything that might be in his stomach time to work through." Again that mild smile. "Check with us after dinner."

"We'll do that," Joss said, and he and Evan went out into the Customs hall together and looked around at the tourists for a moment, while they collected their thoughts.

"One of these people could have planted it on him," Evan said. "I wonder."

"That seems to be stretching it a bit. Usually cabin crews don't have much contact with the passengers, except to tell them what they're seeing out the windows."

"All the same," Evan said, "it might not be a bad idea to get a copy of the passenger manifest."

Joss nodded. There was certainly no harm in it. "Let's go over to Administration," he said. "I want a quick talk with Dorren Orcieres."

SHE WASN'T IN HER OFFICES WHEN THEY GOT there, though, and wasn't answering her page. "Lunch," said her assistant, a handsome young man in a dark skin-tight. "It's her rule: she never mixes business and food. She says it's the only way she stays sane. Might there be something I can help you with? She told me we were to give you anything you wanted."

"We were wondering," Joss said, "if you might be able to put us onto someone responsible, in research, at one of the drug companies. I have some questions I want to ask them. Though I'd prefer it wasn't someone at BurJohn. I don't want things to get confused."

The assistant thought for a moment. "There are a few research scientists working here that freelance to the drug companies," he said, "at least if I understand the situation. They're officially on grants from Earthside, as a rule." The young man turned to his datapad and tapped at it a moment, frowned, then tapped again and said, "Here, try Dr. Laurentz. I think he was doing some work for the station, actually—environmental-health stuff." He

touched another control on his pad, and hardcopy with the
address-coordinates and a small map of the area in question slid silently out of a nearby hardcopier. "Here you
are," the assistant said, handing the sheet to Joss.

He glanced at it: apparently the scientist worked from
home in a nice neighborhood not too far from here.
"Thanks very much," he said. "Please tell Dorren we're
sorry we missed her."

"I think maybe it's mutual," the young man said, and
then became very busy with his desk.

Evan looked at Joss with amusement as they walked
out. "And who have *you* been cultivating while I've been
downlevel?" he said.

Joss smiled a little. "Helps, sometimes, to have a friend
in high places. Actually, nothing's happened. No time."

"Don't know what she's been telling her staff, then."

Joss laughed. "I just hope it's complimentary."

They caught a slidewalk toward the port axis of the station, in a direction they hadn't been before. "There used
to be a forest over here," Joss said, "some time back,
when the place was trying to do its own paper production
instead of paying the exorbitant prices for import. All soft-
woods." He looked around and down from the high via-
duct structure on which the slidewalk ran. "There it is,"
he said, pointing.

It was much as he remembered it; there was still a slight
haze over the treetops in their long, straight lines. The
forest followed the curve of the fiver's wall right up and
around, toward the sky-window. Evan made a little amused
sound at the sight of it all. "Looks like parts of Scotland
did," he said. "That's no forest; that's a plantation. For-
ests don't line the trees up like soldiers for the felling
machines."

"It's the best they can manage here," Joss said, just a
touch defensively. But he had to admit that there was a
certain ruthless quality to the orderliness of it all; it wasn't
the kind of forest that made you particularly want to walk
in it.

They slid on. Here there were more residential islands
rising up from the "floor" of the fiver. That floor might
conceal levels and levels of mean corridors and dwellings,

but there was no sign of it here. The islands came in groups, staggered as to height. Parks and little lakes were scattered among them, usually with a towerblock or group of other small residential buildings nearby on the same island. Some islands were nothing but towerblock, some nothing but park.

The one they were heading for was mixed use: industrial—the drug company, Willis, had its corporate HQ and labs there at the top of the island's main towerblock; and residential, for its employees and dependents, along with some outside renting and leasing, holiday properties mostly. It was a pleasant-looking place, the towerblock's presence softened by trees of surprising age and size. "Wonder how much it cost them to bring those in," Evan said.

Joss shook his head. "They might have been forced," he said. "Some of the gardeners working in low gee have been able to do some pretty surprising things in the cloning department."

"Ah, it's beyond me, at any rate," Evan said. "Nice place, though."

They stepped off the slidewalk at the exit marked for the Willis island, and showed their ID to the security guards at the drawbridge entrance to the place; the guards waved them through. "Bit of a drop down there," Evan said, as they walked along the bridge between the slidewalk and the island. There was a clear drop of nearly four hundred feet to the next island, or another two hundred to the island after that, if you should miss the first one.

Joss looked over the edge and twitched slightly. Under some conditions he was a touch acrophobic, and this was one of them. "Think I'll pass," he said.

They made their way to the towerblock and consulted the map. Dr. Laurentz apparently lived around the back of it, in a little grouping of bi-level country houses called "the Cottages." They walked around the towerblock, through landscaped gardens and more trees. "That's never cloned," Evan said, looking up at one of them. "That's a hundred-year-old monkey-puzzle, or I'm a regular."

Joss looked up at the huge, rough-barked tree with its

snakelike branches, and said, "Would have mistaken it for something from Mars, myself."

Evan snorted at him in a good-natured way as they came around the curve of the pathway leading back to the Cottages. It was as calm a place as one could think of. The fake sun's light fell through maple trees and tall oaks onto well-trimmed grass, where children played, bouncing and "moonwalking" across the grass in the light gravity. Mothers pushed baby strollers along the path and nodded and smiled to Joss as they passed, though most of them looked a little dubiously at Evan. The children were fascinated, though, and pointed and stared with big eyes, not at all hostile. Evan began to smile a little.

The Cottages themselves were almost cute enough to give a man an attack of diabetes—so Joss thought. They were arranged around a series of cul-de-sacs, and were actually *thatched*, and how much the builders had paid to import real thatching reed from Earth, Joss didn't want to think. In structure the houses were more like townhouses than anything else, but the outer finishes varied from golden "stone" through fake-Tudor black and white exposed-beam architecture. "Whoever designed this place," Joss said softly, "studied in California."

Evan laughed at him. "A little odd, yes," he said. "Especially with the microport dishes sticking off the sides of them. Not very Tudor. Come on."

They found the house in question: two floors under its thatch, with "brick" outside and leaded-light windows. There was no doorbell or other signal that Joss could see, so he knocked on the door and folded his hands in his best "nonthreatening sop" stance.

The door opened for them—it was that old-fashioned that it actually had hinges. Standing in the doorway, looking at them curiously, was a young girl dressed in Earth-style casual baggies, somewhat stained with what looked like paint. She had a strong, square jaw that seemed too large for the rest of her face, but otherwise was extremely pretty—in her early teens, dark-skinned, with gorgeous great brown eyes and a delighted smile that spread and spread as she looked at them.

"Good afternoon," Joss said. "We're looking for Dr. Laurentz. Is he at home?"

"Hello!" the girl said, smiling, if possible, more widely.

She didn't say anything else, though. Joss was slightly nonplussed. "Hello!" he said back.

She looked at Evan, then, and the expression of delight grew even more intense as she looked him up and down. "Hello!"

"Hello, young lady," Evan said, glancing with mild bemusement at Joss.

"Coming, coming!" said someone inside the house. Footsteps hurried toward the door. "Excuse me, Beval." And then there was a man standing there too; in his late fifties or early sixties, with short grey hair and beard gone salt-and-pepper, a little pot-bellied, dressed as casually as the young girl. He looked at Joss, and then at Evan, with growing surprise. "How can I help you gentlemen?" he said. "Solar Police, surely?"

"Yes, sir," Evan said. "Officers Glyndower and O'Bannion. The station Administration office suggested we should talk to you. We were hoping you might have some advice for us on a case we're working on."

"Certainly," he said. "Please do come in, gentlemen. I'm Haral Laurentz. Oh," he said, "this is my daughter Beval."

"That's a lovely name," Evan said, smiling at the young girl. She smiled back and said, "Hello!" There was no other response; just simple delight—no sense of any understanding of what was going on.

Joss's heart twisted in him a little, as it always did when he met someone who seemed mentally disadvantaged. It always seemed unfair to him somehow, that he should be all right, and someone else should be crippled of mind, however slightly.

"My daughter is retarded, as you'll have guessed," Dr. Laurentz said. "She's caught at about age three, developmentally. That's one of the reasons I work at home." He led them into the house, through a small anteroom and then into the living room. It was quite comfortably furnished in the modern style, with three big comfortable deep-padded loungers gathered around a low central table. A mock fireplace made up the fourth side of the square. "You go ahead, Beval," Dr. Laurentz said. "You were painting. Do you want to paint?"

"Okay," the young girl said, smiled beautifully at Joss and Evan, and headed off through another doorway, a bit clumsily.

"Please sit down, gentlemen," Laurentz said. "Can I get you anything? Coffee, tea?"

"No, thank you very much," Joss said.

Laurentz sat down across from them. "How can I help you?"

Joss felt about in his pocket and came out with the cellophane-wrapped "sweet." "This is a sample of a drug that's being smuggled into the station," he said. "The one called 'blast,' among other names."

Laurentz took the little wrapped candy with surprise, turned it over, opened up the wrapping. "Inside this? Sugar coating?"

"Yes. What we'd like to find out, if we can, is if this sample gives away any hints about where it was made."

Laurentz looked up at Joss. "That's a tall order, Officer." He stood up, frowning. "Nonetheless, there are usually impurities in a drug, no matter how carefully it's made, that will give away something about its provenance." He headed toward one side of the room, and another doorway. "Would you come this way?" he said. "Possibly I can give you at least a rough idea to go on with."

The doorway led to a staircase to the next story. They followed him upstairs, and found themselves standing in a hallway with more doors leading off it. The right-hand door opened to show a large room filled with lab equipment; several sinks and steep tables were lined up along the walls, and there was the heavy gimbal mounting of a small deep-field electron microscope.

"Goodness me," Joss said, moved almost to jealousy as they followed Dr. Laurentz in. It was the kind of playroom that every chemist dreams of: all new equipment, only the best brands, and everything in lovely order. Laurentz looked over his shoulder at Joss, smiling slightly. "You've worked in the field?" he said.

"Yes, and always wanted a lab like this." Joss looked around and tried to command his equipment-lust to subside.

"There are advantages to being perceived as successful," Laurentz said, "and to also being freelance. The companies give you interesting incentives to work for them . . . all unofficial, of course. No one wants to be seen as giving you anything so coarse as a *bribe*." He chuckled quietly as he put the piece of candy down on a small lab tray and gave it a healthy whack with a reflex hammer to break it open.

"Heaven forbid," Joss said. Evan looked around the room; Joss watched as Dr. Laurentz took a tiny dental scoop and a metal slide and took just a microscopic bit of the white powder, half a pinhead's worth, tipping it onto the slide. "Now then," he said, and carried it over to the electron microscope.

He slipped the slide into the vacuum chamber; there was a moment's hissing as it evacuated. "I may be guessing," said Dr. Laurentz, "but is this somehow connected with the young woman who overdosed the other day?"

"Only tangentially," Evan said. "We just have some questions about this particular sample."

Laurentz fiddled with the controls on the tall column of the microscope. "There," he said, "that should do it. Let's have a look."

He touched a control on a nearby pad, and the microscope's foot-square screen came to life. Joss was even more impressed. "Color, too," he said.

"It's false-color imaging," Laurentz said. The three of them looked at the scatter of big crystals, like three-dimensional snowflakes, that lay across all the field of vision. "There's half your question answered, at least," Laurentz said. "This stuff was made in very low gee, probably less than a tenth. Look at the crystal structure. You can't get that trilateral symmetry in anything but an orbital environment."

Joss and Evan looked at one another. "So it's being

made in a fiver," Joss said, "and presumably not this one. Makes no sense to be smuggling it in otherwise."

Evan nodded slowly. "What are the odds of this being made on the Moon?"

"Too much gravity by far," Laurentz said. "Now," he said, "I am going to have trouble isolating the actual location of manufacture for you, I'm afraid. This stuff looks very pure indeed. I'll run some analyses on it for you, and see what trace elements might be present. That's the best I can do."

"If you would do that, we'd be grateful," Joss said. "We're at the Hilton if you need us for anything."

"Hmm," said Laurentz, gazing at the sample and looking at one of the readouts on the screen. Then he shook his head and laughed. "Let me see you gentlemen out," he said, "before I get too interested in this." He smiled a bit. "I always did like detective stories. Never thought I'd be in one."

Joss smiled too as they headed down the stairs. They were met there by Beval, brandishing a frayed paintbrush and smiling happily. "Come paint?" she said to Joss and Evan.

"Not right now, sweetheart," Evan said, "but maybe some other time."

"Grey," Beval said to him, her eyes shining as she stared at his armor.

"It is that," he said, and grinned a bit. "You be good, now."

They made their way to the door. "Doctor, do call us if anything comes up," Evan said. "We need all the help we can get at this point."

"No problem at all," Laurentz said, and opened the door for them.

They waved goodbye to Beval; Dr. Laurentz drew her gently inside and shut the door. "Sweet child," Joss said. "Pity about her."

"Indeed," Evan said.

"She's painted you, you know that?" Joss said, glancing at Evan's back.

Evan laughed. "Maybe she thought grey wasn't my color. It's no big deal."

They sauntered across the bridge, looking around them. A lark flew by overhead at about thirty klicks per hour, hardly needing to move its wings in the low gravity, and trilling as it went. "I get a feeling someone back home has an Uncle Evan who's used to being painted and so forth," Joss said.

"Oh, aye." Evan waved at the security guards at the end of the bridge as they went by. "My sister's three like it when I come to visit—they brag about me to the other kids. 'Our Uncle Evan is the biggest, strongest—' " He broke off, laughing. "Once I actually heard the youngest one, that's Ian, he's five, saying to one of his playfriends, 'You have to let me play with your spaceship or I'll have my Uncle Evan shoot it with his gun.' "

Joss chuckled. "The family enforcer, hm?"

"Seems so." They walked on to the slidewalk, paused there a moment to let a crowd of people all bunched together get off it. "You've none, have you? Family."

Joss shook his head. "My parents died early. No brothers, no sisters. A cousin or two, but we were never close."

"Must be strange," Evan said, stepping onto the slidewalk. "I can't imagine not dreading the letters I get from the family when I tell them I've been posted to some strange new place, and they come back at me insisting I should stand up and demand some nice peaceful job on Earth. Must be interesting to be able to make up your own mind about where you're going, what you're doing, without that pressure on you. What the family will think."

Joss shook his head. "It's hard to imagine anyone even asking me that kind of question," he said. "I'm so used to doing it on my own."

Evan nodded, watching the forest as they passed it. "They really ought to put some hardwoods in there," he said. "Never mind. Listen, my lad: what are we going to do about this mess?"

Joss sighed. "If the stuff is coming from another fiver, the question becomes, who passed it to Jensen?"

"Or planted it on him."

"You think he might be telling the truth?"

"Until we've established that he's lying," Evan said, "I

suppose we ought to keep the idea open." His tone was dry.

Joss made a face. "You're right, of course." He hefted his pad, tapped it into active mode, and gazed at the opening menu for a moment. "We'll go see him, I guess."

"I had that in mind."

Joss suddenly saw that one of the tags on the menu was flashing. "Mail waiting," he said.

"Who from?"

He smiled a bit. "Dorren Orcieres."

"Aha," Evan said, and gave Joss a knowing look. "I shan't ask, then."

Joss scanned the message. "No, she just wants to have dinner."

"For two, I suspect."

"I suspect so. She says hello to you, though."

"Nice of her," Evan said.

"Hmf." Joss hit the clear control, but another message header came up. "Hmm—"

"What?"

"Something else." Joss looked at the audit trail on the message header. "Looks like it came from a public terminal." He tapped at the pad again. "It's just a file," he said. "No message. Just numbers—" He stopped.

Evan looked over his shoulder. "What, man?"

"It's all credit amounts," Joss said. "Here, hold this for a moment." He handed Evan the pad. Evan held it out so that Joss could tap at it with both hands.

"Compare files—," he muttered. "Evan, I think this is from Trevor. Or maybe someone doing him a favor. Whoever it is, they're being cagey. No ID at all. But I think I've seen this before—"

There was a moment's silence. Then Joss said, "And the duck comes down and gives you a hundred dollars. . . ."

Evan looked wry. "I'll give you a duck, my lad—"

"Calm, calm. Look at this." Joss turned the pad around, so that Evan could see the readout. He had split the screen down the middle. One side showed a column of figures—deposits and withdrawals in a bank account. The other side showed the same list, but with additions:

all large, round amounts of credits, and never less than
four figures. "Well, well," Evan said softly. "So this is
the unedited version of Przno's bank account." Joss nodded.

"Now watch this." He turned the pad again and tapped
at it. "I'm telling the machine to correlate this with the
shifts Przno worked in the past couple of months, and his
off time. Also his accesses to the system on days when he
didn't come in." There was another pause.

The data came up, and Evan peered down at it. "He
staggered his shifts," he said quietly, "but every time there
was a leak, he was either there that day, or had access."

"That's what threw us off before," Joss said. "He was
doing some of those accesses from home . . . probably
calling in to the main comms computer and waking up
some routine he had buried in it earlier. I'll ask Trevor
what we can do about finding hidden routines. But in any
case, each time there was a leak, each day he added something to the data squirt going out, there was a payment
made to his account. Without fail." Joss smiled a bit.
"Someone was punctual."

"The payments cleared the same day, too," Evan said.
"So, either cash, or electronic transfer."

"Transfer, I think. Cash deposit still needs a signature
of some kind. Electronic deposits can be made without
leaving a trail, if it's cash you put in the machine. It just
counts it and tests for counterfeit; it doesn't care who's
putting money *in* accounts. Just who's taking it out."

Evan nodded. Joss cleared the screen and tapped out a
quick note to Trevor's hidden mailbox, thanking him for
the help. Then he stood a moment and just thought. "You
could make a case," he said, "with this data, that what
Przno was doing was sending out the illicit data, getting
his payment, buying the drug, and having himself a nice
little blast. Because, look here—after this transfer, and this
one, he had scheduled days off. This one was a 'sick day';
here's another scheduled one."

"All very well," Evan said. "But this leaves us with
another question. The man didn't blast *while* he was working, if this was any indication. Maybe he thought he would
be caught. Or who knows? But if this is the case, *why* did

he blast at work, that last day, while you were there? Possibly even two days, since the way he behaved the first day we were on was rather like the way he was when only you were there.''

Joss mulled that one over. "You've got me. But it would be a break from the pattern."

"Increasing addiction," Evan said. "From what Doctor Orlovsky was telling us, the tip over the addiction threshold can happen fairly quickly."

"It would," Joss said. "Overuse a couple times, and the change in the receptor sites is profound. In fact, it's a good question how long Przno would have lived if he hadn't been shot."

Evan looked grim. "I wonder if anyone else knew that?"

Joss was startled. "What are you thinking?'

"Suppose he had some piece of information someone needed? And they wanted to get it out of him in a hurry, before he fried his brain like a white pudding?" Evan was frowning. "Or perhaps someone was worried he was so close to collapse that he might give something vital away while he was in hospital, but before he died. So they hurry the process a little—and make it look as like a robbery as they can—"

"It's pretty circumstantial," Joss said.

Evan sighed. "I know. All the same . . . it makes me think that something had gone wrong for Przno. Very wrong. I just wish we had a hint of what." He trailed off a moment, chewing his lip, and then said, "And what about Jensen?"

Joss stared at the pad for a moment and then shut it down and tucked it under his arm. "I'm not so sure of his involvement with the comms problem at this point," Joss said, "but the drugs, now . . ."

"There's a connection," Evan said, "there's *always* been a connection, I think. But we were never meant to find it."

"Possibly neither was Lon," Joss said. The thought made him slightly cold; they certainly knew more, in general, about what was going on here than Lon did . . . and therefore were much better candidates than he had been to be killed as quickly as possible.

"Quite," Evan said. And then added, "Haven't we passed our stop?"

Joss looked around him in surprise. They were halfway down the length of the river, down into farm territory again. "Oops, maybe we did. Where were we going?"

"I don't think we'd solved that. A bite to eat? And then Customs?"

"Sounds like a good idea to me. I want a nice talk with Captain Jensen, indeed I do."

Evan smiled slightly. "I'll join you. Now about this duck—"

CUSTOMS WAS A LITTLE QUIETER WHEN THEY got down there after supper; the shuttle passengers were all gone to their hotels, and the Customs people were mostly off doing paperwork. Pat Higgins was leaning over the reception desk inside the doors of the private part of Customs, and nodded to them as they came in.

"Anything more of interest?" Joss said.

Higgins shook his head and leaned against the desk. "Jensen's still singing the same old song," he said. "He claims he never saw the candy, never set foot off the shuttle except in the terminal—and to do him justice, that seems to be true, from some calls we've made. He was hardly off the ship long enough to have a smoke. In fact, apparently that's what he was doing."

"A lot can happen in a cigarette's worth of time," Evan said. "How have you been working him?"

"Oh, the usual; good cop, bad cop." Higgins glanced over at a young fairhaired man who was tapping out a report off to one side. "Kuvolik there has been being bad cop. He was also in charge of the body search."

Kuvolik glanced up as his name was mentioned. It occurred to Joss that the young man would be good at being bad cop. His face was at rest at the moment, but its lines indicated that it could become positively satanic if its wearer wanted it to. "Sir?" he said.

"Nothing, K-Mac, you finish that up. But we might want you later." Higgins turned back to Joss and Evan. "You gents want a turn in the barrel?"

Joss chuckled. "I suppose we'd better."

Higgins took them back to the little room where Jensen was being held. Its door was a one-way mirror, and they looked in to see Jensen sitting, looking most uncomfortable indeed, across from another young officer, this one a slender, pretty woman, who was asking him kindly questions. Jensen was answering her civilly enough, but he looked rather frayed around the edges; which, Joss thought, was probably all to the good. The room was another of those with the body-search facilities—the cans of spray-on glove were in evidence—and the toilet with the sieve in it had apparently just been used. The facilities showed signs of having been recently sprayed down.

"That's our Meg Davis," Higgins said. "She's only been in there a little while; I'd like to give her a few minutes more, if you don't mind. Meg's good at what she does."

"Your game, sir," Evan said.

So they sat down on chairs in the hallway, and waited for Meg. It was about fifteen minutes before she came out. The door slid shut behind her, and she keyed it locked and leaned against the wall beside it for a moment, looking at Higgins and Joss and Evan. "Gentlemen," she said. To Higgins she said, "Pat, he's holding the line. He exactly reproduced the chronology he gave K-Mac and Jody earlier."

Higgins shrugged. "Once more for luck, then. Gentlemen? Do you want to see details of what he's said, or try it yourselves?"

"We'll take it cold," Joss said, and "No, thank you," Evan said, both at once.

Higgins laughed. "You sop teams," he said, "it's true what they say about you." He walked off.

"What do they say?" Joss called after him, bemused. But Higgins was already in another room.

"Here, sir," Davis said, and handed Joss the keycard for the room. "If I'm not around when you're done, leave it with Pat." She headed off down the hall after Higgins.

"What *do* they say?" Joss said to Evan.

Evan laughed. "Come on."

They went in. Jensen looked wary but slightly glad at the sight of Joss. But when Evan came in, ducking a little to make it through the doorway, Jensen blanched. It didn't improve his appearance. Jensen had the sort of rugged good looks, with distinguished-looking silvered hair, that the shuttle companies liked to use in their publicity. But now he just looked prematurely old, sweaty and frazzled.

"Captain Jensen," Joss said, "you won't mind, I'm sure, if we ask you a few questions."

"Officer, you spoke to me earlier," Jensen said in some desperation. "Surely you must know I wouldn't do anything so stupid as running drugs. I'm a professional, I'm six months off my retirement and my pension—"

"Perhaps you would tell us," Evan said, his voice rumbling in the helm, "all your movements from the time you left the station yesterday."

Jensen sighed the sigh of a man who has told a story twenty times, and is about to tell it for the twenty-first, and began. Joss took notes, and let Evan ask the questions.

Jensen said that he had been awakened by Poole's call saying that he was needed for duty. He had dressed and come straight to the shuttle facility, and started his usual pre-flight procedure, going over the computer plan for fuel and load distribution, checking the freight manifests, and so forth. When the freight was about half loaded, he did his float-round, checking the integrity of the craft from the outside, and then got on board and started his interior craft checks with his copilot, who arrived about a third of the way into the process. They had finished about fifteen minutes early, boarded their passengers, and the craft had been pushed out at the beginning of their available launch window. They had made a good run to the orbital facility at the Moon, had lain over for an hour while the cabin crew changed some personnel and some of the passengers left; had taken on more passengers, and left the orbital facility, again at the beginning of their window, for Earth. A normal landing, a normal checkout Earthside, and Jensen had gotten out into the shuttle terminal to stretch his legs and rest his eyes a bit.

"And did you have your bag with you?" Evan said.

"No!" Jensen said, in the tone of voice of a man who is getting sick of being asked this particular question. "It was in the closet on the flight deck."

"And it had been there since you got on the shuttle originally, in Freedom?"

"Yes!"

"And no one had touched it, or gone near it?"

"No. It was in the stowage locker, as I told your other friends out there."

"That locker was secured?"

"With my combination. I've never had anything stolen, but there's no point in taking chances."

"And no one else has the combination?"

"Of course not. What use would it be if anyone *knew* it?"

"So the bag was with you, or secured, from the time you got into the shuttle until the time you debarked again at Freedom."

"Yes!"

"Was it with you *all* the time," Joss said, "from the time you left your apartment until the time you got into the shuttle?"

"Yes," Jensen said, very annoyed. And then suddenly he said, "No."

"No?"

Jensen's voice was bemused. "No," he said. "I put it down on a desk when I was in the shuttle facility. When I was picking up the pre-flight parameters."

"Was it ever out of your sight?" Joss said.

"Well, no," Jensen said.

"Not ever? You never took your eyes off it for a second? When you were reading a screen, when you were talking to somebody—"

"Well, don't be silly, of course I did—" Jensen suddenly fell silent.

"All right," Evan said. "After you got back on the shuttle, what then?"

"They mounted us on the sled, we ran our pre-flights,

and we hit our window and made orbit again." Jensen looked a little disgusted. "Doesn't happen that often these days," he said, "making all the windows like that without a hitch. And then *this* happens."

"And you exited the shuttle, and the package of 'sweets' was found in your bag when the Customs officer searched you," Evan said.

"Yes." Jensen fell silent.

Joss glanced at Evan. "Thank you, sir," he said. "We'll be wanting to talk to you later about your comms account." He ignored, for the moment, the man's ashen look, and he and Evan got up, and Joss keyed the door.

When the door closed behind them, Higgins was there waiting.

"According to him," Evan said, "there was at least one chance for something to have been successfully planted on him."

Higgins nodded. "A chance, yes."

"This batch was made in orbit," Joss said to Higgins. "You knew that?"

"That's what our chemist says," Higgins said. "Yes."

They looked at one another in silence for a moment. "Someone wants us to think that this stuff is coming up from Earth," Joss said. "Or at least from somewhere else."

Higgins folded his arms, scowling. "There have always been rumors about illicit drug factories on Freedom," he said. "Cookshops. The only problem is, they're not our bailiwick. They're police business."

"And the police—well," Joss said, and trailed off. Higgins was gazing absently at the ceiling.

"Well," Evan said. "Yes. Any cookshop would be hidden well down in the downlevels."

"A man could get killed down there," Joss said softly. "If he began to suspect something, and got too close to it."

Evan and Higgins both looked at him. The expression on Evan's face was too still to be read. Higgins nodded slowly. "They never did find your buddy's notes, did they?" he said.

Evan shook his head. "Bits and pieces, nothing more.

He thought,'' and the words came out with great deliberateness, ''that his communications had been compromised. He never committed any of whatever he suspected to the networks.''

Higgins nodded again. ''Well. Gentlemen, I have to admit at this point that I'm going to have to let Jensen out of here. He seems to have genuinely been an unwitting carrier for someone.''

''He does go before a judge,'' Joss said.

''Yes, but I'm going to have to recommend release. At the very least, bail. I have no grounds on which to keep him in here. Suspicion of involvement isn't enough when the man's record is genuinely clean and his story checks out.''

''However,'' Evan said, ''there would be no harm in running some checks on the people in the shuttle offices . . . would there?''

''That's your right at this point,'' Higgins said. ''And ours. Do you want to go first, or should we? I don't want to step on your toes.''

Joss glanced at Evan. Evan shrugged. ''You go first,'' Joss said. ''Administratively you know this territory a lot better than we do . . . and it's possible that you'll find something we can use while we're following up other business that you're not empowered to handle.''

''That's fine,'' Higgins said. ''We'll let you know the minute we find anything interesting.''

They thanked him and took themselves off out of Customs. On the slidewalk back to the hotel, Evan stood with folded arms, frowning, for most of the run.

''Penny for them,'' Joss said eventually.

Evan's frown got deeper. ''This is not working out,'' he said. ''I'm used to things starting to sort themselves out fairly early on. Instead I feel like I know less about what's going on in this place now than I did at the beginning.''

''Want to shoot something?'' Joss said. ''I do.''

Evan's face relaxed a bit. Finally a little chuckle came out of it. ''I suspect we'll get our chance shortly,'' he said. ''I'm going downlevel in the morning. Want to come along and try out your body armor?''

''Officer,'' Joss said, ''I would be delighted.''

"Officer *what?*"

"Officer *sir.*"

They both laughed. "Your wretched accent—," Evan started to say.

"Glund*oooooo*r," Joss said.

Evan punched him very lightly. "Racist. You need to be reported, Officer O'Bunion."

It was probably the oldest jibe Joss had learned to deal with. He smiled. "Now, now," he said. "Your blood sugar."

"That was a rotten dinner," Evan said, "much too rushed. I think I will have another."

"And I think I will take Dorren Orcieres out for a drink," Joss said.

Evan waggled his eyebrows at Joss. "Don't let down the Force," he said. "Or anything else."

Joss smiled and didn't deign to answer.

A SOP DIDN'T HAVE TO WEAR UNIFORM WHEN he was out on the town, but Joss felt like dressing to impress—he did it so rarely. Solar Patrol mess uniform was quite tidy, too; all black and silver, with its white jabot at the throat, and black tights and softboots. Walking out of the hotel, he saw the heads turn as he passed, and for once was slightly relieved that it wasn't because people were staring at Evan.

Dorren had suggested they meet at a bar-and-grill down on one of the "play" islands, the dedicated leisure facilities. It was accessed by a lift up through one of its support columns. The lift door opened onto what appeared to be a tropical jungle, with mist in the air, waterfalls whispering through the flowers and greenery, and tables set out with flickering bamboo lanterns and grass-skirt "tablecloths."

Wonderful, Joss thought. *Fantasy Island, in the flesh.* He strolled through the greenery to the entrance of the bar-and-grill. It was entirely an open-air affair, with huge palm trees in potted plants separating the tables, and a bar that looked to have been carved out of the bottom of a monster baobab, one that was still in leaf and had vines suitable for a Tarzan hanging down from its branches.

Dorren was sitting at the bar, dressed in a simple golden-colored skintight that appeared to have been sprayed on by someone on a budget. She was sipping something out of a coconut. "The only thing that's missing from this picture of hedonism," Joss said, "is a little paper umbrella."

She smiled at him and pushed the next chair out for him to sit down. "So it doesn't rain in my drink?" she said.

Joss chuckled and turned to the barlady, asking her for a Frog Fur. While it was mixing he looked around and said, "Somehow I wouldn't have thought you'd go for someplace quite so . . ."

"Touristy?" she said. "Garish? Tacky?"

"Ahem," Joss said. "Populist?"

"They teach you diplomacy, too, I see." She sipped at her coconut.

There was a motion off to one side that Joss just caught out of the corner of his eye. He turned his head, and was more than slightly surprised to see a three-foot-long iguana making its way down the bar toward him. "Uhh," he said.

Dorren laughed. "That's Gorgo. He's the owner's pet; he has the run of the place."

"More like the walk of it, I would think," Joss said. A burst of speed did not seem to be on the iguana's menu. "Gorgo, huh. I like it. Here after the barflies, is he?"

"Ouch. Here," Dorren said, and took the straw out of the coconut, feeling around in it. "Here, Gorgo," she said, "have some mango."

The iguana made its way deliberately toward the slice of mango Dorren put down for it, and began to eat it in short, sharp bites and leisurely gulps. "Does the name mean something?" Dorren said. "I thought it was something Polynesian."

"Oh, yes, it's from an old vid." Joss's drink came; he toasted Dorren with it. "Cheers."

"*À votre santé.*"

"Is 'Orcieres' really French, then?" Joss said.

"Oh, back a few generations." She poked around in

her drink for another piece of mango. "Quebecois and Irish mixture, actually. An unholy alliance."

"Interesting, at least." Joss looked around through the greenery. Some levels up, perhaps a quarter mile away, the Administration island and its tower were visible, the lights on in some of the windows through the increasing artificial dusk. "Have things quieted down in the office since the other day?" he said.

Dorren looked a little tired as she nodded. "It's hard. None of us tend to think of one of us just dropping dead on the floor—" She shook her head. "Poor Joanna. She was always kind of a loner. A lot of the people in the office are wondering now whether it was something they did that drove her to it—" She took another long drink.

"Sorry," Joss said.

"No, it's all right." Dorren shook the coconut and put it down.

"Another?"

"Yes, thanks." Joss nodded at the barlady and indicated the coconut. "Listen," Dorren said, "I'm sorry I missed you in the office today. But apparently Richie got you the information you needed."

"Oh, yes," Joss said. "Dr. Laurentz was pretty helpful."

"Did you meet his daughter?" Dorren said. Joss nodded. "Isn't she a sweetie? Kind of a shame about her."

"That's what I was thinking."

Dorren's drink arrived. "Thanks," she said, toasting Joss with it. "Yes. Her father is terrific with her, though. Some of the bigger drug companies have made him huge offers to go private somewhere else, but he keeps turning them down. He told one of my people that they haven't offered him anything that would be worth disrupting his daughter's life."

"Doubtless," Joss said, smiling slightly, "something like this is excellent PR for the station."

"Well, frankly, yes," Dorren said, "and I don't mind exploiting it where it does some good." She put her drink down for a moment, and Gorgo began slowly walking over to it, probably with an eye to putting his head in and ducking for mangoes. "We can use the business, believe me."

Joss nodded. "It was something I'd been noticing," he said. "Somehow the place doesn't seem quite as—lively— as it did when I was here in college."

"You mean it's a wreck," Dorren said, and then looked a little annoyed with herself.

"All this is off the record," Joss said.

"Yes, well, if you'd been here before, you could hardly not have noticed. We had some major capital losses over the past few years. Companies that were offered better leasing deals on other fivers, Paradise for example, found ways to break their leases with us—and there go the taxes, the employment, the cash flow. And then the law changed, and Paradise and Farflung were allowed to establish free- trade areas, with minimum corporate taxation—" She sighed. "Mostly the major corporates that are here are staying because they're in financial trouble themselves, or because no one else has yet made them a better offer. To entice people in we have to offer them lower rents and leases than are really tenable." She shook her head. "So the place has become a freelancer's paradise. You take Laurentz, now: he came here on a grant, originally, from the Wessobrun-Berne Institute; the ones who fund re- search into retardation."

"Seems appropriate."

"Yes. But their grants don't make you wealthy. There aren't many other places where Haral could live as com- fortably and take as good care of his daughter as he can here. He can do his work for them and at the same time freelance—for us, among other people—and make a pretty nice sum. So not everyone suffers."

"The downlevels, though . . ."

Dorren nodded and looked glum. "Not my favorite part of this place. You don't know what we go through, keep- ing the tourists out of there." She snorted softly. "I had one nutcase from Earth who wanted to come up here and organize 'hunting trips' in the downlevels. For *people*! If I hadn't thrown him out of the office, he probably would have asked to take trophies home, next. Runner rugs. I ask you." She took a long drink.

"Seems a little strange," Joss said.

"You don't know the half of it," Dorren said. She

sighed and leaned her head on her hand. "Sometimes I wish I could just seal off everything south of level eighteen or so, and jettison it." Her smile went a little sour. "But then we'd just get a ticket for space pollution."

"Section six-oh-four of the Unified Code," Joss said sadly. "Anyone who shall knowingly chop off a large chunk of their L5 habitat, or shall aid and abet such chopping off—"

Dorren laughed at him. "They teach you a sense of humor, too? Or do you provide that yourself?"

"Don't know if there's any provision for it in the EssPat budget," Joss said. "Not that some parts of the budget itself aren't pretty hilarious."

"All of us," Dorren said, "underpaid and overworked. And your friend in the tin suit probably has a backache from carrying it around everywhere he goes. Is he really as ferocious as he looks?"

"Evan? He's a pussycat." Joss smiled a little and thought, *But all the same, you don't pull the cat's tail when it's holding a machine gun or two.*

"Hard to believe, the way he goes stalking around, always frowning and being serious."

Joss shrugged. "It's just his way. He can be a lot of fun."

Dorren nodded and said, "And what about you?"

Joss did his best to look modest. "I'm told," he said, "that I have some slight entertainment value."

Dorren put up her eyebrows. "Have another drink?" she said. "This one's on me."

Joss smiled.

IT WAS LATE WHEN HE GOT BACK, AND HIS PAD was flashing. Joss got that instant *Uh-oh* feeling in the pit of his stomach that meant the message was something bad. He almost hated to pick the pad up, but he did, and hit the display control. The screen cleared and said in caps:

CALL ME IMMEDIATELY. L.

Uh-oh, Joss thought again, and with more feeling. *She must have gotten the expense account report. . . .*

He hit the pad's voice account link and told it, "Call Lucretia." Then he sat and sweated for about half a minute, while the connection went through.

"Esterhazy," the sharp voice said. There was no video. Joss shuddered: he had seen this before, to his upset. Lucretia sometimes had moments when she decided that she didn't want to waste bandwidth looking at your face, and it almost always boded *very* ill. "About bloody time you called in, O'Bannion."

"We've been a little pressed, ma'am," Joss said. There seemed no harm in being a little formal when she sounded like this.

"Well, so have I. The High Commissioner has been getting complaints from BurJohn and their friends on Freedom that you two haven't yet managed to produce a result. They're still having leaks. Now naturally I told the High Commissioner, and he told the BurJohn people, that you were doing the best that could be done with an extremely complex situation. In fact, seeing that they're corporate types," and Lucretia's voice got a rather wicked edge to it that Joss didn't entirely trust, "I suggested to the H.C. that he show them your expense accounts, to reassure them that we weren't nickel-and-diming them."

Oh, no, Joss thought. *Here it comes.*

"They were somewhat mollified," Lucretia said. "But now *my* ass is in a sling with the H.C., whom I told I was sending two of the absolute brightest and best, and who now has quite reasonably been asking me why I gave you two permission to spend the better part of the EssPat budget for the next year? 'We have spacecraft to buy, you know,' he said to me. I was at a loss to think what to say to the High Commissioner, O'Bannion. Not a nice position to be in."

"Uh, well, yes," Joss said. "Evan has been doing some resource work—"

"Joss, I don't care who he's been bribing. I'm sure it's necessary, but he needs to show a little *restraint*, for pity's sake! Now you get it into that thick head of his!"

"Uh, yes'm."

"You're a team, remember? You have a responsibility to keep him on track. Yes, I know he's upset about Lon, but I won't have that prejudicing the work you went there to do. Understood?"

"Understood."

"And as for *you!* Are you done with sifting through every bank and comms account on the station? Can you imagine what will happen when the civil-liberties crowd get hold of this, if you haven't produced the result of the leaks by the time they do?"

"Uh, yes."

"Then you'd better get on the stick, Joss my son, and produce, or your ass is going to be in this sling with mine. And the sling is tight, it *squeezes,* and parts of you are going to regret it. *Capisce?*"

"Uh, yes. *Capisco.*"

There was silence, then a faint chuckle. "Damn you," Lucretia said, "you are a bitch to discipline sometimes, you and your damn trivia and your way with languages. Never mind. Is there anything you want to add to your report?"

"Nothing at the moment," Joss said, feeling rather chastened.

"You're not doing too badly," Lucretia said, "to tell the truth. It's a nasty row you have to hoe up there. Anything new on the shuttle pilot?"

"No. At least, not as far as whether or not he's been smuggling data. There was some other business that became a bit more noticeable."

Another short silence at the other end. "Yes, this interesting little connection you suspect. Which I think you are probably correct about. Well, I have some news for you about that, too, from down Earthside. A great deal of that commodity has suddenly became apparent in the streets of NYork, Moskva and London, not to mention other places, over the past couple of days. There has apparently been a major shipment. And if it came from up there, as I think you're beginning to suspect, then it went out right under your noses. And Customs', I assume."

"Oh, jeez," Joss breathed.

"Yes, that fact has been noticed here and there," Lucretia said, "and you two had better find out something about it *before* the H.C. asks me, or someone else, to send more sops up there to investigate it separately."

"Oh, Lord, Lucretia, don't do that!" Joss got up and started to pace. "It would blow to pieces everything we've been doing."

"Then get moving, my man. The sling is waiting. And I want your stainless reputations as The Best The Force Has To Offer to remain intact. Like mine." She had gone sardonic, now; it was probably going to be all right. "But for the most part, you're doing good. Just do good *all* the way now, all right?"

"We'll get out there and make you proud," Joss said.

"Don't get cute with me, O'Bannion. Just do the job." Still sardonic. It *was* all right.

"Yes'm."

"And stop staying out so late. You'll ruin your complexion. Off."

Joss killed the pad with some relief. A second or so later, there was a knock at the door between his room and the suite's sitting room.

"Come on in," he said.

Evan leaned around the doorway and said, "She leave any skin?"

"Enough so it won't show when I've got my uniform on," Joss said, undoing his jabot. To his astonishment, it was as wet as a washrag. He tossed it aside.

"She has a gift, that one," Evan said. He sat down in the chair by the bed, and sighed a long sigh. "Still, she has her points."

"She's right, too."

"Right? Disgusting, but true for you." Evan was wearing the amazing cashmere bathrobe, and a frown. He rubbed his face and groaned a little. "I'm going to put the pressure on my lads downlevel tomorrow," he said. "Or start demanding refunds."

"*That* should be interesting."

Evan chuckled. "And what do you have in mind for tomorrow's new accelerated schedule?"

Joss sighed. "Back to my surveillance, possibly. I'll get in touch with Trevor first, see if he has anything else for

me. Then back to station comms . . . since at least one of
us should seem to be doing what we were sent here for.''

"Right you are." Evan leaned back in the chair. "And
what do you think you'll find?"

Joss shrugged out of his mess jacket and sat down in
the other chair, thump. He was very tired all of a sudden.
"Probably bugger-all," he said, "but a sop must be seen
to keep on doing his duty, mustn't he?"

"So I hear." Evan scratched his head. "How was your
evening—if one may ask?"

"Mostly gossip and iguana-feeding," Joss said. "She's
a nice lady. But she's so committed to her work . . . she
can barely unbend."

"Nothing like you, of course."

"Of course not." It was Joss's turn to rub his eyes now.
"Sweet heaven, when was the last time I even looked at a
vid?"

"Yes, you never did finish telling me about this bat-
thing. Or what was the other one? King Kang?"

"Kong. How can a sop have such a bad memory for
names?"

"People's names I remember," Evan said. "Giant
monkeys, now—"

"Apes."

"Never mind. Take your silly machine out and show
me some of these cultural high-water marks."

"Look in the case over there," Joss said, pointing at a
bag he had never gotten around to unpacking. "Do we
have anything to drink?"

"We could send for something, I suppose." Evan pulled
out a stack of vid solids and began looking at the neatly
lettered titles. *"Meder,* look at these," he said. *"I Love
Lucy. My Mother the Car."* He paused. "Goodness, a
classic. *Pobol y Cwm.* You have *some* taste. But *Battlestar
Galactica*? What in the good God's name is that?"

"Ah, educational. Very." Joss took the solid from him
gleefully. "Get on the pad and call room service. We'll
have one night of enculturation before we go back out into
the fray with the forces of evil."

"The only thing frayed around here is your brain," Evan
said. " 'Enculturation' indeed." But he pulled his chair

around to face Joss's portable player, and pulled his pad over to type in an order for the room service people.

"Now watch this," Joss said, and turned the player on.

Evan sat there for a moment, then said, "That horse is singing. And we haven't even started drinking yet. It's unfair, that's what it is."

"Just you wait," Joss said.

JOSS WENT BACK TO STATION COMMS THE NEXT morning in a thoughtful mood. He and Evan had been up late talking, after they got tired of looking at ancient vids, and they had both come to the conclusion that they were at something of a dead end regarding the leaks, for the moment.

"Considering the way Przno's payments were passed to him," Evan said, rather glumly, "I'm wondering if maybe all my investigation into cash passes has been wasted."

"You'd better hope not," Joss said. "Not after that last call from Lucretia. But think about this, Evan. It *can't* be all tidy account-transfers like that. There's should be only so much account-editing you can do before it gets noticed—"

"I would have thought there shouldn't be *any* that wouldn't get noticed," Evan said. "Which leaves us with another problem that Trevor hasn't been able to answer. *Where* is that editing being done? Who has the access, and the talent, and the knowhow to do that kind of fiddling?"

"Programmers again," Joss said unhappily. "I think we both missed our calling. We should have gone into programming and made our fortunes."

"Now, now," Evan said, "don't despair. Let's ask Trevor to do some more work about that. But in the meantime, if large amounts of a drug are physically being shipped to Earth, that means someone, probably a number of someones, are physically handling it. And if there's a factory here, it has to be in the downlevels."

Joss sat back and thought, staring into the scotch he was drinking. "If I were a drug baron," he said, "I wouldn't want to have to move my drugs very far to the shipping point. Less chance it'd be spotted; or the people who were working for me."

"Makes sense."

"Fine. So I would try to put something near the cargo handling areas. Not too close, but in the nearest area where I knew the cops wouldn't go."

Evan looked thoughtful and pulled over his pad, calling up a map of Freedom and rotating the long, cylindrical shape of it until he found the place he was looking for. "Down here," he said, pointing at a spot about two-thirds of the way down the cylinder, toward the shuttle facility. There was a large near-zero-grav cargo and storage pressure there, the second-to-last pressure in Freedom before the facility itself. "Now, look," he said. "The pressure is in the middle—has to be, for the gravity. Then here—" he pointed to an area about halfway out from the center of the pressure "—the sealed levels start again. This is all labeled as industrial. Fine. But we know that from about here—" and he pointed to an area about two-thirds of the way out to the outer hull "—is abandoned downlevel. Or rather it's been taken over by downers. Access to cargo wouldn't take long from here."

Joss nodded. "All right. You're saying that probably some of the cargo people have been paid off. And it would make sense that the drug would come up that way to them—along with their payoffs." He frowned at the map. "And where was Lon killed?"

Evan touched a control on the pad: a spot lit up. It was on the fringes of the block of downlevel that they were considering.

"Could be coincidental," Joss said, playing devil's advocate.

"Could be. The Teekers, the gang that killed him—that area is at the fringes of their own territory." Evan touched a few more controls on the pad to sketch out the Teekers' area. It just touched the downlevel area where they thought the drug was being manufactured.

They were both silent for a few moments, looking at the map. "That's a lot of ground to cover," Joss said eventually.

"It is. And we're going to get shot at a lot."

Joss nodded. "Has to be done, I suppose." He sighed. "Well, as I said, I'll do my surveillance as usual. But after that, I think we'll go borrow a sniffer from the Customs people, and go take a walk in the downlevels, eh?"

"Bring the body armor," Evan said, looking momentarily grim.

"No question."

"But before that," Joss said, "I think I'll visit Laurentz, after the shift at comms, and see if he has anything worth telling us."

"You could just call him."

Joss tsk-tsked at Evan. "Now, now. You know what they told us in training. 'No call over the communications media has the effectiveness of a personal interview. Cues that might be missed over even a video link are elicited when questions are asked in person. In addition, the subject has no chance to dissemble when confronted with—' "

"Damn it all, man, did you *memorize* that bloody textbook? Haven't you anything better to think about?"

"Singing horses?"

"Oh, do shut up."

SO JOSS DID HIS SURVEILLANCE, ON DAY SHIFT this time, and it was stupendously boring, and revealed nothing whatsoever. The staff in comms had ceased to take any particular notice of him, which was probably an advantage; but none of them were doing anything he could identify as illegal, which was no help to Joss at all. Trevor's tag was in his pocket, but not once did any hunch wake up and suggest anyone for him to fasten it to. The best he could do was to leave it on and linger at one or another of the terminals, trying to pick up something that might be of use. He got depressed, and was glad when end-of-shift came and he could head out of there to the forested end of the fiver again.

He was standing on the slidewalk when his pad went off. "O'Bannion," he said.

"Uh, yeah," said a voice he didn't recognize for a moment.

"Cooch?" he said then.

"Yeah. Look, wanted the other sop."

"Don't know where he is just now," Joss said. "Can I help?"

"Don' think so, man," Cooch said, and sounded slightly apologetic. He also sounded very upset. "Got no time for soft options."

Joss laughed softly. "If you say so. Leave a message?"

"Uh." There was a pause. "Look, need somebody. Got some trouble here."

"Distance it," Joss said. "Come see me. Know where island eighteen is? Port axis. Willis Company."

There was a short silence. "Take a little time."

"Take it. I've got another appointment. Listen; the island has two bridges. There's a park just before the bridge to the southern side of the island. Wait for me there."

"How long, sop?" Cooch said. He sounded more nervous by the moment.

"Not too long. The appointment's a quick one."

"Right—" The connection broke.

Joss thought for a moment. Laurentz wasn't expecting him; there was no reason he shouldn't simply go straight to the park first.

He changed slidewalks a couple of times to come at the park without having to go through the island itself. The park was on a small island of its own, with several accesses from other levels of the fiver; a pleasant little place, with more of the old trees that abounded on the Willis island. *Corporate charity,* Joss thought as he crossed onto the park island and looked around. The edges of the island proper were built up with protective hills and moats to keep people from dropping off; those hills were thickly covered with brush and trees to cover up any artificiality in the setting. A very calm, rustic sort of place it was; even the benches and gazebos scattered around were made of wood with the bark left on. There were quite a few people enjoying the place after work. What seemed to be a playgroup of ten or fifteen children off to one side were busy in a huge sandbox, gathered in small groups, digging

and shouting, while a couple of well-dressed ladies off to
one side sat and watched them with lazy benevolence.
Other people went by pushing prams, or jogging gently,
bouncing in the low grav.

Joss looked around for any sign of Cooch. The island
was arranged and landscaped so that it was hard, if not
impossible, to see all the accesses at once. He settled for
a spot where he could see the one he had suggested to
Cooch, and another two; there he sat down on a bench
with his back to a venerable beech tree, and waited.

About five minutes later, the sound of footsteps from
behind him brought his head around slowly. It was Cooch.
The boy had put a coat on over his usual rather flamboyant
clothes, perhaps feeling that this area was a little upmarket
for him. "Got trouble," he said immediately.

"What kind?"

"Somebody did me," Cooch said. "You gotta do
something. Word got out that I—"

The sound of the slugfirer registered before anything
else, and Joss simply flung himself down sideways and
took Cooch with him. *Oh, God*, Joss thought, as the
screaming began. He rolled clear of Cooch and came to
his knees in front of the bench, looking over the back of
it. Something shadowy moved in the rhododendrons and
manzanita some hundred yards away, near a small hill,
and there was a crackling and rustling of brush. *Doesn't
know how to be quiet in the woods, thank heaven*, Joss
thought. *A downer—* He pulled the Remington, picked a
spot and fired.

More screaming behind him, but he couldn't spare time
for it. The figure, dressed in something between urban
camo sweats and downer wrap-rags, went plunging out of
the bushes for one of the accesses. *Oh no you don't*, Joss
thought. *I have some questions for you.* He adjusted the
Remi's range, and took the gunner in the arm, high. He
fell, rolling, then scrambled to his feet again.

People were still running and screaming, but some of
them were just standing there frozen. "*Get away!*" Joss
shouted at the top of his lungs, and then added "*Solar
Police! Freeze or be stopped!*"

The gunner kept going—right at one of the people who

had frozen, one of the figures over by the sandbox. *Oh, God, please no!* Joss thought, sprinting after the gunner. But he was too far behind, by a hundred yards. The gunner grabbed the small frozen form and screamed at Joss, "She dead, sop! You freeze now!"

The gunner's gun was against the girl's head. Joss froze, because it was always wisest—and as the gunner was screaming *"Drop it!"*, Joss pretended that he was back in the range on the Moon, sighted very carefully but very fast on the eye shape on the target, held his breath, braced and fired.

The eyes on the targets were always black. This one started out some other color, but instantly turned black, and then burst into flame. The target jerked convulsively and fell over. There was a muted *crack* as the residual heat and expansion of the pressure-cooked brain inside the target's head cracked its skull open from inside.

Joss stood there amid the screaming and the weeping and the shouting, and felt the sweat come bursting off him, all at once, as if he was a sprinkler system. He turned around to look for Cooch: he was still sprawled on the ground by the bench, watching Joss, and shivering.

"Get out of here," Joss called back to him. "Go to the Hilton. Wait there for me—tell them I said you should. I'll call them and tell them it's all right."

Cooch scrambled to his feet and ran.

Joss holstered the Remington and went to the dead gunner and the girl.

She was standing there staring, not at the body, but at him. "You okay?" Joss said to her as he came up. And then paused.

"Hello!" she said to him, and smiled.

It was Beval Laurentz.

"Hi, honey," he said to her, glancing away for a moment at the gunner. Very dead. Female. Half her face was burned off, which at the moment suited Joss entirely. He turned his back on the corpse and drew Beval with him. "Remember me?" he said.

"The nice sops," Beval said.

Joss had to chuckle a little, even in the present circumstances. "That's right. Officer O'Bannion."

"Mmmbnnyn," Beval said, with great pleasure.

"Close enough for jazz," Joss said, and keyed his implant on as a woman came rushing from the rest of the playgroup toward him. "Tee?"

"Right here."

"Call the Hilton for me? Tell them a young gentleman is going to be there asking for me shortly. It would aid me in my investigations if they would please take him into the manager's office and make him comfortable there. And tell them to augment their own security, because there may be some trouble. And call Evan for me. I need him bad."

"Right away. Oh, listen, Analysis—"

"Later."

The lady who had been with the playgroup stopped about six feet from Joss and said, "Officer—"

"O'Bannion, ma'am. Sorry about this." He glanced briefly behind him. "Are you in charge of Dr. Laurentz's daughter here?"

"Oh yes, she always comes out with our group twice a week, he works so hard and she—" The woman was dressed in the kind of Earth-fashion baggies that are worn to impress others with how much one can afford to pay for imports, rather than the kind that simply come in on the back of the wearer. She went white, then flushed, probably at the thought that Joss was about to accuse her of being irresponsible about the child. "Oh, Officer, I didn't know she was going to—"

"Madam, there was nothing you could have done," he said. "I just wanted to let you know I'll take the child back to her father as soon as the regular police get here. No need for you to stay if you don't want to. Doubtless the other kids need seeing to."

"Thank you," she said, and fled straight back to the wailing crowd of children; she and the other woman shepherded them hurriedly away.

"Come on, Beval," Joss said, "let's go get my pad." He took her hand and walked back to the bench with her. She bent over and picked it up, and started turning it over and over in her hands. "Daddy," she said.

"Does your dad have one like that? Want to hold it for me? Here, hold it so I can type on it. That's right." Joss touched the code to bring up the comms directory, then touched the code for the station police.

"Police, Sergeant Redpath," came the reply.

"Sergeant, S.P. Officer O'Bannion here. I'm in the park south of Willis Towers. We have a dead person here. Armed attack, attempted hostage-taking. I'd appreciate it if you would send the local patrol to assist."

"You're on, sir," said the voice on the other end. "ETA four minutes."

It was nine, actually. Joss sat down on the bench and chatted with Beval, while keeping an eye on the body in the field and making it plain by his looks at the over-curious that their attention wasn't needed. When he saw the three officers came loping over the nearest footbridge with weapons drawn, Joss got up, leaning over first to tap in the combination that locked his pad. "Here, honey," he said. "You sit here and push all the buttons you like, okay?"

She nodded delightedly and began hammering on the pad in the beginnings of a test-to-destruction. Joss turned and walked away across the field to where the cops had just stopped by the body.

He looked at their drawn guns and said, "Thanks, but there was just the one."

They holstered up, a little sheepishly, Joss thought. "What happened?" said the most senior of them, a woman in sergeant's stripes.

"I was meeting a contact in the investigation I've been conducting," Joss said, "and this lady came after one of us, or both. We weren't given time to find out. She broke and ran, then grabbed the young girl over there and threatened to kill her. She's the daughter of Dr. Haral Laurentz, but I doubt this lady knew about that, or cared; I think she just wanted a shield." Joss let out a long breath. "I didn't let her have one."

The cops looked down at the corpse. The sergeant said, "How far away were you?

"Maybe a hundred yards."

The younger cops looked at each other. "That's all there was to it," Joss said. "Will you be needing anything else from me? Formal recorded statement? I'll file one for you if you like, but in the meantime I'm expected elsewhere.''

"No, that's all we need," said the sergeant. She pushed the corpse disdainfully with one boot-toe, then looked up at Joss. "Nice shooting, Officer."

"Personally, I'd rather have stayed in bed," Joss said. "But thanks anyway."

He went back to Beval, who was banging the pad eagerly against the bench by this time, and singing something tuneless to the rhythm. "Come on, Tondelayo," he said, gently reclaiming the pad, "let's go see your dad, huh?"

"Daddy!" Beval said, and jumped up and took Joss's hand.

THE DOOR TO LAURENTZ'S HOUSE OPENED, AND the doctor looked out at Joss with extreme surprise, and more surprise when he saw his daughter there. "Why, Officer—Beval? Where's Mrs. Maloney?"

"There was a shooting in the park, Doctor," Joss said. "No one was hurt except the person who was doing the shooting, fortunately. Since I was coming this way anyway, I thought I would bring your daughter home."

"Why, I'm glad you did, I have a little more data for you—but tell me what happened! Come in, please—"

Joss came in and sat down, and was privately glad of it. He had hit that reaction-point where his knees were beginning to shake, and would continue to do so until he had something to eat. It was strictly a placebo reaction, he knew, but it worked—that was the important thing. By the time he was finished telling Laurentz what had happened in the park, he was feeling a little steadier, but it was Laurentz who was shaking now.

"My Lord," he was whispering, "my Lord, how can such things happen?" He looked over at Beval, who was hammering happily on Joss's pad again. "To think that because I didn't take the time to take her out, my daughter was almost shot or—or—"

"It wasn't your fault, sir," Joss said. "She had just wandered a little ways off from the group she was with."

He wasn't sure if Laurentz was listening to him. "It's hard," the man said, "having to hold down a job and take care of the child at the same time. I do the best I can for her, but she needs other children to play with—"

"Of course she would," Joss said. "Everything turned out all right, sir. Don't deprive her of her playtime because of this. It really isn't your fault."

"The mother would have said it was," Laurentz said, running his hands wearily through his hair. He sighed. "And she would have been right. I carry a recessive gene for Kreunatz-Viggen syndrome."

Joss shook his head. "I'm not familiar with it, unfortunately."

"A nonglandular psychoneural affective syndrome," Laurentz said it in the kind of voice that made it plain he had done this recitation too many times before. "The associational networks in the brain never 'set up' properly in the fetus—there are chronic misfires in the chemical neurotransmitters. So the brain grows, and physically it's complete, but large parts of it don't talk to one another the way they should. Usually not motor functions, thank heaven. But the higher corticals . . ." He trailed off.

"I'm very sorry," Joss said softly.

"Yes, well." Laurentz sighed and sat back on his lounger. "She may be retarded, but at least she's not dead. I owe you a great deal, Officer."

Joss went all hot. "Sir, thank you. Even though I can safely say I would have done it for anybody."

"Understood." Laurentz sighed and straightened up a bit. "It's very sad," he said, "the way this place is deteriorating. When we first came here, crime of this kind was almost unheard of. Or what there was, was strictly white-collar. Now, though . . ." He shook his head. "All kinds of horrible things. Thefts and burglaries and murders and spying and I don't know what else." Joss opened his mouth, but Laurentz wasn't looking at him, he was watching Beval pounding on Joss's pad. "Just last week it was, one of the people up here at Willis, the head of their chemical processing department, got fired for industrial espionage, they said it was. Seemed he had been fired from two previous jobs, for something similar, and they found out that somehow he had managed to falsify his employment records.'' Laurentz shook his head and looked back at Joss. ''How do they do that kind of thing?'' he said. ''They always tell you that there's no way to manage it any more.''

Joss shook his head. ''Some of the naughty people out there are very creative,'' he said. ''Keeping ahead of them is a challenge.''

''Yes, as you say. Which brings me to that sample you brought for me. I ran all the checks on it I could manage, Officer. There were some faint traces of carbon residue. Also some dust, mixed with very small amounts of heavy hydrocarbons, the kind of benzene-ring structures associated with—''

''—liquid fuels,'' Joss said, ''the kind of thing you put in a shuttle's maneuvering jets—''

''Exactly. You're a chemist yourself, are you not?''

''I have been.'' Joss thought for a moment. ''That's still not much for us to go on, I'm afraid.'' He stopped himself before he said out loud that it suggested that the drug was packed or processed near a place where shuttles, or some other liquid-fuel using vehicles, were kept.

He heaved a great sigh and stood up. ''Well, sir, I thank you for your help, though I'm not sure it's going to do us much good at this point.'' He turned to Beval and said, ''I have to go, honey.''

''Bye,'' Beval sang, whacking the pad on the table to keep time, ''bye, bye, bye, bye—''

''Oh, heavens,'' Laurentz said, but Joss laughed. ''Never mind,'' he said, ''it's still under warranty. Come on, darlin', give it here.'' He took the pad gently. Beval continued singing the byebye song, her eyes shining at him.

''Thanks for your help, Doctor,'' Joss said. ''If we can think of any more weird questions for you, we'll be in touch.''

''You'll be most welcome,'' Laurentz said, seeing Joss to the door. ''Officer—thank you very much indeed. *Very* much.''

"My pleasure," Joss said, going hot again. He waved to Beval and made his escape.

HE FOUND EVAN WAITING FOR HIM AT THE HILton when he got back: standing there in the lobby, looking tall and grim and faintly worried. "Are you all right?" Joss said to him as they headed in toward the hotel manager's office. "You look a little strung out."

Evan laughed softly. "An interesting afternoon," he said. "A few of my contacts in the downlevels seem to have come a cropper."

"Pardon?"

"They're dead," Evan said.

"Did you help?"

Evan rolled his eyes. "I did not. Someone else did. Several someones."

In the little anteroom to the manager's office, the hotel manager himself was standing and going over something on his own datapad. He looked up as they came in. The hotel manager was cast in that older mold that Joss was familiar with from many old vids. The man managed to look as if he was wearing a tuxedo, even though he was actually wearing a tightly-buttoned singlet and a kilt; and his expression indicated that anything untoward that happened on his shift would be managed with the utmost grace and tact . . . and gossipped about amongst upper management later, over port and cheese at the club.

"Sir," Joss said. "Was my communications tech in touch with you?"

"She was. The gentleman—" and there was the slightest stress on the word, making it plain that the manager was giving Cooch the benefit of the doubt "—is inside my own office. Is he going to need to be there for long?"

"Not very," Evan said. "Do you have any rooms in the hotel that are specifically secure? This gentleman has been most helpful to us . . . and I would rather not throw him in a jail cell to protect him until this matter is resolved. It strikes me as discourteous as best, not to mention uncomfortable."

The hotel manager nodded. "We have a limited-access floor," he said, "which we use for management staff and corporate business. I could arrange something up there."

"Thanks muchly. Please add it to our bill. And please ask your people to see to it that the young gentleman is made as comfortable as he can be. Someone just tried to kill him."

The manager's eyes widened slightly. "Certainly, Officer. Is he going to have to stay very long?"

"Not too long," Evan said. "We're close to wrapping this one up."

Joss thought to himself that Evan wasn't above spreading rumors that would heat things up for both of them; but at the same time, it wasn't a bad idea to misdirect anyone of bad intent who might be listening. He tapped at the office door; it was opened from the inside by one of the hotel security people. Inside, on a fat leather chair behind a littered desk, Cooch sat looking very small and scared and out of place.

"It's all right," Joss said to the uniformed security guard, who nodded and left in a hurry, looking relieved to get away from such a dangerous-looking character. Joss rolled his eyes slightly and sat down on the edge of the desk as Evan came in and touched the door shut behind him.

"Any problems on the way here?" Joss said. "See anybody coming after you?"

Cooch shook his head. He was trembling. "Word's out," he said. "You're dead . . . anybody who talked to you gonna get shot up."

"Hmm," Evan said, in a thoughtful tone, sounding not at all upset. "Interesting. We must have hit a nerve, Joss."

Joss nodded. "Look, Cooch," he said, "you don't want to be dead? Huh? Well, neither do we, but if we don't start getting some information that means something, we're gonna be as dead as that first sop, and then they come for *you*. We need your help. You need to go up to this safe room where they're going to take you, and we'll leave a recorder with you, and I want you to tell it *everything* you know about the downlevels and the trade down there. Who's passing, how you think they do it, *everything*. Understood? You need anything, you call the manager—*not* the desk—and ask him. He'll have his people get you anything you need. Just stay calm, talk to the machine, and don't panic.''

''Pretty panicked already,'' Cooch said.

Evan smiled slightly. ''Shouldn't last much longer,'' he said.

''Okay,'' Cooch said, but he sounded a little skeptical.

Joss gave him a little salute and touched the door open. To the security man outside, he said, ''This gentleman will be going up to one of the secure rooms. Would you escort him up there and see that someone from the security staff keeps an eye on his door? He's not confined. We just want to make sure no one gets near him that he doesn't want to.''

The security guard nodded, and Joss and Evan headed out of the hotel offices. ''How many tried to get you while you were down there?'' Joss said.

''Four.''

Joss sighed. ''We *did* step on someone's foot.''

''Just hope we didn't shoot ourselves in it,'' Evan said drily. ''How was *your* day?''

Joss told him, and told him also about the encounter with Dr. Laurentz afterwards. ''The thing that interests me,'' he said, ''is that he seemed very forthcoming for some reason. Gossipy. As if he was trying to misdirect me somehow. He went out of his way to mention the lab manager at Willis.''

''Well, probably we should look into him, then,'' Evan said. ''So far Laurentz has been reliable; I'd like to see if this pans out too. And I still want to go back to talk to Jensen about the business with Przno before he died.''

Joss sighed. ''We could split up to do it,'' he said, ''but I have this weird feeling that that way we're just more likely to be shot at separately. What's your preference?''

''Misery loves company,'' Evan said. ''And you still don't have your body armor on.''

''Shortly. Let's get over to station Admin and see what they know about this situation before they close.''

WHEN THEY GOT OFF THE SLIDEWALK TO AD-min, they did so through a great crowd of people getting on: closing time had already happened. "Damn," Joss said, "they'll have shut the place down."

"You're the one who's been cultivating the PR lady," said Evan. "Wangle something, for pity's sake."

Joss nodded thoughtfully, and they made their way up to the Admin offices. But there were more people on Deimos, or on Pluto, for that matter, than were in the offices at that point. The place was a desert of deserted data terminals and scoured-off desks. A bored-looking building security gentleman sat at the front reception desk, reading a copy of *The Spectator* on his pad and cracking his chewing gum every few seconds. Joss winced and said, "Is Dorren Orcieres in?"

"No," said the security guard, not looking up.

"Except she's right back there," said Evan, looking pointedly at one of the glass-enclosed cubicles toward the back of the office, where Dorren and a man in his late thirties, thin, tall, balding on top, were having an animated argument. Dorren had just slammed her hand down on the back of the chair and turned her back on the man.

"We're closed," said the security guard, still not looking up.

"Son," Evan said, "we're Solar Police. You want to find out how closed you are, you just keep sitting there ignoring us. We'll close down this whole station, and after that's happened, and people find out why, the only place you're going to find employment is at a fertilizer works on Triton. As the fertilizer." He smiled gently. "Hear there's a lot of demand for a young man high in nitrites out in that part of the world."

The security guard looked up for the first time, saw Evan's suit, and Joss's uniform, and blanched. He got up and fled headlong from the desk toward the glass cubicle.

"Now *where* did you find that accent?" Joss said under his breath.

"That vid you showed me. Clint Westwood, was it? The one with the great big—"

"Never mind that," Joss said. The security guard flung the cubicle door open, said something very fast. Dorren looked out; the man did too, then looked back at her, and his expression was hard to decipher. It might have been annoyance, or shock. Dorren looked away again, then said something to the wall. Joss sighed. He could lipread, to a certain extent, but not through heads.

The tall thin man turned his back on Dorren and walked out of the cubicle, out of the office, and out of the building, past Joss and Evan. He glanced at them without meeting their eyes—the kind of look Joss had been trained to understand by beat sops and customs men; the kind of look that said "I am innocent" but meant the person definitely wasn't. The security guard went away into the back of the building—to the euphemism, Joss thought—and Dorren came out to them. "You gents are working late," she said.

"No such thing as 'evening' in space," Joss said, in inaccurate paraphrase of one of the old EssPat mottoes. "We were wanting to get into the Admin records to do a little digging."

Dorren shrugged gracefully. "Most of our comps people are gone, gents . . . sorry. I'm no good with the master system, and even if I were, I couldn't get at it this late. The computer chief has the code keys."

Joss shrugged. "It can wait till tomorrow. Does Iain Maughan often come up here to chat at the end of the day?"

Dorren looked mildly amused at that. "We see one another every now and then," she said. "He's had business problems, but that's no reason to assume he shouldn't have a social life."

"And you two are social?"

Dorren looked at him with a flash of anger that abated after a second. "Is it your business?" she said. And then added, "We were, once. It's hardly a secret." She sighed. "But it got better. Unfortunately, our mutual business throws us together on occasion."

"After hours?" Evan said.

"Officer," Dorren said, very coolly, "some contacts are judged more politic not to take place during business hours. Surely you must understand that.'' She sighed and added, ''Iain and I had a child on contract. We don't see each other much any more, except here, under circumstances like these.''

''Can't manage it socially,'' Joss said.

''Couldn't stand to meet the man socially,'' Dorren said quietly. ''Gentlemen, is it urgent? Must I recall the whole department and pay them overtime? Or can it wait until the morning?''

''It can't really,'' Evan said. ''But the one person who can get the system open will do nicely. We needn't keep you.''

Dorren looked in annoyance at Evan. If he noticed, he never showed it, and the armor shed the annoyance like rain, or cosmic rays. ''Very well,'' she said, ''I'll call her back.'' She turned from them long enough to bend over a hushed data terminal and speak to it; then she straightened. ''She's breastfeeding her baby at the moment,'' Dorren said, ''but she'll be with you in about fifteen minutes. I'm heading out to dinner. Joss—'' She nodded at him and was gone.

''Cheeky bint,'' Evan said, and looked sideways at Joss. ''What was all that about, then?''

''Iain Maughan there,'' Joss said, ''was the lad I was telling you about. The lab manager from Willis. I had a look at his picture a little bit ago.''

Evan whistled softly. ''Some chance meeting,'' he said.

''I find it mildly significant,'' said Joss. ''We'll see how significant it gets when we get at this information.''

So they sat down and they waited. The front-desk guard emerged after a little while from the back of the office and took his place again, glaring at Evan when Evan wasn't looking; he glared at Joss whether Joss was looking or not. Joss smiled to himself and sat there with his arms folded, staring back and feeling mildly belligerent.

After fifteen minutes or so a young blond woman came swinging in the front door, with a baby slung over her shoulder in a carrier. The baby was blond, too, and looked at Evan with grey-eyed fascination.

''Evening,'' the lady said. She was dressed in the first smock Joss had seen on anyone since he came to Freedom—a soft flowy white dress in a floral pattern, that made her look wonderfully old-fashioned. "I'm Caroline Smyth. You gentlemen need to get into the Admin system?"

"Yes, ma'am," Joss said, standing up to greet her. "If you'd be so kind."

She smiled at him. There was annoyance in it, but not too much. "Right. What are you after?"

"Employment records and history on Iain Maughan."

Caroline lowered herself into a seat at one of the terminals and stroked her fingers over it, a motion more like someone petting a cat than working with a computer. "Spell that?"

Joss spelled it.

Caroline stroked the input pad again, and the terminal blanked, then showed her two or three lines of print. "Sorry," she said, "those records are under seal."

"What?"

"Look right here," she said, pointing to the screen. It said: ACCESS LIMITED TO ADMINISTRATIVE PERSONNEL ABOVE LEVEL 8 AND DEPARTMENT HEADS. auth: D. ORCIERES.

"Wwrion an dabh," Evan said softly.

Joss put his eyebrows up. "Nothing you can do about that, Caroline?"

"Sorry, gents," she said, and touched the pad again. The screen went dark. "Was that all? Jason here needs to get to bed pretty soon . . . otherwise his schedule gets mixed up." She grinned up at Evan. "Hate to have to call *you* to do the 2 AM feeding. Though," she added, "it'd be a treat for the neighbors."

Evan laughed. "Thank you, madam, but no. Thanks for coming down."

"Least I can do," she said, "and it's overtime anyway. Night, gentlemen."

She got up and swung out again, with Jason blinking at Evan as she left. When the door closed, Joss said, "Not nice of Dorren, that last little stunt."

Evan laughed a little. "I could catch her, if you like."

"No, I'll do it."

"Ah, no," Evan said. "We may want good-cop-bad-cop with this one, and you're good. Let me go be the heavy. I suspect I can find her.''

Joss stretched and sighed. "All right," he said. "But what will you do with her when you catch her?"

Evan's grin got wicked. "Just bring her back here, and our friend Caroline too. Something's up."

"Well, call it as you see it," Joss said. "I'll head back to the hotel, unless you need me."

"Go, and sin no more," Evan said,

"How can I sin no more when I haven't sinned at all yet?"

Evan leered. Joss burst out laughing at the look. "I'm going," he said.

JOSS STROLLED OUT OF THE ADMIN BUILDING and got onto the slidewalk in unhappy mood. *Something's about to happen,* he thought. *Evan was right: it* is *about to pop. I just hope it doesn't kill us both doing it.*

The slidewalk was emptier than it had been not too long ago. There was a perceptible rush hour here, something that Joss had no memory of from his college days. *Or is it just that we were on a different schedule, and didn't notice the workday one?*

Without really thinking about it he changed slides at the Four-cross, a multi-level slidewalk crossover, and slipped up several levels toward the college's islands. Freedom U was nothing special as colleges went, a mostly technical branch of the Cambridge/CUNY system; it turned out techies and electronics engineers and pilots and chemists of more than middling quality. The islands of it were small, supporting tall, fairly ugly buildings, designed by some anonymous student of Mies van der Rohe. One of them, a dorm building, had a stainless steel Tree of Life in front of it. The legend among the students who lived there was that on spring nights, coeds danced around it and scattered ball bearings.

Joss smiled a little as the slidewalk took him past the main entrance bridge to the central island, past the tall grey consteel structures with their narrow little windows.

Where were all the kids he had gone to classes with? He could hardly remember their names, though their faces were still fairly immediate. A long time ago, it all seemed. But anything seemed a long time back, he found, on a day he'd been shot at.

Joss looked around and down from the slidewalk as it carried him past the college. This had always been a rather seedy area, the islands growing fewer as the end of this pressure drew near. The next pressure was farm country, as he had showed Evan. But the end of its central area, above the farms, was taken up by a long core of zero-gee storages. It had no slidewalks, but rather a cable transit system that ran up and down its outsides and center; you hung onto one of the nylon cables, and were pulled along where you needed to go. There had been some wild parties in those cargo areas when Joss was younger. They were never locked except when something was being stored in them; sometimes not even then. Not that it mattered, since it was mostly container cargo that was stored there, all combination-locked, or padlocked to someone's palm-print.

Joss looked up at the central core, feeling vaguely nostalgic. *Why not?* he thought. *Just to have a look, before I go home.*

He changed slidewalks at the end of the second pressure and found the little cable-pulled car that led up to the center core, like a vitamin capsule on a pair of strings. The big capsule, the one used for cargo transit to the slide and island level, was up at the core. He got into the smaller capsule and touched the go-pad; the door of the capsule slid shut.

He held onto the handholds, his stomach and ears adjusting to the loss of weight and gravity without consulting him for advice. When the capsule stopped, Joss pulled himself out and grabbed a nearby cable that ran to the master cable rosette at the center of the storage core.

It was very quiet up here. Surprising how quiet it could be, with a quarter million people living not a quarter mile below; sound never seemed to travel the same way it travelled in atmosphere, on Earth. Little artificial wind from any of the farms made it up this high. Everything seemed still, hushed, at the center.

Joss came to the center of the cable rosette and let go of the one that had been towing him, catching instead one of the cables that ran down the inner surface of the great hollow cylinder. He immediately began to pass large empty cargo storages; big barnlike segments of the cylinder, with sealed cargo containers magneted or strapped to the white steel walls. *This one, right here,* he thought, *that was where we had the party the night before I left. The whole batch of us who were graduating—*

There was a sound from up ahead, a soft scuff. Joss had been letting the cable carry him along; now he began hand-over-handing backwards, at some speed, to maintain his position until he dropped some forward velocity. After a few seconds of this he let go of the cable entirely, drifting forward only a little. He was good in zero-gee, but even in his college days he had never been able to leave himself completely motionless after one of these maneuvers. There was always a little inertia left over.

He drifted, kicked out a little ahead of him to minimize what drift was left. *Where did that sound come from?*

It came again. *Section after next,* he thought, and considered his options. Catch the cable back? Pause here and wait?

One more scuff, a slightly different note. Either someone moving, or a different person. In which case sitting still was useless, and going back was foolhardy.

Hell with this, he thought, seized the cable again, and began hand-over-handing along it as fast as he could. The Remington was loose and ready in the holster: he checked it as he went. As he came level with the storage he was interested in, he threw himself off the cable and toward it in a slow controlled curve, tucking himself into a ball to make the most of the inertia.

Like a cannonball he flew at the open storage. The entrance was fifteen meters by fifteen at least; no particular danger of him running into the walls on either side. There was a lot of container cargo stored in here, the big grimy white or grey shoeboxes nudged up against one another.

Joss spread out his arms and legs to slow himself down,

fetched up against one of the containers and grabbed it by
a hold-handle. He held very still, held his breath.

Scuff. Scuff, bump.

It was hard to localize the sound. Joss tracked with it,
thought he had identified the source: the third container
back, between it and the next one, where there was a bit
of a gap. *All right,* he thought, and as quietly as he could,
began pulling himself along the containers' handholds toward it.

At the far corner of the third container he paused and
peered carefully around the corner of it. Nothing: but a
faint, faint scent, of someone who hadn't washed recently.

Behind there, he thought. *If I were them, I would try to
sucker me down between these two containers—and then
push.*

Scuff, came the noise, from just behind the left-hand
side of the two containers, about ten meters away.

Indeed, Joss thought. He went up the "front" side of
the left-hand container, over onto its top, and slowly, silently along the top of it, trying to move his body as little
as possible.

And about halfway across, the container came loose—
vertically. Something underneath it was pushing it, harder
and harder, upwards toward the ceiling of the storage
module. Joss looked up and gulped as he saw the ceiling
two meters away, a meter—

He rolled sideways off the container, down its left-hand
side—and right onto two of the people who were helping
push it. They collided, and hands tried to grab at him.
Joss had a first impression of nothing more than dark
clothes, black and camo rags, and a bad smell. He struck
out, his zero-gee training reasserting itself. There was a
crunch as he connected with something solid, and his hand
came back wet and red.

It only took a second for him to get his bearings. Three
of them, he could see now: youngish. One had a knife,
one had what appeared to be a piece of metal pipe; no one
he could see yet was carrying a gun. *Good,* he thought,
and pulled the Remington and holed the nearest one, the
one with the pipe, neatly through the knee. There was a
small explosion of smoke and boiling bursal fluid, then

blood, but not much. The pipe went spinning out of control to clank against another of the containers, and the downer, clutching his ruined knee, curled up into a retching bundle and floated away.

Joss spun, kicked against the next container to realign himself on the second downer he saw, all in dirty grey, the one with the knife. *Right,* he thought, and burned it out of the girl's hand. The charred-pork stink in the air got stronger. The girl fainted straight, not particularly to Joss's surprise, considering how much pain a hand wound could produce.

He grabbed a handhold on one of the non-moving containers, and listened.

Scuff.

Not this time, he thought, and stayed where he was. The container he was hanging onto was strapped tight to the floor of the cargo section; the next one along might move, but not this one.

He held still, breathed softly.

Held still.

Held still.

Movement, at the far side of the container he was holding onto. A hand gripped the corner of the container; someone started to swing around. Joss sighted on where he thought an eye could produce itself.

A head began to inch out. And another hand, this one came grimy side-of-palm first, as if the butt of a weapon were held in it.

The gun showed, a big nasty showy slugthrower. *Now,* Joss thought, and aimed the Remington at the gun. It exploded in its owner's hand.

Screams. Joss held still, listening for anything else.

No scuffs.

He held still a moment more.

Nothing.

Joss slipped out and away from the cargo container and began to look around it. The two he had disabled first were still useless, both heaving with pain or curled up into little balls. The third was bleeding freely and spectacularly into the air from where his hand had been, red blobs of blood dancing away and blotting onto whatever they touched.

Joss made his way over to that downer, an ice-blond young man in soft green and grey camo, curled around himself and clutching his wrist.

'You," Joss said, "here." The boy had a rough canvas belt on. Joss whipped it off him, wrapped it around the wrist-stump and tightened it enough to stop the worst of the bleeding.

"Now," Joss said. "Whose idea was this?"

"G'off me, furg," said the boy, pushing feebly but ineffectively at Joss. "Y'gonna be dead."

"Not before you," Joss said mildly. "Who paid you?" He raised the Remington.

"G'off—"

"This is bleeding too much," Joss said thoughtfully, though the bleeding wasn't really threatening. "Better cauterize it."

"No!"

"Who paid you?"

"No—"

"Really *is* bleeding too much," Joss said, and carefully pointed the Remington at the biggest bleeder he could see.

"The lady! The lady!" screamed the young downer.

Joss looked at him quizzically. "Which lady?"

"Lady from the station! Said, follow you, get you dead. Make it look like an accident. We came up the other way—"

"Her name, son." Joss pointed the Remington again.

"Orseers, something—Dorn—"

"Thank you," Joss said, and pushed the downer away. He keyed in his implant. "Tee?"

"Where you been, buddy?"

"Busy. Forward a call to the station medics for me. Injured in core three inner, number—" he paused to squint up at the number on the ceiling "—sixteen. Level three injuries. And call the police and tell them to come too. Multiple arrests, assault with a deadly weapon and so forth. I'll swear out the warrants later. Right now I've got other business."

"Before you start that," Tee said, "what about this stuff from Analysis? It's been sitting here for hours."

"Sum it up for me?"

"It's mostly that datasolid you sent me. What was left on it seems to be a map."

"My God," Joss said.

"Also, there was a piece of paper that you had sent along. Someone had written something on a piece of paper in the pad several sheets above it. It said 'fourteen'."

Joss shook his head. "Never mind that now. Get that map unloaded to my pad, quick. Tell Evan I'm on my way back from the cargo pressures . . . and I have a little surprise for him."

"Right. I have a message from him for you. He says to meet him at BurJohn. He's talking to your young friend Trevor."

"On my way."

Joss pushed himself away from the cargo containers and the writhing, groaning downers, out into the hollow corridor.

Fourteen? he thought, and grabbed the cable for the run back down to the island levels.

TREVOR'S OFFICE WAS ALL BUT DESERTED. ALL the normal, shift-working people had gone away for the night. Only Trevor sat tapping busily at his pad, with Evan leaning over him, looking down with fascination at what he was doing.

"Ah," Evan said as Joss came in. "Been in trouble again, I see."

"Can't let me go anywhere by myself," Joss said. "It's awful. What's up?"

"I have established intent of the local authorities to defraud or block an investigation," Evan said formally, "and have therefore begun measures to complete said investigation in due course."

"You decided to break into the system," Joss said delightedly. "Sounds good to me. How are you, Trevor?"

The boy was grinning slightly. "I always wanted an excuse to do this and not get caught," he said. "It's a party."

"So you're in the Admin computers?" Joss said, pulling up a chair.

"Sure," Trevor said. "Nothing to it." And he chuckled. "I mean, *I* designed their security."

"So what have we found?"

"Well," Evan said, folding his arms and leaning against the nearby wall-divider, "first of all I looked up our young friend Iain Maughan. And he has been a *naughty* boy." Evan shook his head and *tsk*ed. "Something like eight different counts of industrial espionage in his history. And there are two versions of his work history in the computers: one accessible and one—the real one—not." Evan smiled at Trevor. "Well, usually not."

Joss rested his head on his hands for a moment. "The second one kept for blackmail purposes, I guess."

"Seems likely. Then, considering what we had been thinking about storage areas in the downlevels—"

"Don't forget the core."

"A good point. Trevor, be a good lad and run that same check on core storages. Joss, what a surprise we had. We found that there are storages down in the downlevels with most peculiar names-of-license on their records. They're no names identifiable with any corporate tenant on the fiver. Or any *regular* tenant, for that matter. But can you guess who pays their rents?"

"Illuminate me," Joss said.

"The station's own management account. And you know whose name is on all the payment authorizations?"

"Dorren Orcieres's?" Joss said, and smiled.

"What a perspicacious gentleman you are," Evan said.

"Stop talking dirty."

Evan laughed. "I think we should go see this lady, don't you? Not socially."

"After this," Joss said, "I don't think I should care to see her socially anyway."

"And quite right, too," Evan said righteously. He looked over at Trevor. "How are we doing?"

"I'm in," Trevor said.

"In what?" said Joss.

"Station comms. I found a back door." Trevor looked wicked. "Your buddy Przno left it. Evan authorized me to break into his electric mailbox accounts. The passwords were just lying there.''

Trevor then actually lifted his hands off the datapad long enough to rub them together in glee. "What'll we do?"

Evan's eyes half-closed in thought. "Kill Dorren Orcieres's comms circuit," he said.

"Nothing to it," Trevor said. He touched the pad and began calling up screenful after screenful of data. He typed at one of them for several minutes, then hit one last key and said with satisfaction, "Done."

"Fine," Evan said. "How about that core-level search?"

"The machine should be done with it—oh, right." Trevor hit another key. Joss leaned in to see the words that began to fill the screen. Evan looked too, and was satisfied.

"Yes," he said, "it's the same fake names. There's our setup, Joss. They manufacture the stuff in the zero-gee areas; they ship it down and store it in the downlevels; then they move it on to the shuttles."

"All we need to know now," Joss said, "is how. . . ."

Evan smiled gently and touched a nearby comm pad, picking out a number on it.

"Yes?" said a woman's voice.

"Dr. Orlovsky," said Evan, "it's Officer Glyndower. Might we be able to borrow a spray pressure injector from you?"

"Certainly. Come on down and you can take your pick."

"A big one," Evan said.

"I've got one I use on horses."

"Perfect. We'll be down shortly."

THEY STOPPED BY ORLOVSKY'S AND PICKED UP the injector. It was indeed big enough for a horse, and she looked at them strangely when she saw with what satisfaction they examined it. "Want anything in it?"

"Normal saline, please," Joss said.

She looked even more strangely at them then, but

shrugged and filled the thing up. "I hope it's in a good cause," she said.

"No question," Evan said.

DORREN ORCIERES'S FLAT WAS IN COMPANY-sponsored housing not too far from the Admin island; a beautiful building on its own island, with its own park surrounding it. The security woman at the slidewalk end of the drawbridge let them through without question, nodding amiably at Joss.

Evan looked sidelong at that, but Joss just laughed. "You have a suspicious mind."

"Keeps me alive," Evan said. They went into the building, greeted the security man there, and called for Dorren via the comms panel. There was no response.

"Seems to be out," Joss said guilelessly to the security officer, who shrugged and said, "You gents go ahead: I know what outfit you're with."

"Thanks," Evan said.

They took the lift up to the sixth level of the building and found the discreet silvery door to Dorren's flat. Joss knocked on it.

The door slid aside. Dorren was standing there looking at them with a mixture of annoyance and dawning shock. "Oh, no—"

"Yes," Evan said, and seized one of her arms in the gauntlet of his suit, a grip that steel could not have denied, and human flesh was in no position to resist. He steered her backwards into the main living area, and sat her down forcibly on one of her couches, a plush thing of real suede leather. His hands locked down over her shoulders from behind, and there he held her while Joss sat down in front of her.

"*You* had my comms killed," she said. Astonishment was there, but anger was coming to the fore now. "This is a violation of my civil rights, I—"

She stopped, and the blood drained suddenly from her face, as she saw the pressure syringe in Joss's hand; saw the size of it, and the big loading ampule full of something clear.

"Yes," Joss said, "we found a nice big batch of this the other day on poor Jensen. He's been doing other things that we'll have to deal with separately—" and Joss kept his face quite straight to conceal the guess "—but *this* wasn't his fault at all." He looked Dorren in the eye. She stared back at him, her face gone passionless with fear.

"The problem is," Evan said softly, "blasting may make you clever, very clever indeed, for short periods . . . but it doesn't make you thorough. There are always these sloppy spots. Like Lon Salonikis's apartment, for example. Trashed thoroughly enough to make someone think everything of use in it was lost. And indeed, after you and your tame downers were through tearing it apart, *your* poor police weren't able to find anything that would help them in understanding what was going on. If you paid them better," Evan said, "they wouldn't have to go on the take, would they? They wouldn't need to be such a wretched, run-down lot, who don't really care about anything but their paychecks."

"Doubtless that works to your advantage, though," Joss said, looking rather philosophically at the syringe. "No matter for that. We're here to do justice. It's in our brief, after all. We will have what we want to know, or you will die of what killed poor Joanna Mallory, and a lot of other people on this place. And no one will ever question what happened to you if we swear that it was necessary."

The passionlessness of that face was breaking, but only with cunning at the moment. Joss could see it behind the eyes. "I trusted you—" she said.

"If you had been trustworthy yourself," he said, "this wouldn't be happening."

"We want to know," Evan said, "the location of the production facility for the mindblast leaving this station, and the location for its storage in the downlevels. We want to know how it has been successfully leaving the station under the noses of Customs, in such huge amounts. And we want to know it now."

"There's no way in *hell* I'm going to tell you!" Dorren said, writhing ineffectively in Evan's grip.

"Which way you go is your business at this point," Joss said, and reached out with the syringe. She tried to squirm out of the way, but Joss pressed it to her forearm and squeezed the trigger. The little *puff* of the syringe, and Dorren's little grunt of terror, came at the same time.

Joss looked at the syringe: its level was down by about half. "Knowing your emergency services the way you do," he said, "I should think you know you have a fairly limited time left to discuss matters. If they get you on a catalysis in ten minutes or so—"

"Look, it wasn't my fault," she said quickly. "Other people got me started. It was easy to do. I didn't—"

"The storage area," Joss said, thinking of the map from Lon's last datasolid. And he added, "I suggest you cooperate quickly before we change our minds. The man behind you lost a good friend to your tame downers. He's flexible at the moment, but I doubt he'll much mind seeing you die blasting your brains out if you insist on being difficult."

She was panting and flushed now. This was fortuitous. Joss knew that this was only a result of a largeish injection of saline, but it would easily be mistaken for the first effects of mindblast by someone who didn't take the drug often, or at all.

"Fourteen down, radius six," she gasped. "That's the downlevel storage."

Fourteen, Joss thought, and thought of that piece of crumpled yellow paper. "And the core storage?"

"One radius three, portside," she said, gulping. Joss glanced up at Evan, nodded. It was not all that far from Willis . . . some of whose chemists seemed to play fast and loose when they got a chance.

"Now, then," Joss said. "The shipping. Some tons of this stuff are obviously going out each week—"

Dorren had been gasping like a fish; suddenly it began to taper off. She looked at Joss with something like growing triumph. "I'm not blasting," she said.

Uh-oh, Joss thought. *Not quite fast enough.*

"I don't have to say anything else to you," she said. And she glared up at Evan. "You have to either arrest me or let me go."

"Ah, then," Evan said, "we'll arrest you. By the authority vested in me by the Solar Patrol, I invoke 'predominant status' and place you under arrest, to remain in durance and *incommunicado* until it is deemed necessary to alter your status." He picked her up like a toy and tucked her under one arm, glancing over to Joss. "Where shall we stow her?"

"Station police will do," Joss said. "They're not going to help her escape . . . not with *their* paychecks."

THE POLICE WERE AT FIRST ASTONISHED TO see Evan and Joss bringing Dorren in; but then a kind of stillness settled about the faces of most everyone there, a very carefully concealed relish. Evan and Joss signed the obligatory order, requiring Dorren to be kept completely *incommunicado* pending other investigations, and then headed back to the Hilton for a last consultation before they moved.

"Tee?" Joss said.

"I was beginning to feel ignored," she said.

"Tell Lucretia for me that we've made our first arrest. The thing is cracking."

There was the muted sound of applause, some hundred thousand kilometers away at Telya's console. "This one took a while," she said.

"It's not over yet. This last part is going to be the worst."

"Well, shout if you need me. The last of the stuff from Lon's solids is in your pad for you when you get back."

"Thanks."

They got back to their room, and Joss went for his pad. When he had fetched it, he found Evan already poring over his, nodding slowly.

"Fourteen," he said. Joss brought up his own map of the station, starred the spot on it that Dorren had indicated, and then added the spot where Lon had died. They were fairly close, a matter of a few hundred yards.

"So," Evan said. "It should be exciting, breaking into those. They'll both be very well guarded."

"Not well enough, I don't think," Joss said, glancing at Evan's suit. Evan laughed softly and turned his attention back to the pad.

"We'll see," he said. "I think it might be wise to call the police in on this one. Heaven knows they deserve a little action—the ones who *aren't* on the take have been looking for these facilities for a while. And the extra fire-power won't hurt."

Joss nodded and started paging through the rest of the data from Lon's solid, the nongraphic material. It was patchy, and there were gaps, but not so many that they made it impossible to understand.

Lon's notes were full of references to Przno. He was sure the man was somehow responsible for the apparent leaks in his communications with EssPat. Joss wasn't sure what to make of this. If Lon had had direct evidence, he seemed not to have recorded it. And, unfortunately, Przno wasn't around to ask any more. "If Przno blasted regularly," Joss said to Evan, "I suppose he might actually have stumbled across a way to subvert Lon's comm frequencies, while he was hyperprocessing."

"It could be," Evan said. He frowned. "I suppose we should be grateful it died with him."

"We hope it did."

Joss worked his way down through a couple more pages of materials. Lon had carefully been interviewing his way through every chemist working on the fiver, work that must have taken him months . . . but he stopped abruptly when he got to Laurentz. His notes on Laurentz were much more detailed than on anyone else.

LAURENTZ HAS BEEN WORKING ON CORPUS-CALLOSUM-SPECIFIC DRUGS FOR SIX YEARS, said the notes. THIS RESEARCH IS NOW LARGELY IL-LEGAL ON EARTH, POSSIBLY PROMPTING LAU-RENTZ'S MOVE HERE? There was a break, then: FREELANCING FOR MAINTENANCE WHILE US-ING GRANT MONEY TO PAY FOR PRIVATE RE-SEARCHES INTO C-C DRUG THERAPY.

Joss sat quietly for a moment, breathed out. He looked over at Evan.

Evan was reading, too. He looked up at Joss and put

his pad aside with a frown. "It's a fool I feel," he said. "Here I've been assuming that the person behind all this is some rotten greedy druglord fat with cash."

"And instead," Joss said, "what we get is a man who's been looking for something to cure his daughter's associative disorder. He pulls up roots on Earth, moves here, settles in to work . . ."

"And since the research he's *really* interested in is a bit on the shady side—something for which the big drug companies wouldn't advance him funding—he starts testing the drugs he invents on himself."

"And invents blast," Joss said. "Probably while looking for something else. Anything that would do his daughter good would have to artificially increase the connectivity between the various associational networks in the brain. He found something—but also found out about how debilitating it is. It was no use to her."

"But it might be,' Evan said softly, "to other people. They would pay for it. The side effects would be their business."

"And there would be more money, afterwards, for his research. . . ."

Joss put his pad aside. "I'm betting you," he said, "that his bank account will confirm it. He's got to be taking either a royalty of some sort, or lump payments for when a shipment is correctly produced. We'll check that later, after we make the arrest. But Evan . . . we've still got to find out how that stuff is leaving here. If he doesn't tell us, we never will. It's obviously thoroughly enough hidden to fool professionals of any stripe."

Evan nodded. "If all this is true," he said, "the man is all the more dangerous for being guilt-driven. He gave you the key. His wife said it was his fault: that's why she left him. Perhaps it *was* his fault. But he loves that child, and he'll do anything to cure her."

"Even kill other people," Joss said, "as many of them as it takes, until he has enough money to fund the research that will make her better. . . ."

Evan stood up. "Let's go find out if it's true," he said.

"And if it is? What about his daughter?"

Evan had no reply.

THE BIRDS WERE SINGING IN THE TREES SUR-
rounding the Cottages when they got there. There were
children playing on the central lawn, and one of them was
Beval, enthusiastically helping another child hammer a
rock into the turf with another rock. "Sops!" she shouted
the minute she laid eyes on them, and jumped up and ran
to them.

"Hi, Beval," Joss said. "Where's your dad?"

She pointed at the house, and then looked at Evan and
said excitedly, "Paint!"

"Ah, no," he said, patting her head. "Not today."

Joss had to smile a little. "We'll see you in a while,
honey," he said, and they went to the door and knocked.

It took several minutes before there was an answer. Laurentz
looked out at them, then, and was surprised. "Gentlemen!
Come in."

They did, and Laurentz made them comfortable in the
living room. "I was hoping you might come by," he said.
"I ran a few more checks on that sample you brought me.
There were very, very tiny traces of a very specific contam-
inant, an iridium compound that literally didn't show, last
time, for the dust. I think I know the source location—"

"One radius three, portside?" Evan said quietly.

There was a long pause as Laurentz looked from one of
them to the other. "Sorry?"

"We know where the processing facility is, Doctor,"
Joss said. "We know that you've been assisting with the
production of the mindblast drug, and taking large cash
payoffs from the wholesalers who buy it from you and pass
it on to other people, here and on Earth. We are going to
be arresting you. But we would like to talk to you about
exactly how the drug is being shipped off Freedom. How
much you tell us freely will have some effect on your final
sentence."

Laurentz sat there and looked simply stunned, his handsome face almost a blank. "You mean—"

"Sir, we know near everything," Evan said. "It would
go better with you if you tell us what we want to know."

Laurentz rubbed his face. "And who'll tell me what I

want to know?'' he said to no one in particular. "What about my child?''

Joss and Evan looked at one another.

"She's all that matters," Laurentz said softly. "Don't you understand? When she was born impaired, I couldn't just sit there. I had to do something. I had to do whatever it took. I was responsible for her being the way she was—''

"Sir," Joss said, "I was meaning to ask you about that. The gene you're carrying is only capable of being passed on in one out of six hundred cases . . . unless the mother also has the necessary reinforcing pattern of recessives. More than one of you was to blame, if blame is to be assigned at all.''

"Well, that's your job, isn't it?'' Laurentz said. There was a sort of bitter edge of humor coming into his voice. "Assigning blame? Surely you can understand when a man has to do it to himself. It was justified. And there was no use trying to wiggle out of it afterwards. Better to spend the time doing something worthwhile, to try to correct the problem." Laurentz smiled. "I'm good with receptor sites, if I do say so myself. Not good enough yet . . . or not lucky enough. But it won't take much longer.''

He began to be almost animated. "I'm quite close to it," he said. A note of pleading was creeping into his voice. "I've found how to match to the neuotransmitter sites in such a way that the 'drain' effect, the catastrophic firing and collapse of the sites, doesn't occur any more. All I have to do is find how to make the chemical stable—''

"Doctor," Evan said, "you need to talk to us, or else the case against you is going to be a lot rougher than it needs to be. Please tell us about how the drug is shipped out of the station. It's not going in its usable form: we know that—the Customs snoopers are set for it and are turning up nothing—''

"You don't understand," Laurentz said. "I don't have time for your case. I'm close to solving the problem that I've been working six years on—''

Evan stood up. Joss did too, but (he thought) not quite as tall as Evan did. It was amazing the way the man could loom when he wanted to. "Doctor," Evan said, "we are going to have to arrest you, I'm afraid. Does your daughter have somewhere you would prefer her to go, to a friend or relative on the fiver, who can be responsible for her until a guardian can be appointed?''

Laurentz went ashen. ''No, she can't leave me, that's what I was telling you—''

Joss was wrung with pity. It was becoming plainer and plainer that the man was operating at diminished capacity, on quite a few levels at least. Talking to him much further was probably a waste of their time at this point. ''If you won't help us,'' Joss said, ''we'll have to manage it ourselves.'' He looked at Evan. ''Orlovsky, perhaps?''

Evan nodded. ''Doctor,'' he said, ''please get your things together. We're going to have to go down to the police station.''

The little man seemed to shrink in on himself. ''This is all, then,'' he said. ''Everything ends here.''

''I'm afraid so,'' Evan said, not without sympathy. ''Please get your things, sir.''

Laurentz stood up and just wavered there, frozen for a moment, then turned to the wall unit nearby where his pad and some other paraphernalia lay.

Behind them the door opened. Joss looked over his shoulder to see Beval come dancing in, shouting ''Daddy, paint the sops!''

—and then Evan's gauntlet came around and clubbed into him and knocked him flat, out of the path of the spread of needles that would have been enough to kill him several times over had they hit.

From the floor Joss saw Evan move with incredible speed at Laurentz. Laurentz fired again, and Joss covered his head: more needles burst from the gun, shattered on Evan's armor and scattered everywhere. Then it was over— Evan had the gun, and put it aside for evidence, though the look on his face indicated he would have liked to crush it like a bug. He grabbed Laurentz, none too gently, and shook him.

''No, don't!'' came the cry from behind him. Evan looked over his shoulder, this time, as Joss got up from the floor, being careful to avoid the poisoned needles. Beval's face was twisting into an expression of terrible unhappiness.

"All right," Evan said. "Doctor, come along. Joss?"

"I'll take her down to Dr. Orlovsky," Joss said. He was torn: they had caught the people they wanted . . . but it didn't feel as it should have, not triumphant, not glad. He took Beval by the hand and said, "Shall we go for a walk, honey? I want you to meet a nice lady doctor. She has lots of flowers in her yard."

"Okay," Beval said. "Bye bye, Daddy . . ."

From behind him Joss heard the sound of a man weeping.

He hardened his heart and took the child away.

THE POLICE WERE SURPRISED BY THE SECOND delivery, and sat in on the debriefing of Laurentz with growing delight. When Joss arrived, he found Evan having very little trouble. It was as if taking the man out of his house, or away from his daughter, or both, had left him shattered. *Then again,* Joss thought sadly, *the fact that she's probably going to get no better than she is now—and that it's his fault, in a way, for real this time—is probably quite enough to do the trick. . . .*

Laurentz spent a good long while implicating numerous people on Freedom, most particularly Dorren Orcieres. She had found out about the manufacture of the drug at its very beginnings and had decided that she wanted a part of the profits. Since her position enabled her to be privy to almost everything that happened on the fiver, both through its news services and less usual channels, she was in a perfect way to make sure that anything about the drug trade that needed to stay hidden, did so. She had been able to cover up all manner of things, and her cut of the drug profits had helped her buy silence in many places: at the banks, in the comms network where Przno had been her chief deputy; in the rental allocations department, which handled where cargo was stored and inspected . . . many other places.

Jensen, it turned out, had been innocent of everything. The sweets had been planted on him at Dorren's orders by a confederate on the fiver. It was no more than an unhappy accident that had caused Przno, quite routinely, to be responsible for turning off Jensen's comm account. Dorren didn't mind of course; it meant there was another suspect when she killed Przno. He had been destabilizing; she was afraid of what he would give away.

The information leaks had been just one more way to make money to invest in the drug business. The leaks were either produced by outright bribes or by payments-in-kind of the drug, and Przno handled their transmission—either by way of hardware implanted in the shuttle, or the disguised software squirts that Trevor had helped them find. With the breakup of the drug cartel, those would stop. Joss sighed at the thought that, since they had managed to solve the case they had been sent to investigate, Lucretia wouldn't kill him over the cost of the investigation. EssPat didn't mind what worked, as long as it worked.

But the best part, for Joss, came when Laurentz told them—in the same flat, tired voice he'd been using since his arrest—how the drug was being shipped Earthside. He and Evan immediately went down to Customs to find Pat Higgins.

The man was looking harried—a shuttle had just arrived and his people were stretched thin—but he took a moment for them. "Can we go over to the nearest cargo hold?" Joss said to him.

"Certainly."

There was a sealed cargo area at the back of the shuttle bay. When they arrived, Evan looked around and picked a container at random. "Let's have that one open, shall we?" he said.

Higgins looked bemused. "All right."

He went to the container, a small one about three meters by three, and touch-keyed its top lid open with his Customs authorization. Inside were numerous packages, sealed in polymer foam against vacuum, since only certain cargoes went pressurized. The packages were all nestled in the usual mass of insulating and cushioning polymer chips.

Joss reached in and came out with a double handful of these. "Now, then," he said. "Do you have a microwave in your kitchen?"

Higgins's face was astonished. "Of course. Come on."

They headed back to Customs, Joss attracting some bemused stares as they went. Higgins led them through the back offices to a battered little coffee room with a microwave built into one wall. "Here," he said.

Joss dropped his handfuls of plastic chips onto a towel, put the whole business in the oven, and turned it on low for a few moments. "Do you know what a clathrate is?" he said to Higgins.

Higgins shook his head, mystified.

"It's a chemical structure like a little cage of atoms," Joss said. "It occurs a lot naturally. There are numerous minerals and so forth that cage other substances inside their structure—water is a favorite candidate for being captured this way—and you get a substance that has entirely different qualities than either the one that's the cage or the one that's trapped."

The oven went *ping!*, Joss opened the door and brought out the plastic towel. There was nothing on it but a heap of white powder.

"Laurentz built himself a clathrate with a tailored polymer," Joss said. "At the end of the manufacturing process, each molecule of the drug gets surrounded by a little cage of polymer. When it's heated, like this, the polymer simply sublimates off."

Higgins began to smile: not a nice smile, either, but very pleased. "And when these cargo containers are cracked open on Earth," he said, "someone in the know just comes and sweeps the plastic chips up and takes them away."

"And sells them for about five hundred creds a gram on the street, about half an hour later," Evan said.

Higgins looked like a man who wanted to dance. "Oh, my," he said. "The overtime we're going to have this week."

He went bustling out into the Customs hall to talk to his people. Evan and Joss smiled after him, and left.

WHIPPING THE REPORT INTO GOOD ENOUGH shape for Lucretia to approve their leaving took some hours more. They first had a word with Cooch, still shaking in the Hilton, and Evan offered him (as he was authorized to do) a considerable resettlement bonus. Freedom would probably not be healthy for him any more, and it wasn't EssPat policy to leave people who had assisted it worse off than they were when they started. Cooch accepted the bonus and was out on the next shuttle, for Farflung.

When the report was ready they called Lucretia together, voice, and submitted it to her formally. There was a long pause while they watched their screen dump its many screenfuls of contents to hers.

"I'm supposed to read all this while you're waiting, am I?" the amused, annoyed voice came back after a moment. "This thing goes on for about a week. Take a couple days off and then get back here. There must be something else I can find for you two to investigate. Somebody illegally selling real estate in a swamp on Triton or something."

"Yes'm," Joss said, and glanced over at Evan.

"You two just pulled this business out of the fire to keep me from calling you on your expense account," Lucretia added. "Don't think I don't know."

Joss and Evan cleared their throats at one another and said nothing.

"All right, never mind," Lucretia said. "Thick as thieves already. See you in a couple of days." She broke the connection; their screens went blank.

"Just how thick *are* thieves?" Joss said, bemused.

"I'll explain it to you some day." Evan stretched and began shucking out of the armor, piece by piece. "Two whole days." he said, "of our very own. What in the worlds will we do?"

Joss pondered for a moment. "I have this vid collection at home," he said. "Did I ever tell you about Pigs in Space?"

"Sounds unusually pertinent," Evan said, chucking another piece of armor across the room. "Let's blow this joint."

Joss groaned at the slang suddenly appearing in that lyrical voice. "Never mind," he said. "I'll check the shuttle schedule."

"You never *did* learn it," Evan said. "Hopeless creature that you are. Years, it's going to take to train you."

Joss laughed a little and started to pack up his life . . . leaving a little extra room.